D0766353

A Fight For

Freedom

Oliver Murphy

LIBRARIES NI
WITHDRAWN FROM STOCK

GULLION PRESS

First published in 2015 by Gullion Press

Copyright © 2015 Oliver Murphy
All rights reserved.

This book is sold subject to the condition that it shall not, by way of trade or otherwise, be lent, resold, hired out, or otherwise circulated without the publisher's prior consent in any form of binding or cover other than that in which it is published and without a similar condition including this condition being imposed on the subsequent purchaser.

ISBN: 978-0-9931917-0-1

Cover design by Patrick Clarke
clatrickparke@gmail.com

The lines from "Epic" by Patrick Kavanagh are reprinted from *Collected Poems*, edited by Antoinette Quinn (Allen Lane, 2004), by kind permission of the Trustees of the estate of the late Katherine B Kavanagh, through the Jonathan Williams Literary Agency.

gullionpress@gmail.com
@gullionpress
www.facebook.com/gullion.press

This novel is dedicated to the memory of my father, the greatest man I have ever known, and to my mother, the kindest lady I have ever known.

And old McCabe, stripped to the waist, seen
Step the plot defying blue cast-steel –
'Here is the march along these iron stones'.

– Patrick Kavanagh, *Epic*

A Fight For

Freedom

1

Things had changed since Seanie's last visit. There were loose slates on the roof. The outside walls hadn't been whitewashed for some time. The little side garden seemed neglected. Shadowy movements reflected on the gable wall were sheep in the orchard huddling together, as if sensing something was wrong. Seanie knocked on the front door. Pink blooms ripped from a Clematis shrub arching over the entrance lay strewn and trampled on the ground. Moans came from inside the house. He knocked harder.

A woman's frightened voice shouted out, 'Who's that?'

'Seanie O'Rourke.'

No one answered. The voice said, 'Push the door.'

Seanie forced the door open. Screwy Bennett was rolling around on the kitchen floor, squealing in pain. The phone on which Alice Bennett had called Seanie hung by its cord. She sat hunched in the corner, slighter and greyer than he remembered. Both arms were wrapped protectively around her body. The pallor of her face indicated she was in shock. When Seanie came near she grabbed him by the arm and said, 'They shot my boy.'

'It'll be all right,' said Seanie. 'I'll take him to the hospital.'

A dresser used for storing the best china had been turned over. Family portraits, the glass in the frames shattered, lay scattered on the floor. Among the debris was a wedding day picture of Mrs Bennett and her dead husband. Alice and her son had been having supper when the attack happened. The table was a mess. Spilt milk and tea dripped off the edges. A slab of butter splashed with blood looked like a slice of some exotic ice cream. Seanie took in the scene. Was this the new Ireland the Provos claimed to be fighting for?

The victim had bled a lot. It was possible Screwy could lose a leg if not treated soon.

'Here, let me help you to the van,' Seanie said.

'Don't touch me,' cried Screwy. 'Go away.'

Seanie knew he would have to sedate him in some way. In films they used alcohol to kill pain. Mrs Bennett seemed to have come around a little bit. He asked her if there was any whiskey in the house. She produced a half-full bottle of poitín. What did the widow want with poitín? Maybe for rubbing on her joints.

Seanie ran out to the van and turned on the headlights. The beam shone through the gate into the orchard. He began searching in the grass. A badger nosing around under the apple trees for windfalls gave him a fright. The lights of the van had blinded it. Then Seanie saw what he was looking for: magic mushrooms, the same shape as a slightly extended umbrella. They always grew here at this time of the year. As teenagers, he and his pals had often experimented with them. A school friend had polio when he was a child, and his doctor told him that some of the ingredients in this type of mushroom were great for pain. He would only use three. Any more might be dangerous.

Back in the house, Seanie poured some poitín into a cup and squeezed the mushrooms to a pulp before stirring them in. Screwy's moaning drowned out any reservations he might have had. There was a packet of salt on the table. Screwy would have lost a lot of fluid. Just a spoonful. Maybe the mixture would taste so bitter Screwy might refuse to drink it. He added a tablespoonful of sugar. It wouldn't dissolve. There wasn't time to boil water. Tomato ketchup. Everyone loves red sauce. Seanie dumped a good dollop into the concoction, thinking that it had to be full of good things anyway. Now the potion was a reddish colour. 'Here, drink this. It'll kill the pain,' he told Screwy. Screwy grabbed the cup and swallowed the mixture in a gulp. He would have drunk poison to relieve his agony.

In a few minutes Seanie sensed his patient wasn't howling as much. 'Let's get you to hospital,' he said, going behind Screwy and trying to lift him up. But if the mixture had dulled Screwy's pain, it was also making him sluggish. Alice was no help. Seanie looked around him. A rug lay in front of the fireplace. He rolled Screwy onto it and dragged the rug out to the van. After much effort he managed to get him into the vehicle, lying askew across the van's floor.

As he drove off Seanie decided the worst part was over. In the rear-view mirror, Mrs Bennett stood in the doorway, a frail, sorrowful-looking figure with hands clenched tight against her chest. Her husband had been killed in an accident shortly after they got married. When Seanie was a boy his mother often sent him over the mountain pass to the widow for eggs. Sometimes she would give him a big blue duck egg, just for himself. In the autumn he would gather blackberries, which she would mash up with a little sugar; then she poured cream over them. The cream had been skimmed from the top of a churn of milk that was kept cool in the dairy. The intense blackness of the hedge fruit contrasted dramatically with the cream's delicate whiteness. During these past few years he had somehow neglected to call and check on how she was keeping.

Seanie had travelled less than a mile when a light materialized ahead. He knew it had to be an IRA checkpoint. The kneecapping wouldn't have happened with the Brits around. Although the Provos claimed their checkpoints were about security and keeping the community safe, they were mainly a propaganda exercise. The message was clear to both the foe and the populace: we control this area.

Seanie pulled up and rolled down the window of the van. Two hooded men in camouflage approached him carrying machine guns. 'Turn off the engine and lights,' one of them said.

It was Leslie McCracken. McCracken had been a member of a juvenile football squad coached by Seanie. He showed promise, but the 'Troubles' had intervened. Ballyduff, like other local clubs, sometimes found it hard to field a team of late for the same reason. Republicans would argue that these missing young people were sacrificing the normal pastimes of youth for love of their country. However, for some there were other factors involved. An Armalite rifle in one's hands gave a bigger buzz than a leather ball. Running around a training ground seemed tame when compared to combat manoeuvres, and what football match could generate the excitement involved in a mission where life and liberty were at stake?

'What's going on?' Seanie asked.

'Just a security check, Seanie,' said McCracken.

The IRA man poked his head into the van and saw Screwy. 'God, Seanie, what are you at?'

'He's in a bad way,' said Seanie. He didn't have to tell him what had happened to Screwy. McCracken might even have pulled the trigger.

Another man materialized out of the gloom. He was Big Frank Ratigan, a bully who loved throwing his weight around.

'Screwy's in the van,' said McCracken.

'He needs hospital treatment urgently,' said Seanie.

'Who gave you a licence to be running an ambulance service?' asked Ratigan.

'Who gave you a licence to be stopping people going about their business?' Seanie replied.

'Don't act the smart ass, O'Rourke. Why are you taking this bastard to hospital?'

'I can take whoever I want to hospital.'

'Get out of the van.'

'Screwy could die or lose a leg if I don't get him to a hospital.'

'Get out of the fucking van or you'll be needing a hospital,' said Ratigan, before turning to McCracken. 'Why wasn't this man out of the vehicle and immobilized?'

McCracken mumbled something about not knowing what to do. Ratigan put his hooded face up to the recruit's face. 'Order this man out of the vehicle and shoot him if he refuses.'

McCracken stood paralysed.

'Do it!' Ratigan shouted.

The Provo gingerly pointed his gun at Seanie. Seanie suspected McCracken couldn't have shot Screwy and almost felt sorry for him.

'Please get out of the van, Seanie,' said McCracken, his voice cracking.

'Ask him where he wants it?' Ratigan barked.

Seanie had no wish to back down. He wouldn't mind getting out of the van for McCracken, but to do so under threat would be capitulation. Was Ratigan crazy enough to shoot a neighbour on the road? That's what the 'B' men did in the past. As boss of the unit he couldn't be seen to lose face in front of the others.

Just at that moment the whirring of a helicopter could be heard. Then a voice from somewhere shouted, 'Take cover.' In an instant everyone had vanished.

Seanie told himself not to panic, but if there was any shooting he was in the middle of everything, and to start the engine might draw fire. God knows how many Provos were lying in the ditch, waiting for the enemy to appear. A watery half-moon came out from behind a cloud and a quick glance around told him that they were on top of a hill. He eased the brake off and the van began to roll down the slope. If a bullet went through his head he wouldn't even know it had happened. A fox darted across the road. For a second Seanie thought he was shot, but there was no sign of anyone or anything. Then, just as he reached the bottom of the brae, he heard the unmistakable sound of machine guns. There were several bursts of firing. Crackles like the sound of a rattle used by supporters at a football match filled the night air. Seanie pulled the van in under a tree. A couple of minutes later he became aware of being hunched almost under the steering wheel. He had heard stories of cattle being killed by stray bullets half a mile from a firefight. Farmers claimed compensation for the loss of animals in such instances. It was not unknown for old unproductive stock to be shot by the farmer himself if he was lucky enough to have a gun battle near his farm. While neighbours might be jealous of his good fortune, anything that drained the British exchequer was to be welcomed as an act of patriotism. One guy in the claims department of the Northern Ireland Office said that if only half as many Provos as cows were shot, the Troubles would be over in a week.

The shooting only lasted a few minutes. Perhaps there hadn't been an engagement between the two sides. It could have been random firing at a helicopter in the off-chance of bringing it down.

After about ten minutes of silence, Seanie started up the van and moved off. In the back, Screwy was having a conversation with a goat. Then it struck Seanie, if there had been a firefight and the Brits saw Screwy, they would think he was a casualty being taken to hospital by a comrade. If they were stopped, and Screwy discovered, there was a high risk of being summarily shot. He couldn't go back the way he came because there would be checkpoints everywhere after the ambush. An alternative might be to pull up at some house and ask them to take Screwy in, but the injured man still needed hospitalization urgently. Seanie decided his only option was to continue on.

Headlights were flashed at him by oncoming traffic. A helicopter flew high overhead. Seanie could read the signs long before coming upon a tailback of traffic. The checkpoint was still half a mile away. He had to keep advancing. To turn around and be stopped somewhere else, further from the hospital, could look even worse because it would be seen as an escape attempt. At least this way, if the soldiers took time to listen, he could tell them the truth.

Slowly, the vehicles in front inched forward. Seanie tried not to think that he might be edging towards his own death. Then he noticed in his rear-view mirror that the driver in the car behind him was a priest, whose passenger was also a priest. It had Free State number plates. Seanie put on the handbrake, jumped out of the van and ran back to the priest's car. He yanked open the rear door and was sitting in the back seat before the occupants knew what was happening. 'Stop for a second, Father,' said Seanie.

Frightened by the sudden intrusion, the priest managed to say, 'What's going on?' In the confusion he stalled the engine. He was young with curly fair hair. The other man was in his late fifties and had a well-fed appearance. A little Jesus statue was stuck to the dashboard and a St Christopher medal hung from the rear-view mirror. Alongside it was pinned a prayer expressing a wish that the car be used as a means of helping others.

Seanie blurted out his story. When he had finished the older priest wanted to know what they could do. Seanie asked if he would accompany him through the checkpoint and tell the soldiers that Screwy had a farm accident and he was administering the last rites.

'That would be a lie and a sin,' said the priest.

'It's not a lie,' said Seanie. 'He needs the last rites and the shooting happened on a farm so it's a farm accident.'

The priest didn't reply. Seanie could tell by his accent he was from Wexford or somewhere down the east coast. He imagined the cleric was thinking that it was no business of his what this Northern crowd did among themselves. The younger priest stayed quiet.

'You have to help me,' Seanie begged.

The clergyman took a white handkerchief from his pocket and rubbed his brow, and then used it like a towel to dry his hands.

'Please,' Seanie said. 'Jesus would help if he were here.'

The priest still didn't reply. The driver in the vehicle behind blew the horn, wanting them to move on. Then, abruptly, the young priest turned to Seanie and said, 'I'll do it.'

'You can't,' protested his colleague. 'You're not ordained yet.'

'Who's to know?' said the car driver, almost cheerfully.

'God will know.'

'I'll sort it out with Him later. You take over here, Father Rogan, and wait for us on the other side of the checkpoint. While you're there, ask Him to help us out. Let's go.'

He opened the dashboard and extracted some prayer books before getting out of the car.

They were next in line approaching the checkpoint. Seanie clenched the steering wheel, his palms sweaty. Behind him, Screwy was mumbling about digging ditches. The trainee priest knelt beside him on one knee. He was holding Screwy's hand, and reading aloud from a missal in his other hand.

'Licence please,' said the soldier. 'Have you anything on board?'

'Farm accident,' said Seanie, pointing behind him. 'He got caught in a thresher. We're trying to get him to hospital but it's likely too late. He'll be leaving a big family behind him.'

A couple of the soldiers opened the rear door and looked in. There was blood all over the floor. The decoy priest ignored them. He blessed himself in a measured way and continued chanting prayers in Latin.

One of the soldiers said, 'Poor sod,' in a Manchester accent, and closed the van door.

It's who you happen to encounter, Seanie thought as he moved off. The seminarian left Screwy's side and moved up to sit in the front. Seanie asked him his name. He said it was O'Shea, and that Rogan must have been praying for them. Seanie responded that his friend was scared, but O'Shea argued that people have different strengths and weaknesses, that maybe his colleague's role in this affair was prayer. Seanie asked him what Rogan's boss would have to say about how the priest performed his Christian duty.

'Rogan is the boss,' was the reply. 'He's a bishop.'

After leaving Screwy in hospital, Seanie drove back to the widow Bennett's. On the way he wondered what his strengths and weaknesses were. Perhaps his independent streak was a weakness because it often got him into conflict with others, not least with his dad. But in his heart he knew that had more to do with trying to get out from under the shadow of his legendary Republican father.

Mrs Bennett was relieved when Seanie said the doctors told him her son would be fine. She had started to tidy up the mess in the kitchen. 'How did all this start?' he asked her. 'Screwy never got into trouble before.'

'They were stealing cars, draining petrol from tanks, drinking, getting into fights. He's easy led,' said the widow, 'and it's getting me down terribly. The doctor has me on anti-depressant tablets and says I should go out more. But where is there to go, and times so bad? Anyway money is scarce.'

'What about getting a part-time job? It would be good for you and earn you a few extra bob.'

'I would love that. But I've only ever worked in a shop and there's unlikely to be any of that kind of work about.'

Alice had been trying to stick together the wedding day picture. Seanie picked it up and said, 'I have glue at home that'll mend this. Leave the part-time job idea with me, and we'll see what I can do. Who else is involved in this crowd Screwy is running around with?'

'There's a gang of them, but they're not touched by the IRA. Only my son, who's not as smart as the rest.'

'Do I know any of them?'

'I'm not sure who else is involved.'

'Do you think they're local?'

'They pick him up here at the house sometimes.'

'It's a pity you never asked him about them.'

'I did, but you know how it is with young people. They'll tell you nothing.'

'Yeah, I know.'

'Anyway, as far as I can tell the ringleader is Josie Ratigan.'

'Big Frank Ratigan's brother?'

'Yes.'

'Are you sure?'

'Yes, I think the Josie lad is the youngest of them Ratigans.'

'I'll make a cup of tea,' said Seanie, getting out of the chair.

'Why did you shake your head when I told you who the ringleader was?' asked Mrs Bennett.

'No reason really,' said Seanie, 'but I have a crow to pick with Big Frank.'

2

Seanie sat in his HiAce van watching the brickies on the scaffolding. They were building an extension to the local school where Eileen worked. It was just over a month since Seanie and Eileen had married, and today they were going to Seanie's home to check the attic for things he wanted to bring with him to their new bungalow.

As Eileen came out of the school door, some construction workers on a nearby building site launched a barrage of wolf whistles and shouts of, 'Lizzie, Lizzie, Lizzie.' She hurried on, not looking up, and jumped into the passenger seat of the van, her face flushed.

'What's all that about?' said Seanie.

'Pay them no heed. They come in for hot water to make tea sometimes, and one of them said I looked like Elizabeth Taylor.'

'I always said you could pretend to be Elizabeth Taylor, that's if you could act.'

'Did I ever tell you what my father said about you the first time he saw you?'

'No.'

'He said you reminded him of a donkey because of your big ears.'

'Did he indeed?'

She reached over and gave him a peck on the cheek.

'Don't mind him, I love you the way you are. And anyway, my mother said big ears were a sign of intelligence.'

Seanie glanced over. Her figure was perfect for the blue jeans and open-necked blouse she wore. The sun shining through the windscreen caused the darkness of her hair to shimmer like will o' the wisps at night in the bog.

The attic room contained old clothes and books, Christmas decorations and long-abandoned toys. Seanie's mother didn't go into it very often because she would have to be in the mood for the nostalgic feelings it was sure to evoke in her. It might be the expensive coat that got stained at a wedding the first time she wore it, the Christmas lights from when the children were small, the discarded dolls belonging to the girls, or the brush handle she made into a horse for Seanie. This stuff should be termed 'memories' rather than rubbish, Seanie thought, but then decided maybe most memories are just junk anyway. He pulled at a linen sheet protecting a pile of long-playing records and forty-fives. A dust-covered Bing Crosby album of Christmas songs had slipped from the top of one stack. He never liked Crosby's phony Irishness. Ruby Murray, Eileen Donaghy and Michael Holliday records were scattered about. A Gallowglass Ceili band album lay on top of an album entitled *Bridie Gallagher – The Girl From Donegal*. Also exposed were a number of gramophone seventy-eights that came from America. The top one was a collection of cowboy songs by Gene Autry. The records had belonged to his granny. When he was a child, he had often stayed with her during the summer holidays. If it was cold in the little bedroom at night she would warm the horsehair mattress with a brick wrapped in a sock that had been heated by a turf fire. His job was to pump the bellows to fan the flames, and when he was lying in bed she would wind up the gramophone and sing along with the cowboy songs by the light of the candle until he fell asleep. His granny had told him before she died that she wanted him to have the records. He would have to take them with him to his new home.

Then Seanie noticed the trunk. Unpleasant memories flooded his mind. One was particularly vivid. He had fallen off his new bike, a present from his parents on his sixth birthday. His face was cut and needed stitches. His father was livid at the accident happening. His fear was that there would be a scar left on Seanie's face, which would always be an identifying mark if he was wanted by the British authorities. As a little boy, he felt responsible for having the accident and causing his daddy to be angry.

'What's in the trunk?' Eileen asked Seanie.

Seanie knew what the suitcase contained before he lifted the lid: a pair of big black boots and old mackintoshes – rain weather gear to combat elements likely to be experienced on the hillsides. He hated 'Dad's army stuff'. When he saw his father take it out it meant he was going out to be with his unit and he was secretly afraid his dad wouldn't come back.

'Just some old stuff.'

'Is it of any use now?'

'No, but we'll have to take it with us.'

'Why?'

'It's part of my inheritance you might say.'

There were four customers in the bar. A picture of Francis McIver, grandfather of the present owner, hung above the open hearth. He was dressed in the uniform of the old IRA. Affixed to the opposite wall was an ancient copy of the Declaration of Independence, torn at the edges. Photos of local football teams decorated a third partition. Beside them was last year's calendar. Old accordions, fiddles, bandoliers and bits of uniforms worn during the War of Independence gathered dust on nooks and window sills. Mixed among them, though much less dusty, were a couple of rubber bullets and some empty CS gas canisters. On one of the window sills lay a mahogany box with a glass top which contained a blood-stained piece of white material. Next to it, a cross made from bog oak bore the inscription: *The sheet used to bandage the wounds of Rory McCarty, aged 21, staff captain, Óglaigh na hÉireann, shot dead by British Occupation Forces while on active service, January 12 1972.*

Slash McMahon, Mousey Reilly, and Wee Pat – all permanent fixtures in McIver's – were sitting at the bar. Joe 'Sober' McGee sat dozing in a corner. Wee Pat was reading the *Irish News*. Mousey was watching the racing on TV. Slash, the unofficial spokesman for the group, busied himself studying how much liquid remained in his glass. The television, placed behind the bar where nobody could get at it and fiddle with the dials, rested on a shelf that still had a strip of Christmas tinsel stuck around its edges. As he dozed, Sober leaned forward on the table in front of him. His glass of beer had gone flat and a thin column of smoke spiralled upwards from a Woodbine butt in an ashtray.

Slash welcomed Seanie like a long-lost brother and demanded to know what he was having. Wee Pat, having studied Slash's tendency to immediately offer to buy newcomers a drink, reckoned the odds were about ten-to-one they would respond with something like, 'I'll get this one, what are you drinking?'

Slash's strategy proved successful again. Seanie ordered a round for everyone and had a glass of beer for himself.

'What's the craic?' he asked.

'The Screwy kneecapping and the calf rustling,' said Mousey.

'Why was Screwy shot?' said Seanie, pretending not to know much about it.

'Nobody is sure,' said Mousey. 'There's rumours about who's stealing the calves.'

'Cahill is mentioned,' said Slash.

'Talk is cheap,' said Wee Pat.

'People went to kneecap Cahill,' said Slash. 'He was milking at the time and he escaped so they kneecapped the cow instead.'

'Imbeciles,' said Seanie.

In the corner, Sober woke up muttering, 'I'm sober, I'm sober.'

'What do you think, Sober?' asked Slash. 'Should cows be kneecapped for antisocial behaviour?'

Sober tried to focus on who was speaking to him.

'Kneecapping is an IRA punishment,' said Wee Pat.

'We know that,' said Mousey.

'Who's to say when a kneecapping is warranted?'

Mousey looked away from the racing. 'Whoever does the shooting decides.'

'Somebody has to provide law and order,' said Slash.

'Shooting a cow or someone like Screwy can never be justified,' said Seanie.

Just then the door opened and Big Frank Ratigan and Lazy McGuire came in. Slash immediately said to them, 'Hello boys, how's it going?'

The two men nodded towards everyone and took up a position slightly apart from the rest. Lazy ordered two pints. Nobody was speaking. Then Sober shouted over, 'Who shot

Screwy?'

Slash took a drink from his glass and said nothing. Wee Pat turned another page on the paper. Mousey concentrated on the television screen.

'He was shot in his own home,' said Seanie.

Sober was fumbling with a Woodbine and a lighted match. He kept sucking and drawing on the cigarette, but the two objects weren't meeting. McIver set the two pints in front of the newcomers and said, 'The old people would tell you we're in for a bad winter next year because of all the blossom on the hawthorn.'

'I heard that before,' said Ratigan.

Sober got up. After knocking a chair over he stumbled his way to the bar. 'Give me a light,' he said to Seanie. Seanie struck a match and held it to the tip of the Woodbine.

'They're putting too much saltpetre in the fags these days, that's why they won't light,' said Sober, before starting to splutter and cough. When he got his breath back he said, 'Why would anyone shoot Screwy?'

'I don't know,' said Seanie.

'Sometimes I think there's too much drinking going on,' said Sober, before repeating, 'Why would anyone shoot Screwy?'

Seanie took a long swallow of beer. 'Cowardice,' he said.

Slash butted in straight away. 'I'm not so sure Seanie. You can never know the whole story.'

'There's another side to everything,' agreed Mousey. 'It's bad to jump to conclusions.'

'There's one thing I know,' said Seanie. 'Unarmed people can't shoot back.'

'Hi McIver, turn up the television a bit,' Lazy McGuire shouted.

'In my opinion, only a know-nothing would shoot someone who is simple minded,' said Seanie.

McGuire set down his glass with a bang on the counter and turned to Seanie. 'You have a lot of opinions, O'Rourke.'

Lazy was a bigmouth and would be unlikely to tackle Seanie if he didn't have Ratigan to back him up.

'What business is it of yours?' said Seanie.

'Don't bother about him,' said Ratigan to Lazy. But Lazy was determined to make an issue out of it.

'We can make it our business,' he said, walking over to Seanie. Being six feet in height, he was about an inch taller than Seanie.

'I'm not simple minded,' warned Seanie.

'What do you mean by that?'

Seanie set his glass on the table. 'If the cap fits, wear it.'

At that point McIver intervened. 'Listen,' he said, 'if you two have any arguments please conduct them elsewhere.'

'Leave it, Lazy,' said Ratigan, taking McGuire by the arm.

Seanie suspected Ratigan didn't want another confrontation with him so soon after the road incident, and Lazy backed off. Everyone stared at the television screen. A pop group was performing. Slash said, 'I hear on the news they are going to put up everything in the budget. Cigarettes, drink, tax on betting. The working man will be hit again. Why is it always us they come after?'

'They won't have any trouble finding you,' said Mousey.

'Or you either,' said Slash.

After a little while, Ratigan said loudly to Lazy, 'We better be heading off if we don't want to be late. The others will be waiting on us.'

When they had gone, McIver explained to Seanie that in the circumstances he had to be firm. Seanie said, 'No problem.' He knew McIver made his living off the community. The bar owner wouldn't want to antagonize the Provos.

Cormac Farrell and Seanie's father came into the bar. Cormac was Seanie's boyhood friend and groomsman. They worked together, dealing and smuggling goods across the border between the North of Ireland and the Republic. Smuggling, partly because of its anti-authority nature, partly because of its tax free status, and partly because it turned the hated border separating the two parts of the island into an economic advantage, was a highly respected occupation in South Armagh.

'Ah, hiya Paddy O'Rourke,' gushed Slash. 'It's great to see you. Seanie is just after expressing his views to Lazy and Frank Ratigan. You should have been here.'

'I'm glad I wasn't,' Paddy said. He had the stance of an army man, upright and stiff. 'I had a calf stolen last night. I'd love to know the culprits.'

Two youths selling Easter Lily badges entered the premises. 'You'll be our first customer today,' one of them said to Paddy.

'Gladly,' said Seanie's father, his concern about losing a calf quickly forgotten about. 'It's good to see the spirit of my comrade Tom Williams is alive and well.'

At the mention of Tom Williams, Seanie smiled wryly to himself. He had heard the deceased hero's life story repeatedly when he was a child. 'He died a martyr's death that Ireland might be free,' his father would say.

Paddy O'Rourke put a pound in the Easter Lily box. Seanie and Cormac each put in fifty pence, but Seanie didn't take an emblem. When he noticed his son's refusal to sport an Easter Lily, the older man's expression changed. 'God almighty, Seanie! When are you ever going to stop embarrassing me?'

'I'm not trying to embarrass you.'

'Cormac, can you talk sense to him?'

Cormac had tousled fair hair, and wore a perpetual grin even when he was angry. But friends knew his laid-back demeanour and smiley face concealed a steely determination when required. Paddy knew Cormac loved Seanie like a brother.

'Any oul' scoundrel can pin an Easter Lily to his jacket,' said Cormac.

Paddy straightened himself up to his full height and said to Seanie, 'When I was doing my bit, your mother might have been glad to receive money raised by Easter Lily donations.'

My mother again, thought Seanie. His father would often accuse his wife and shift the blame to her. It was as if he couldn't bring himself to believe that a son of his wouldn't be dedicated to the cause.

'It's only a badge, Seanie. Pin it on and say nothing,' said Cormac.

'I can't.'

'Why can't you?' asked his father.

'You know what it represents,' said Seanie, fiddling with some beer mats.

'Seeing as you're so smart, you tell me.'

'Physical force.'

'Jesus! Republicans are only responding to physical force, a thousand years of it.'

'That's not the point.'

'What's the point?'

'Physical force is just a nice name for the killing and maiming of people.'

'There are some things worth dying for.'

Seanie paused. Forearms on the counter, he kept cutting the drip mats like a dealer at a card table. 'If someone is prepared to die for what they believe in that's fine, but they shouldn't expect others to die also.'

'Did Tom Williams take anyone with him when he walked to the scaffold?' replied his father. 'Did Kevin Barry take anyone with him? Did the heroes of 1916 take anyone with them when they were executed?'

'Only people who were involved got executed.'

Paddy ignored this response. 'What has a simple badge got to do with this airy-fairy attitude of yours?'

'A poppy is also only a badge.'

Paddy O'Rourke let himself collapse into a chair. 'Jesus,' he said. 'What kind of a son has your mother reared?'

Cormac intervened. 'Will the two of you shut up?'

Seanie built pyramids with the beer mats. He knew he was wrong to have mentioned the word 'poppy'. His father detested anything British. He didn't like the British Empire. He didn't like British royalty. He didn't like soccer, rugby or cricket. From his perspective, the religious feast of Easter, occurring in a fortnight's time, and the 1916 Easter Rising were equally sacred. Especially, he didn't like the British Army. They were an occupying force.

3

Old Bob Murphy's clearance sale attracted a huge crowd. The farmer's livestock and contents were being sold off. In the makeshift sale ring a florid-faced auctioneer balanced himself on a beer case, while next to him, a young chap recorded details of each sale. A man with a hawthorn stick kept the cow moving within the circle of people so that everyone could get a proper view.

Big Frank Ratigan stood beside Dick Fleming at the forefront of the crowd. Fleming, a middle-aged cattle dealer, wore a hat and overcoat matching the colour of his footwear. The brown boots, as essential to a cattle man as a peaked cap to a policeman, had just the right amount of cow dung around the edges. He had a cane in his hand and every so often he'd strike a pebble on the ground with it like a one-handed golfer.

Donal Cahill and his son took up a position near the back of the throng. Cahill was the man suspected of the calf rustling. Seanie thought it significant that he had his offspring with him, and that he kept himself somewhat inconspicuous. The drover herded another animal into the ring. After the auctioneer had finished his usual spiel about the beast's finer points, he asked for bids. Cahill stuck up his hand. 'I'm bid fifty pounds at the back,' said the man on the beer box. As soon as Cahill bid, Fleming the cattle dealer raised his cane.

Somebody else at the front bid next. Fleming didn't respond, but Cahill did. The price of the animal now stood at fifty-four pounds. Fleming put up his open hand and closed it twice, thus representing fifty-five. The third bidder signalled another bid. Fleming failed to react until Cahill bid. Seanie came to the conclusion that Ratigan, in his self-appointed role as law keeper in the community, was using the cattle man to make a statement: Cahill would be frozen out. At the end, only Cahill and Fleming were bidding, and the farmer could not compete with a cattle dealer.

Seanie tensed up for a moment when the young Provo, McCracken, came up beside him, accompanied by Dickie Stone. Stone was reckoned to be an important guy in the IRA.

'Hi Seanie,' said McCracken.

Seanie greeted the two men. He knew the young fellow hadn't wanted to have a falling out with him at the checkpoint. Ratigan had caused the aggression. Stone asked Seanie if he had played any football lately. Seanie said, 'Some,' and enquired if Stone was still togging out. Stone said he hadn't kicked a ball since the day Seanie got him sent off.

'You should have been red-carded much sooner,' said Seanie, and pulled up a trouser leg to show him a scar on his shin.

The IRA man glanced at it saying, 'A total accident. Don't let your father hear you mention red cards or he'll think the GAA has been infiltrated with soccer rules.'

'I don't think he would even know what we're talking about,' said Seanie. 'He has never watched a soccer match.'

'He's an amazing man,' said Stone.

'Do you know, when we were young and listening to a game on the wireless, everyone had to stand for the National

Anthem.'

'I know other houses where the same thing happened. What's going on here? Any bargains to be had?' asked Stone. Another cow was being herded into the makeshift sale ring.

'From what I can see, not for certain people,' said Seanie.

It was the same as before. Once Cahill was seen to make an offer, Fleming bid next. Seanie felt like asking Stone if what was going on had official clearance, but decided to mind his own business. Anyway, that's what he might be told to do. Then Stone said, 'Would you look at Big Ratigan. He's so dumb he wouldn't know if he was milking a cow or a goat.'

Seanie was surprised at Stone's comment but said nothing. In the end, the animal was knocked down to the cattle dealer who, in a disinterested manner, studied his cane to see if there was a slight curve in it.

The final cow was herded in. Cahill bid sixty pounds. This was followed by a bid of sixty-one by Fleming. Then Cahill bid sixty-two and Fleming bid sixty-three. Stone edged his way to the front and said to Seanie, 'Isn't milk supposed to be good for you?'

'That's what they say,' said Seanie.

The IRA man caught the salesman's attention and stuck up his finger.

'New man in,' said the auctioneer. 'Sixty-four pounds I'm bid.'

'What are you at, Dickie?' said McCracken.

'I'm thinking of becoming a dairy farmer.'

Seanie shifted himself into a better viewing position. Feuds between neighbours frequently began at auctions, and sometimes lasted for generations. The bidding process could also be seen as a test of masculinity.

'You're not serious?' said McCracken to Stone.

Cahill bid sixty-five pounds. Fleming bid sixty-six. Stone struck immediately with a bid of sixty-seven. Cahill bid sixty-eight. Now it was up to Fleming again. He made no move. The stockman kept the Friesian going round in a circle. There was little noise, only the auctioneer rattling on. 'Sixty-eight I'm bid.'

A baby crying in someone's arms caused Seanie to look around him. The crowd had got noticeably bigger. As a rule, only dairy men would be interested in the cows. Stone's involvement in the drama taking place between Cahill and Ratigan was being spread around by word of mouth.

'It's on the market,' said the salesman, meaning he was about to bring down the hammer.

Then at the last moment, after a nudge from Ratigan, Fleming waved his cane. 'Sixty-nine bid. The bid's at the front,' declared the auctioneer. 'Still cheap for this prime animal.'

Stone made it seventy pounds.

'Seventy I'm bid,' said the auctioneer. 'You're out at the back and to my right at the front.' Then Cahill came again. 'Seventy-one at the back. Still a long way to go.'

Fleming was waiting for instructions when the cow at the centre of attention suddenly discharged a spew of fresh grass scour. The gush of watery clap almost caught the drover, and the sight of him jumping out of the way broke the tension for a couple of seconds. Young McCracken commented, 'More shit.'

The auctioneer took no notice. He was getting great publicity. This auction would be a huge topic of discussion even if behind closed doors. 'Still the best value today. The bid's at the back. You're both out at the front,' he declared.

Fleming bid seventy-two. Following this bid, Stone stood

out in front of the crowd and shouted, 'Seventy-three pounds.' This was the equivalent of challenging Ratigan to a duel. A hush descended. The auctioneer hesitated for a couple of seconds. Then slowly in a lower more official tone, he said, 'Seventy-three pounds I'm being bid for the Friesian milk cow on offer.'

The child cried again, reminding Seanie of the way a child suddenly screeching in the middle of Mass seems an affront to the proceedings. Then the auctioneer, his jocular attitude totally subdued, stated, 'I have now been bid seventy-four pounds at the back.'

After Cahill's bid, there was no move from Fleming. Everybody's eyes were on the auctioneer. He said the cow was going to be sold. He asked if there were any more offers. Finally, he held up his pencil, which substituted for a gavel, and while watching for a signal from Fleming, intoned, 'If all done, I'm selling at seventy-four pounds. All done at seventy-four. All finished. Going, going, gone. Cahill, at the back,' he shouted, as he hit the pencil off the notebook.

A buzz of noise erupted. Young McCracken almost started to clap. 'What am I at?' he muttered to himself.

Seanie turned to Stone. 'You done a good job there.'

'There's things going on that shouldn't be happening,' said Stone.

'I know,' said Seanie. 'Kneecapping Screwy Bennett is hardly going to get rid of the border.'

'Don't look at me,' said McCracken. 'I'm just a foot soldier.'

'It's bad publicity,' said Stone. 'We're doing the *Daily Mail's* job for them.'

'Do you see Ratigan's face?' said McCracken.

'He doesn't look happy,' said Seanie.

'Cahill has Collie pups for sale in the paper,' said the young fellow. 'But if he's not allowed to purchase a cow, I don't see him having a rush of buyers at his front gate.'

That evening, Seanie told Eileen about what happened at the auction. Eileen wondered at Ratigan and Stone having the run in. Seanie said Stone's intervention had nothing to do with him feeling sorry for Cahill; he had some other agenda.

'Why would he do it so publicly?' asked Eileen.

'Who can say? I'm sure vindicating Cahill had nothing to do with it, if only because most people think Cahill's a thief.'

When Seanie told Eileen about Cahill having Collie pups for sale, she begged him to get her one. Seanie at first acted reluctant, as if he didn't want anything to do with Cahill, but then pretended to give into Eileen's pleas. His interest in buying a pup would give him a chance to talk to Cahill face to face. Maybe he was just being nosey in wanting to see first-hand how the alleged thief at the centre of so much attention was reacting to it, but he could convince himself he had a genuine reason because of his father's calf.

The mother and five young pups were in a nursery cubicle beside a number of other doggie pens. The one Seanie decided to buy ran to meet him. It had a white collar that made him stand out from the others. Whiskey would be a suitable name. Perhaps that wasn't very original, and also Black and White wasn't an Irish whiskey. Eileen could decide. Cahill explained that the pup was almost weaned. After agreeing the price, Seanie had a beautiful little puppy to take home.

When he got home, Eileen couldn't wait to pet him. 'Oh I love him,' she said. 'Look how inquisitive he is, sniffing about. He'll make a great guard dog, won't he Cormac?'

Cormac was lying on the sofa with his hands behind his head. 'Guard dog, how are you! He's probably crying for his mother.'

Cormac's flippant remark reminded Seanie of his meeting with Cahill. There were calves bawling then, although nothing unusual struck him about that at the time. Now when he thought about it, calves do bawl for their mother. When Eileen left the room he said to Cormac, 'Tomorrow morning we're going to confront Cahill about my father's calf.'

As Seanie and Cormac drove into Cahill's farmyard, the cobbled stones caused the van to shake and shudder. A row of stables with red half-doors looked forlorn. Not a single horse's head poked out. An old style loft, with a door high on the gable side, contained bales of straw. Farm machinery and a tractor were under cover inside a barn. The barn's blue roof gave an indication of the farm owner's religious persuasion. Where the yard ended, a grey two-storeyed dwelling house with huge bay windows and a front portico could be seen. Hydrangea in the front garden reminded Seanie that his granny used to call them Protestant flowers; maybe because they were blue. The cobbled stones, the stables and the house all hinted at a minor class of gentry. Fifty years ago, this yard would have been a hive of activity with ploughmen, yardmen, milkmaids, huge horses clinking their harness, and the smell of fresh dung in the air.

Cahill emerged from the barn's shadows with a pitchfork across his shoulder. He was a well-built man of around forty.

'We have come about a very delicate matter,' said Seanie.

'State your very delicate matter,' said Cahill.

'My father has had a calf stolen. Can we inspect yours?'

'Why would you want to inspect *my* calves?'

'Can we see them?'

'What is there to see?' said Cahill. 'My animals look no different than anyone else's.'

'Let's not play games,' said Seanie. 'You know very well why we want to look at them. My father puts a special mark on his stock. If it is not on any of the calves in those houses we will apologize and leave you in peace.'

Cahill jammed the fork into the ground in front of him. 'You're *not* seeing my calves.'

'Donal Cahill,' said Seanie. 'I am accusing you of stealing my father's calf.'

Cahill pulled the fork from the ground and gripped it with both hands across his body. 'Get off my property.'

Seanie made a move towards the outhouses but was blocked by the farmer, who jabbed the fork at him in a threatening manner. Cormac jumped between them. 'This is getting us nowhere,' he said.

After a stand-off lasting several seconds, Cahill said, 'Do you want to know what really happened?'

'I know what happened,' said Seanie. 'You stole my father's calf.'

'There are two sides to every story,' said Cahill.

'The main side is, you're a thief.'

Cormac, still standing between the two men, intervened. 'Wait a minute, Seanie. Let's listen to what he has to say.'

'All right,' said Seanie, glad of any respite. 'Say what you have to, but it won't change the facts.'

'About a year ago,' said Cahill, 'I got the better of Lazy McGuire in a pub brawl. Ever since, he has been bad-mouthing me. Then certain people decided to shoot me. When I escaped they shot the cow. Do you know what it's like to live in fear of being shot? Plus, I cannot afford to lose a milk cow.'

'My father didn't threaten to shoot you, and neither did he shoot the cow,' said Seanie.

'The people who did the shooting have nothing. To make up my loss, I took the calves from those who are indirectly responsible.'

'How is my father indirectly responsible?' asked Seanie.

'You're all from the same litter.'

Neither Seanie nor Cormac answered. Cahill continued, 'My father and his father before him have been on this land for generations. The soil of these fields is soaked with their sweat. Now upstarts who have never worked a day in their lives think they can do what they like because they have guns. They will not get away with it. I'll get my own back whatever way I can.'

Nobody spoke, then Cormac said, 'Where does the shooting of Screwy Bennett fit into all this?'

'I know nothing about Screwy Bennett. Ask Big Frank why he is trying to put the blame for the antics of his younger brother onto simple-minded people like Screwy.'

Seanie didn't know what to do. He squatted down on his hunkers and lifted a clump of straw lying at his feet. The rich gold stalks felt warm and crinkly in his hands. He began fashioning them into an old-fashioned tie band the way his father had taught him. There was silence in the yard. A flock of crows flew overhead. Seanie concentrated on working the straw. After a minute or two, the stillness was interrupted by the braying of a donkey in one of the stables. Seanie stood up and stared at his antagonist. Suddenly, he tossed the straw rope to the ground and said, 'You're wrong about us all being from the one litter.'

Then he turned abruptly towards the van and said, 'OK, let's go.'

The two men walked away. Cahill was left standing in the yard.

'Wow,' said Cormac as he drove out of the gate. 'What did you make of that?'

'I don't know,' said Seanie after a long pause.

'He has a point.'

'Maybe he has.'

'I think it's better to say nothing to anyone and let the entire affair drop,' said Cormac.

'I suppose so,' mumbled Seanie.

Cormac glanced over at him. 'You're not with me.'

'I am. I'm listening to you.'

'He's certainly big into the whole father thing,' said Cormac.

Seanie looked out at the hedgerows speeding by. Cahill was mistaken. Seanie O'Rourke was his own man.

4

Seanie lay naked on the bed face down. 'You'll be the death of me,' he moaned into the pillow.

'Hardly likely,' said Eileen, resting on her elbow and rubbing her nails gently up and down his spine.

The cream-coloured bedclothes were all in a heap. Outside, the dawn chorus had finished. Only a wood pigeon in a clump of trees cooed to its mate.

Eileen stopped the massage and lay across Seanie's back with her cheek resting on his shoulder. Neither of them spoke for a little while. Then Eileen jumped out of the bed, ran naked to the window and pulled back the curtains. Legs apart and standing on tiptoe, she stretched her arms out high and wide to soak in the sun flooding the room.

Seanie was aware that she realized he could see her in the mirror. Her long black hair hung loose down her back. Her eyes were black also. 'Ebony eyes,' he called her, after the hit song of the same name. She stood with her mouth wide open as if to let the sunlight fill her inside. My God, she is so beautiful, thought Seanie.

After a couple of minutes of displaying herself to the bracken-covered hills, Eileen wriggled back into his arms again.

'You shouldn't be running around bare like a brazen hussy,' said Seanie.

'I'm allowed to wear no clothes on my honeymoon.'

'Are you still on your honeymoon? We're married a month.'

'I'm going to be on it for years,' said Eileen, nuzzling his cheek.

The couple hugged each other and were still. At such times, when there was no need to rise early, Seanie sometimes remembered the strategies his father employed to get him out of bed. He would tell him to think of the poor lads compelled to jump out of their beds in the middle of the night when the RUC came raiding. They had to pull on their clothes and escape through the window for fear of being caught, he would say, and go on to describe how the fugitives might have to spend the night living out on the mountain, cold and wet. Seanie turned on his back, and with his left arm under his wife's neck, he gazed at the ceiling. These days it was the British Army that came calling. They rarely gave their quarry any chance of escape, and hiding out on the mountains was a thing of the past – helicopters had put an end to that. Anyway, the Brits largely left him in peace. He gave them no reason to do otherwise.

Eileen gave him a little shake. 'You're away from me again, Seanie. What are you thinking about?'

'Nothing much. My father has asked me to meet someone this afternoon.'

'Who is it?'

'He didn't say. You know he used to make me swallow two raw eggs before my breakfast every morning.'

'Who did?'

'My father.'

'Yuk, were they awful?'

'He had plans for me,' said Seanie.

'What plans?'

Her husband didn't reply. There was a long pause.

'Love me again, darling,' murmured Eileen.

Seanie could see his father pottering in the vegetable patch as he drove into the yard at his parents' house. The garden was Paddy's pride and joy, even if he was in constant battle with the slugs. Sometimes Seanie wondered whether the slugs or the British Army was number one on his father's hate list. Seanie got out of the van and made his way over to watch him sprinkle water over some fragile lettuce seedlings.

'They don't look too healthy,' said Seanie, knowing his father would take it as a personal failure if any of them died; not that too much didn't take in this plot. All kinds of vegetables, from beanstalks to beetroot to cucumbers, were beginning to sprout. The largest area of the garden was planted with seed potatoes.

Potatoes had been the cause of Ireland's population explosion, and because their failure resulted in the famine, his father looked upon the tuber as something to be both feared and revered. 'The potato gave life and it took away life,' he would say.

As he was getting off his knees, the older man said, 'The lettuce will be OK. Every living thing strives to live. They deserve a chance.'

'I was stopped on the way over by the Paras,' said Seanie.

'They're everywhere, the bastards,' replied his father. 'They should all be shot.'

'They were asking about you.'

'What were they on about?'

'They wanted to know if you are a loyal British subject.'

'Don't let them rile you, son. They shot poor Owenie John

A Fight For Freedom

through the head for target practice.'

'Who is this guy that wants to see me?'

'I don't know.'

'You must know something?'

'All I can say is that I was told to ask you to be here.'

'I'm going in to see mum,' said Seanie.

Seanie entered the house and was struck by the familiar smell of home. 'You're baking,' he shouted to his mother, even before he reached the big open kitchen. A dark brown table big enough for ten people took up the centre of the room. Green wallpaper depicting horses and hounds matched the curtains that dropped to the level of the sill on both windows. One wall had family photos on it. Another carried a picture of the Sacred Heart beside a photo of President Kennedy.

Seanie's mother said, 'That's a beautiful morning. What are you at today?'

'This and that.'

'What's this and that?'

Seanie laughed. 'It's this and that.'

'Seanie O'Rourke, getting information from you is like trying to get eggs from a rooster hen.'

Seanie kissed his mother on the cheek. 'You're a nosey parker. I was over at McIver's asking him if he would give Alice Bennett a part-time job.'

'Aw, the poor craythur. Do you remember the time she gave you the blue duck egg and you wanted to know if the inside of the duck was blue?'

'You make up those stories, mum.'

'What did McIver say?'

'You know McIver, one foot on each side of the ditch.'

'I know, and his mind on the till.'

'He was dubious at the start, and went on about Ratigan not being happy.'

'And?'

'I said it would demonstrate that his pub served the whole community and not just one section of it, and that Ratigan wasn't popular anyway.'

'Popular! He's as popular as the Bore Gallighan at a wake.'

'McIver said he would give her a try. When I told Alice she was delighted.'

'It'll do her the world of good.'

'She was wondering if Ratigan came into the bar much. She detests him.'

'Why wouldn't she? Everyone else does.'

'She has more than that to dislike him for, if she only knew.'

'Well, I don't want to know about it if she has. Sit you down and I'll make some tea and a nice piece of fresh bread and butter.'

Seanie's mum was very proud of her baking. It was her opinion that today's wives didn't bake enough for their husbands and families. 'Oh, Seanie only likes his mummy's homemade bread,' Eileen always answered when his mother would enquire if she had done any baking.

Seanie told his mother about the British soldiers mentioning his dad's name. She said she had lived with that type of thing since she first met his father. He'd been involved all his life, and each time there was a flare up, he'd be first in line for attention. 'They know his dream is a United Ireland,' said his mum.

'Dad's dream can cause a lot of trouble,' said Seanie.

'If you don't have a dream, what's the use of living?'

'Do you have a dream, mum?'

'My dream is that I have lots of little grandchildren running around my feet.'

Amidst a blast of heat and the smell of baking, Seanie's mum lifted out a tray of bread. After setting it on the worktop, she turned to Seanie. He was her only son and even now after twenty six years, every time she looked at him she remembered her joy on the day he was born. He had her dark brown eyes and sallow skin. People joked she possessed a shipwrecked Spanish sailor's gene. They were always remarking how much Seanie looked like her. She knew everyone said he was very intelligent and she would boast he took that from her as well. She also knew he adored her, maybe even more than his father, but perhaps that was understandable.

'What's your dream, son?' she asked.

Seanie couldn't think of an answer.

A battered old jeep with two men in it drove into the yard. Seanie recognized Ratigan as the driver. He stayed in the vehicle while the passenger, Seamus Galvin, an American with supposedly Irish connections, got out. He had a burly physique, short hair cut in the army style, a bullet-like head and very little neck. People said he had been a Green Beret in Vietnam, but his appearance didn't fit in with how movies portrayed such people. His name had come up in McIver's just the previous night. In a confidential tone, Slash McMahon told the others that Galvin could jump out of an aeroplane without a parachute, was trained to withstand torture, and could kill a man with his little finger. Ball Malone said he wished they had him playing fullback.

The American's surly expression turned friendly as he walked towards Seanie and his father. His countenance wasn't improved by a livid scar under one eye. He greeted them both and then shook Seanie's hand, saying in a Texas accent, 'I'm pleased to meet you.'

'Had you any problem at the roadblock?' asked Seanie's father.

'A surveillance team kept watch. We got word as soon as it had been lifted,' Galvin said.

Seanie wondered who was doing the surveillance.

'Is there anywhere we can talk?' asked Galvin.

'In the haggard, follow me,' said Seanie's father.

Paddy O'Rourke loved the haggard. On a nice day he could sometimes be found in it sitting on the ditch relaxing. The entire ritual of threshing and the notion of the haggard had a special resonance for country folk.

'Would you believe, we were exporting foodstuff at the height of the famine?' he said. 'Do you know that Trevelyan's policy involved letting people starve so as to teach them a lesson?'

'I'm familiar with the history,' said Galvin. 'The reason I'm here today is to help in the struggle to create a different history.'

'God give you strength,' said Paddy. Seanie said nothing.

The former soldier stood still in the centre of the paddock and ranged his gaze out over the surrounding hillsides shimmering in the afternoon sun. For a minute or two only the humming of a lone bee flitting from flower to flower broke the stillness.

'Walk with me,' said Galvin, giving Seanie's father a nod that told him they wanted to be alone. As they strolled he said to Seanie, 'Why have we lost over there?'

Seanie said nothing, not knowing if he was addressing him or not. Galvin turned around to face him and said again,

'Why have we lost?'

'Vietnam?'

'Yeah, Vietnam.'

'I don't really know much about it,' said Seanie, bending down to pick up little stones from the side of the ditch and flinging them at a whin bush in the next field.

'What do you think?' said Galvin.

'Maybe people at home in the States had enough.'

'Have you heard of the Ho Chi Minh trail?'

'A little bit.'

For a couple of seconds Galvin appeared lost in thought.

'It has to be some operation, going by the newspapers,' said Seanie.

'I'll tell you what it is,' said Galvin. 'It's a myth that almost on its own is beating the most powerful army the world has ever known.'

'You're ahead of me,' said Seanie. He plucked a green shoot from a clump of rushes to chew on. 'I thought it was real.'

'The Ho Chi Minh trail,' said Galvin, 'is a Viet Cong supply line from North Vietnam to the South. We've dropped thousands of bombs on it, so it's real enough, only now it has taken on the power of legend.'

'Oh yeah?' said Seanie.

'Legends win wars.'

'I don't know what you're talking about.'

'Kathleen Ní Houlihan is a fucking legend.'

'So what?'

'People are still prepared to die in her name.'

'I haven't a clue what you're on about, and I don't know what any of this has got to do with me.'

'The Ho Chi Minh trail is, at bottom, a gunrunning

operation. I want to run guns into Ireland and I want you to help me.'

'You're talking to the wrong person,' said Seanie, starting to move off.

'We might create a myth. You could become famous.'

'I'm sorry. I want nothing to do with it.'

'Aren't you a smuggler?'

'What I do and what you're talking about are totally different. They've nothing in common.'

'Both are getting materials from one country to another without the authorities being aware of it. What's the difference?'

'What I shift does not result in people dying.'

'We're not responsible for what people do with the goods.'

Just then a big brown frog jumped out of the grass. It was followed by several more. Seanie wasn't surprised to see them. This area always had colonies of frogs because their breeding grounds weren't far away. These consisted of water dams that had been dug out in order to ret flax, before sending it to the scutch mill. Seanie had taken jam jars full of frogspawn into class at school. The pupils' entire experiments in nature study consisted of watching the tadpoles emerge.

In the haggard a hugely swollen frog, obviously full of spawn, landed just in front of the former soldier. Quick as a flash, Galvin stomped down on it and squashed the creature into a mush of sticky slime. Then, after pausing for a moment to clean the sides of his shoe in the grass, he said, 'Let me explain something to you, Seanie. The IRA is an amateur army up against a world power. While they don't have much hope of winning, without people like me they have even less chance. Hand grenades are just one type of ordnance I can easily access. Those babes would be a powerful weapon in the

Republicans' armoury.'

Seanie, his mouth hanging open, had stopped chewing the rush. He stared at the little puddle of goo at the man's feet for a few moments. 'Listen,' he said. 'I'm not your man. All I do is a wee bit of excise duty avoidance, and all I'm interested in is a wee bit of profit.'

'When we get this thing going, there'll be profit enough for everyone.'

'Why do you need me?' asked Seanie.

'You know the country and you've lots of experience in this business.'

'You're just a mercenary.'

Seanie was about to leave when he saw Frank Ratigan come towards them. He called out cheerfully that if every day was like this, they wouldn't need package holidays to Spain. Galvin agreed with him that Ireland was a beautiful country.

Ratigan then addressed Seanie. He admitted the two of them had some little disagreements, but he said that shouldn't interfere with the bigger picture. Seanie said it wasn't nice being threatened on the road at night. Ratigan told Seanie he was never in any danger. Galvin asked Seanie to shake hands and get on with what was really important. Seanie said he would shake hands, but that didn't mean he agreed with Ratigan's notion of the bigger picture.

'Seanie is reluctant to get involved,' said Galvin.

'Seanie boy,' said Ratigan, 'when I was growing up, your father was one of my greatest heroes. We all knew he was a comrade of Tom Williams.'

Seanie doubted this. The Ratigans weren't known to be an especially Republican family. 'Tom Williams may have become one of those legends you were on about earlier,' Seanie said to Galvin.

'Your father is a living legend,' said Ratigan.

'My father has strong beliefs.'

'You don't get a gooseberry growing on a strawberry bush.'

'That doesn't mean my beliefs are the same as my father's,' said Seanie.

'There's no need to decide anything just now, Seanie,' said Galvin. 'At the end of the day we all want the same thing.'

Seanie said nothing. Then Ratigan said, 'I agree, and if there's a few pounds to be made at the same time, then what's the harm?'

'Where does Stone fit into all this?' asked Seanie.

Ratigan lifted a paling post off the ditch. He held it at arm's length and twirled himself around like a hammer thrower before letting go. The timber stake soared in a high arc far into the next field. 'Fuck Stone,' said the Provo.

Just at that moment, another frog sprang out of the undergrowth. Seanie turned around quickly to leave. 'I have to pick up Eileen,' he said.

Ratigan and Galvin were still talking as Seanie left. On his way out of the haggard he stopped to speak to his father. 'Where did the IRA come across that crazy guy?'

'He has lots of contacts,' said the old man.

'He's a nutter.'

'We can't always choose who we might want to help in the struggle.'

'Ratigan,' said Seanie, 'and that head-the-ball. God Almighty!'

5

The football meeting had been scheduled for the club room, which was just a fancy name for a barrel-shaped corrugated shed. The heating system in its draughty interior consisted of one old Superser gas fire. Forms were set in rows up the centre of the wooden floor. The chairman, a middle-aged man, hadn't been a great footballer himself, but dedicated much of his life to the club. He sat between the secretary and treasurer on decking chairs behind a kitchen table. This year's incumbent as secretary was a youngish guy and still a member of the team. Being fluent in the native language meant his duties included transcribing a list of the team in Irish and presenting it to the referee before the start of each game. The winning team could have the result of a match overturned if they had not properly observed this rule. The treasurer worked in a bank. He even smelled like a bank, according to Cormac. When Seanie asked him what a bank smelled like, Cormac replied, 'Like money.'

Cigarette smoke filled the air. Tin ashtrays advertising Harp Lager, once blue in colour, but now burned black by cigarette butts, were scattered about. Because this was such an important meeting, practically all the club members were in attendance. There were no women present. Besides attending matches and being involved in fund-raising, their role in the club's affairs consisted mainly of catering at social events and washing the team's jerseys.

The chairman called the meeting to order. He said they were there to decide whether to play the final and get badly beaten, or not play the match and thus give the Brits the satisfaction of being able to stop it. He was clearly trying to contain his anger. 'It's been forty years,' he said, 'since we reached a final, and now the British Army are trying to spoil our chances by arresting half our team. Because they have taken so many losses in this area, it would give them satisfaction for Kilshean to beat us. Plus they're convinced the club is a cover for an IRA unit.'

Oul' John Wilson, sitting beside Big Frank Ratigan, was on his feet in a flash. 'What damn right have they to be here at all?'

'Interference by the English in our Gaelic games is nothing new,' said Ratigan. 'Didn't the Statutes of Kilkenny from the fourteenth century have a decree that forbade non-Irish from attending hurling matches.'

'It's ironic,' said Seanie. 'There isn't any difference in that and our rule twenty-seven.'

'Rule twenty-seven, banning our members from attending foreign sports, was a legitimate regulation,' said the chairman.

'We weren't the first to impose bans,' added Wilson.

'It's important to put things into perspective,' said Seanie.

Wilson was becoming annoyed. 'Our past is littered with injustice,' he said.

'I'm just trying to keep the record straight.'

Somebody asked, 'Is this a football meeting or a history lesson?'

But Wilson was on his feet again, almost shouting. 'You have a nerve,' he said to Seanie, shaking his walking stick in anger. 'Why are you defending the bastards?'

'I'm not defending them.'

'It's lucky we have people present who are prepared to do something about it rather than lie down under them,' said Wilson.

'I lie down under no one,' said Seanie.

'Order,' demanded the chairman. 'Dickie Stone, you're keeping very quiet?'

The IRA boss stood up. 'Nobody has done more for the national cause than John.' Before Stone could say anything more, a voice at the back of room interrupted him.

'May I suggest something?'

Like a flock of birds in flight, the entire congregation turned their heads in unison to gaze at the speaker.

'Mr Galvin, I assume. You're very welcome to our meeting,' said the chairman.

'Winning comes from the will to win,' said Galvin. 'If I obtain cooperation, I am prepared to get the team into a frame of mind that will give them a fighting chance.'

'You can't score points with your mind,' said Mousey Reilly, half standing up. 'You have to be able to kick the ball.'

'If your mind isn't right, the kick won't be right,' said Galvin.

Mousey didn't answer, but after plopping down again he whispered to Slash, 'Some of our guys don't have a mind.'

A buzz of excitement filled the room. The chairman asked, 'Do we not have too little time?'

'I will instil in the players a belief in themselves,' said Galvin. 'But on one condition: that Seanie agrees to be my second in command.'

Seanie jumped to his feet. 'I'm sorry,' he said. 'There's plenty of people here better equipped than me.'

Seanie knew Galvin just wanted to get him under his wing.

Galvin said, 'If Seanie won't make the effort, I cannot get involved.'

'Would you reconsider?' the chairman asked Seanie.

'No, I'm sorry.'

Ratigan stood up. 'For the sake of the club, I propose everyone here get on their feet and unanimously endorse Seanie as Mr Galvin's assistant.'

For a few moments no one moved, then the chairman stood up. Almost the entire room followed. Ratigan began to clap and chant, 'Seanie for assistant! Seanie for assistant!' In seconds, everyone was reciting the slogan, and Seanie knew he couldn't refuse. In the general melee it went unnoticed that Dickie Stone wasn't on his feet clamouring like the rest.

Galvin told Seanie that the training sojourn would be for a long weekend, but said nothing about the location. The coach driver only knew where he was going on the morning of the trip. There were rumours of Mosney holiday camp being the destination. The players were looking forward to a few days' holidays in salubrious surroundings. However, as the coach crossed the border going south, the excitement among the passengers changed to anxiety when it took an unexpected turn towards the mountains. Seanie's companion said, 'We're taking the scenic route.'

The landscape did look scenic, but in a barren, isolated way, which made the increasingly nervous passengers ever more apprehensive. Finally, the coach stopped in a clearing between the hills. Galvin stood there on a little rock, dressed in shorts and singlet.

Everyone filed off the coach, and Galvin had them form a line along the lonely mountain pass. Walking up and down the row of men, he barked at them that on this outing there would be no shelter from the weather; sleep would be in the open. If they wanted to eat they would have to catch and kill their food. While all were aghast at this scenario, such was Galvin's personality that it looked as if no one would raise any questions. However, once Galvin had passed him, Gary Mulligan, who always found it difficult to stay quiet, whispered to the man next in line, 'He can't be serious?'

Galvin whipped around in a flash saying, 'Who said that?'

Instinctively, the line-up straightened and each man stared directly ahead.

Mulligan spluttered, 'I did.'

Galvin came back to him with a big smile on his face. He stuck out his hand saying, 'Well done, shake hands.'

Mulligan took the proffered hand. One second later he was down on one knee howling with pain as Galvin squeezed his fingers unmercifully.

'You asked me if I'm serious,' he said, speaking into Mulligan's face. 'Do you think I'm serious now?' Mulligan said he believed him. Galvin paused for a second before releasing his grip. No one else spoke. Seanie felt a shiver up his spine that had nothing to do with the cold wind funnelling through the valley. The former Green Beret walked along the line and roared into the face of each man in turn. 'Do you want to win?'

'I want to win,' was the reply.

'Louder,' he yelled.

'I want to win.'

'Louder!'

'I want to win!'

Eventually, when satisfied with the response, Galvin gave the bus driver the nod to start the engine. 'Now go or stay,' he shouted at the line-up.

They all wanted to go home, but none could be the first to say it.

During the training, each member of the party had their own worst hardships. For some, it was sleeping out in the cold. For others, lack of normal food created problems. The starving men managed to buy or steal some hens and eggs from isolated farmsteads, and at other times they caught strange-looking fish in a lake. For many, the endless running up and down rocky hills inflicted the worst torment. As they ran, they chanted a mantra composed by Galvin. One half of the pack would say one line, and the other half would repeat it. It became embedded in their brains.

We are the meanest football team,
We are the meanest football team,
We hate the sissies from Kilshean,
We hate the sissies from Kilshean,
Cause we love to hear them roar,
Cause we love to hear them roar,
We'll kick their balls until they're sore,
We'll kick their balls until they're sore.

Galvin taught them various ways of slowing down their marker. He pointed out that the testicles were vulnerable and should be seen as a prime target of attack. One's elbow could be used like a spear. A knee in the thigh on exactly the right spot would cause a dead leg. Seanie wondered if Galvin realized this was a football match and not hand-to-hand combat. However, by the end of their time, the fact that they had endured did give the bunch of players a belief in themselves that they previously didn't know existed.

A tricolour fluttered in the breeze at the Athletic Grounds in Armagh city. GAA pitches were among the very few areas where the national emblem might be tolerated.

Galvin appeared in the dressing room just as the team was about to take the field. Under a long white coat he wore shorts and a team jersey. His appearance caused a ripple of confidence to pass through the players.

'We're going for a jog,' he told them.

Kilshean were already on the pitch. Ballyduff were led out by Galvin. 'OK,' he ordered. 'You know the drill. I want it heard in the next townland.' He started them off. '*We are the meanest football team.*'

Bellowing out their training rhyme, Ballyduff jogged around the area where the Kilshean players had congregated. The referee knew of no regulation which forbade this type of thing. When the game started, Ballyduff's psychological attack obviously had the desired effect, because within a short time they were leading by three points to no score. Then Kilshean settled down and fought back. At half-time the teams were level. During the break Galvin subjected his charges to a verbal onslaught that seemed to inspire them for the first few minutes of the second half. But as before, Kilshean soon began to look the stronger side. At one point, Seanie noticed Galvin in animated discussion with the selectors, and shortly afterwards Ballyduff substituted one of their midfielders with Big Barry O'Donnell. O'Donnell wasn't much of a footballer, but Galvin had taken a liking to him during the training weekend, and chose him to demonstrate ways of disabling an opponent. Soon after Big Barry entered the fray, Kilshean lost their key player due to a leg injury. Then Ballyduff had another stroke of luck when the referee ordered one of the Kilshean men off following a melee of players squaring up to each other. Neutrals would probably say he got it wrong. Five minutes later, a second Kilshean player was sent to the line.

With their opponents two men short and a star player injured, Ballyduff were doing well. Yet with seconds remaining, they were still behind by two points. The ref gave them a free. The ball landed near the Kilshean goalmouth. Again the referee blew the whistle, and without any hesitation pointed to the penalty spot. Despite fierce objections from the Kilshean side, he stuck to his decision. Seanie closed his eyes while the kick was being taken. When he opened them, the ball lay in the back of the net and the ref was blowing the final whistle.

The celebrations in McIver's lasted well into the night. Galvin wasn't there. He hadn't come into the dressing room after the match. Amid much discussion about the referee's decision to award a penalty, the cup got filled several times. Slash made a speech. He congratulated the team and said they were almost as good as the team that he played for.

Mousey whispered to Wee Pat, 'Slash was only a sub, and the team won one match in three years.'

Ratigan told Seanie he owed a debt to Galvin. 'You know the old story of there being no free lunches.'

'The team as a whole, not me personally, owes Galvin a debt,' said Seanie.

'Seanie lad,' said Ratigan, 'do you think Galvin has any interest in Ballyduff winning the championship? You owe him.'

After getting home, Seanie and Eileen were preparing to go to bed when a furious banging on the door occurred. Seanie went to investigate. On opening the door, he had it shoved in his face. Several soldiers with blackened faces and guns pointing barged into the house. They frogmarched Seanie into the sitting room, where he and Eileen were ordered to sit down.

Army personnel began rummaging through the rooms. A sergeant said that they were investigating a report that there were terrorists in the house, and began questioning Seanie.

'Ballyduff won the match today,' he said.

'Yes,' said Seanie.

'Are you all members of the IRA?'

'I'm not a member.'

'Your father is an IRA godfather.'

'My father is not a well man.'

'He's fucking well enough to know everything that's going on.'

'He has high blood pressure among other things. You should leave him alone.'

'How many on the team are in the IRA?'

'Why don't you ask them?'

'You're a smart aleck. We can take you with us and you may be more cooperative in the barracks,' said the soldier.

Seanie didn't reply.

'It's said you cheated a penalty,' the soldier said next.

'Referees make the decisions.'

'Was Ratigan there tonight?'

'I think most members of the club were there.'

'What about Galvin?'

'I know nothing about Galvin, only that he gave us some training,' said Seanie.

His questioner obviously knew all about the match and the American's role in their win. Someone was feeding them information.

The partying lasted the best part of a week. Slash didn't sober up for days. One night in McIver's he stumbled over to Seanie and Cormac. He had an empty glass in his hand that he hoped would be noticed. 'Kilshean are taking their defeat very badly,' he said.

'I believe so,' replied Seanie.

'Have you heard the latest yarn?'

'No.'

'They're saying that on the night before the match, somebody went to the referee's house and gave him a parcel. It was supposed to have contained a hand grenade with a note stating Ballyduff had better win. Did you ever hear the likes of it?'

6

Eileen and Seanie were sitting at the table having breakfast. The walls were coloured sunshine yellow. A calendar hanging over the range cooker advertised a local animal feed store. The papal blessing certificate, bestowed on the couple by Pope Paul VI on their wedding day, hung on another wall beside three delft geese, wings spread in full flight. The geese had been a present from Seanie's father. Eileen liked the ornaments and didn't attach any other significance to them. But the symbolism wasn't lost on Seanie. 'Ancient Ireland was lost forever with the Flight of the Earls, the first of the Wild Geese,' he often heard his father lament.

Cormac's car pulled up in the driveway. As he came in the door, Eileen said affectionately, 'Good morning my best man.' Then with concern in her voice, she said, 'What's the matter? You look shook.'

Cormac pulled a chair out and sat down. 'I got stopped by the Brits.'

'What happened?' said Seanie through a mouthful of toast.

'We had an argument,' said Cormac.

Eileen asked him if he'd like a fry, but he said tea and brown bread would be fine.

'We don't want to be drawing attention to ourselves,' said Seanie.

'They were hassling me, and I told them to go back to

their own country, and they said they were in their own country.'

'Will you never learn?'

'There was a tricolour attached to a telegraph pole beside the roadblock.'

'And you told them, that's not the Union Jack, that's the flag of the Irish Republic,' said Seanie.

'I dared them to try and remove it.'

'And they wouldn't go near it for fear of it being booby trapped.'

'Yeah,' said Cormac.

Seanie shook his head in resignation.

'You sure you don't want something more, maybe a small fry?' said Eileen.

'No, this is fine. Anyway what's the situation?'

Seanie told Cormac that the run had to be done that night. An order for fifty cases of spirits brought out the competition, so they needed to be there first. The usual tactics were probably best. If they encountered a customs patrol car it was essential to keep it behind them as far as Minnie's Meadow. This would give them a chance to make the outskirts of town, and once there they could be under cover anywhere. Cormac asked Seanie if they would take the hen gun. Seanie said, 'Yes, just in case it's needed.'

Seanie called into McIver to tell him about the run. The publican could provide an alibi if he encountered a British Army checkpoint on the Northern side of the border. The British security forces might not be too concerned about him smuggling goods into the South, but the less they knew the better. If stopped, he could say the spirits had been purchased in Belfast and were being delivered to McIver.

Almost before Seanie got through the door, Slash asked him what he was having. Seanie said he would have a Black Label and that he would buy the round. Alice was behind the bar. She was proving to be a popular bar maid. Slash said her countenance was like a spring morning after a long winter. Mousey told him that at his age he should be saying the rosary and praying for a happy death, instead of chatting up the widow like something out of that Shakespeare fella.

Alice told Seanie that Screwy's leg was recovering nicely. The regulars sat around the bar while the smell of turf from the open fire created a homely atmosphere. Wee Pat, needing intellectual stimulation, asked Seanie if there wasn't a moral ambiguity to his profession.

Slash almost choked on his pint. 'What is a moral ambiguity?' he spluttered. Maybe a new sin, he decided. He went on to explain that a priest, home from the missions, recently preached about it being a sin not to pay tax, and who ever heard of such a thing? Everyone knew it was a sin to be doing things with a woman, but a sin not to pay tax was a new one on him. Then Mousey said, 'It's not a sin to be doing things with a woman if you're married to her,' but Slash argued that was different.

Seanie told them he was just a businessman. He bought goods at one price and sold them at another. But Wee Pat maintained that dealing in two separate states made a difference. Mousey said that a few miles up the road a man could stand in one country and pee into a different country, and if someone said Finn Mac Cool could do that, they would say it was just another legend.

'What does it matter how far Finn Mac Cool could pee?' asked Slash.

Wee Pat said that many countries in Europe have a similar

type of border. However, Mousey suggested he go back a hundred years and say to people that Ireland is two different countries. 'They would think you were mad.'

Wee Pat countered this argument by saying that prior to England uniting the whole island and making it one administrative unit, Ireland had been divided up.

Mousey insisted it was still all one country, and that there had been no effective administration for people such as themselves who were outside the Pale.

'We're off the subject,' said Wee Pat. 'You never answered the question, Seanie. Is smuggling wrong?'

'Smuggling,' said Seanie, 'is certainly not a sin. Did you know my old Uncle Mick?'

'Ah, a decent and religious man,' said Slash, blessing himself by tapping two fingers in the air midway between his forehead and chest. 'He very seldom got caught. May he rest in peace.'

'He told me, sitting on his knee,' continued Seanie, 'that the pope in Rome himself passed a law allowing people to swear a lie in court if it related to smuggling.'

'Well, that's that then,' said Slash. 'The pope can never be wrong and he knows everything.'

'The pope can never be wrong,' said Wee Pat, 'but he doesn't know everything.'

'If he's never wrong,' said Slash, 'then he must know everything.'

Before he left, Seanie ordered another round of drinks for everyone. Slash shook his hand and told him he was a credit to his parents and to his country. As he was leaving, Seanie heard Slash ask about the Pale. He wanted to know if he was outside it or inside it.

*

On one side of Richie Gilson's farmyard there were four large wooden sheds containing thousands of hens. 'Hiya, Seanie,' Gilson said. 'You must be making a fortune?'

'You might be up one week,' said Seanie, 'and down the next.'

'There's no guarantee with anything,' said Gilson.

'It's good of you to let me have the hens.'

'These are going to be culled anyway. Let's get them loaded.'

Seanie reversed up to one of the hen houses. He reached in behind the passenger's side and pulled a lever. From underneath the floor at the rear of the van, an empty compartment with the back number plate still attached to it slid open like a drawer. It wasn't an easy task getting the hens into it because of all the squawking and flapping of wings. Eventually however, there were about two dozen hens jammed together under the false floor. When Seanie was leaving, Gilson wished him good luck.

'Thanks,' Seanie said. 'In my game luck's important.'

He arrived at the out-farm where the spirits were stored under bales of hay in a shed. The twenty-five acre holding of rocky upland soil and some old outbuildings had been left to him by his Uncle Mick. For the last two years of his uncle's life, Seanie had looked after the old man. The house was cold and draughty, and the fire in the bedroom needed constant feeding. Light came from an assortment of Tilley lamps, hurricane lamps and candles. The bed was covered in old overcoats, which his uncle claimed provided better heat than blankets. Seanie enjoyed his company. Often, as he sat by his bedside, the terminally ill man would clasp his nephew with a quivering hand and tell him in hoarse voice, 'Always do your duty, son.'

Nowadays, Seanie wondered what that meant. His father's notion of duty involved either killing the enemy or being prepared to die for the cause. As a child growing up with romantic notions of heroism, he could accept that. But it was easy then, because the wrongs were all on the one side. It was easy because his school friends were not getting shot through the head for amusement. It was easy because people were not being swept up with yard brushes and shovelled into plastic bags. After his uncle died, Seanie regretted not having questioned him more about what he meant by 'duty'.

Seamus Galvin appeared in the hayshed doorway as Seanie arrived in the yard. The American shouted some kind of cheery greeting. When Seanie asked him about his business there, he said he'd heard things and knew there were cases of spirits hidden under the bales of hay. For a moment, Seanie wondered at this being public knowledge, and then it struck him that Ratigan would know about everything in the area.

Galvin said, 'Can I accompany you on the next smuggling run?'

Seanie refused, and enquired why he wanted to go. Galvin said he was anxious to see what tips he could pick up. He reminded Seanie of their meeting in the haggard and his proposal that they work together.

'I didn't make any commitment,' said Seanie.

Galvin then suggested he might be of help.

'Highly unlikely,' said Seanie.

'Cooperation in a partnership is important,' said Galvin.

Seanie informed him that he had a partner.

'There's no reason why Cormac can't get his share of the spoils also,' said Galvin.

'Where's Ratigan?'

'He takes care of other interests.'

'Get him to show you the ropes.'

Galvin stood silent for a few seconds and looked up at the sky as if deep in thought. 'Did it ever strike you, Seanie,' he said, 'that clouds are the same all over the world?'

Seanie didn't answer.

'It's impossible to tell what country you're in just by looking at a cloud. If it wasn't for the climate, I wouldn't know whether I was in Ireland, Texas, or the Nam.'

Seanie still said nothing. He thought to himself that this kind of talk didn't sound like the real Galvin.

'Let me show you something,' said Galvin.

'I haven't time for this.'

Galvin took out a wallet from his hip pocket. He withdrew a picture from it. The photo was of himself and another guy. Both were in uniform.

'He was my best buddy,' said Galvin. 'On one occasion he risked his own life for me.'

'Then he was certainly a great friend,' said Seanie.

'He's dead now.'

'I'm sorry. What happened to him?'

Galvin didn't answer for a moment. Then he said, 'I guess I could have saved him. I was involved in setting up an ambush.'

Seanie stared at Galvin. 'Why didn't you tell him?'

'We were involved in black-ops at the time, and he had some bullshit ethical qualms about our work.'

A flock of swans flew in perfect formation overhead, their whiteness almost dazzling against the blue sky. 'My God,' said Galvin. 'Did you ever see anything so beautiful?'

He watched them for a few seconds, and then said, 'Seanie, people who don't cooperate have to be persuaded one way or another.'

Everything was set to go. Denis Horan, who was driving the decoy van, had arranged bridging planks in Minnie's Meadow earlier that day. Seanie would drive the run van carrying the spirits and the hens. Galvin sat between Seanie and Cormac with a bag at his feet. He didn't say what it contained. Finally, Seanie said, 'OK Des, let's go. We'll give you ten minutes start.'

Ten minutes later, Seanie pulled out after Horan. Inside the van there was no talk.

A full moon lit up the hedges and fields. There would be very little other traffic. People stayed close to home because of the dangerous times. The smugglers were using routes not officially recognized as legitimate ways of going from one jurisdiction to another. A stranger would only know they had crossed the border by a change in the road's surface. The signposts were also different, but it would be foolish to rely on any of the directions they gave. The people who needed them would be strangers to the area. Not facilitating authorities of any kind was deeply ingrained in the local populace's psyche.

Although the shadow-filled countryside seemed empty of activity, Seanie knew this was not so. Undoubtedly, there were belligerents from the different sides involved in all kinds of undercover manoeuvres. His old Uncle Mick had died before the Troubles reached such a fever pitch. What would he say now about how his favourite nephew was doing his duty?

Thirty minutes into the South of Ireland and the radio on Cormac's knee began crackling. A thin, high-pitched sound emitted from it, and then an excited voice repeated over and over, 'Bait on the hook.'

'That's it,' said Cormac. 'We have to get out of the way fast. There's a laneway up ahead. Pull in there.'

Seanie drove into the laneway. In less than a minute, the two vehicles passed them. The decoy vehicle was about ten seconds in front of the customs car, heading back in the direction it had just come. A van with no number plates and soft tyres, which suggested it was weighed down with contraband, would be a nice catch for the revenue men.

After a little while Seanie started to breathe easier. The road ahead looked deserted and there wasn't far to go. Then as if from nowhere, a customs patrol car appeared in his wing mirror. 'Jesus Christ! Another one. How far is it to Minnie's?' he shouted at Cormac.

'Keep calm,' Cormac said. 'Fifteen minutes. You have to stay ahead of them.'

Seanie pressed hard on the accelerator. The chasing customs car nudged the van's rear several times. If it got in front, the driver could then block the road. A couple more miles of frantic driving and still they managed to keep their pursuers behind them. Galvin tipped Seanie on the elbow. 'Let me out,' he said. 'I'll stop them.'

Seanie pretended not to hear. This was no time to be humouring the American. Another mile and then Seanie nodded to Cormac. 'We're near Minnie's gate, be ready when I come to the next corner.'

Cormac got into the back of the speeding van. 'OK, tell me when.'

'Now,' cried Seanie.

Cormac pulled the lever, and the fowl that had been packed inside were suddenly released. Squawking and squealing they took off. In twos and threes a stream of screeching birds rained against the pursuing car's windscreen. An egg popped out of one in mid-air and smashed on the glass leaving a slimy yellow yolk trailing down. One hen hooked itself on the aerial, its wings flapping like a sheet in the wind. A fowl somehow got its leg trapped under the wipers and frantically pecked at the windscreen. Another bird managed to cling to one of the wing mirrors. Some remaining hens that had been cowering in the false floor also took off. They resembled a second wave of dive-bombers swooping in on the target. The driver slammed on the brakes.

Seanie meanwhile had rounded the corner, out of sight of his pursuers. He wheeled the van through an open gate into a field. A hundred yards into the meadow were two little white flags. They marked where Horan had laid two planks across a concealed swamp. Seanie hit the timbers with a thump, dead centre. Once across the makeshift bridge he and Cormac jumped from the van and picked up the planks.

The customs car swung into the field with feathers, egg yolk and hen shit stuck to the windscreen. A bird was perched on a wing mirror like a parrot on a pirate's shoulder. The men inside the car quickly formed the opinion that their quarry had stalled for some reason.

'They're trapped,' one of them shouted to the driver. 'We have them.'

He hardly finished the sentence when their vehicle hit the swamp. They were stuck wheel-deep in mud. From their vantage point on the other side, Seanie and Cormac could hardly contain their glee at the hapless excise officers scrambling from the car. The advantage of this field lay in the fact that there was another exit at the far side of the swamp leading out onto a byroad.

They drove for a few more minutes and then parked in a

laneway to organize themselves and tidy up their cargo. Seanie noticed Galvin looking somewhat bemused by the whole event, and asked him if he was all right.

'Where's my rucksack?' replied the American.

'Here you are,' said Cormac. 'What have you in there anyway?' He peered into the bag. After a moment he said, 'Jesus.'

'What is it?' said Seanie.

Cormac kneeled down by the roadside verge and gently turned the bag upside down. Three hand grenades rolled out onto the grass.

'I could have stopped those bastards pronto,' said Galvin. 'One of these little sweeties strategically placed would cause a crater in the road and you'd have no need for fucking hens.'

7

Every so often McIver ran a function in his pub centred on the customs and traditions of another country. Tonight's party was being promoted by the publican as an Italian Night. Possibly the only difference in this night and the previous American Night would be plates of spaghetti instead of hamburgers. McIver maintained the aim of his endeavours was to enhance his customers' understanding of other cultures. Most people believed it related more to the enhancement of his own bank balance.

Seanie browsed *Exchange and Mart* while waiting on Eileen to get ready. His attention was drawn to an advertisement for the sale of 1,000 toy donkeys by a factory in Spain. He knew what the donkeys were like as he often saw them in homes where someone had been on a package holiday. At fifty pence each the price seemed cheap, which could be explained by the much lower cost of living there.

Eileen entered the sitting room and sashayed in front of him. She was wearing a print yellow dress and red shoes. Around her neck she had a red bandana, and her hair was tied back in a ponytail with a matching ribbon.

'You look beautiful,' said Seanie. 'Like a butterfly emerging from a cocoon. Only it wouldn't take a butterfly as long to surface.'

Eileen struck a pose, feet apart on the floor. Her fists were up and head tilted back to one side. 'I float like a butterfly, but I sting like a bee.'

'It's a pity you weren't a guy and we could put you into the ring.'

'Would you like me to be a fella?'

'You might make some big money.'

'Do you never think of anything only money?'

'Sometimes,' said Seanie, but then he told her about his plan to buy the donkeys.

Eileen said, 'My father warned me you would eventually go flaky.'

'I have to go to Spain for them.'

'Spain! My God, why didn't I listen to him?'

'Wait till we see his face when I make a killing on them.'

'Would you really go to Spain, Seanie, and things so bad here?'

'What's happening here has nothing to do with me.'

On their way to McIver's, Seanie looked out at the familiar landscape. The whin bushes flamed the countryside in a blaze of colour. Long forgotten famine-era potato ridges on the hillsides lay hidden beneath a sea of dazzling yellow. Seanie knew his father had been prepared to lay down his life for these bare hills, swampy bogs and rushy fields. Earlier generations had imagined that a new republic, liberated from foreign domination, would be some kind of nirvana, but it hadn't worked out like that. Perhaps his father's goal of a United Ireland was a similar fantasy. However, Seanie long since realized that this struggle mirrored his own efforts to release himself from his parents' ambitions. Whereas his father allied himself with history, he sought to loose himself from it. His father wanted a free Ireland. He wanted to be free himself.

Eileen gave him a nudge. 'You're very quiet.'

'Patrick Kavanagh talks about hawthorn being April's ecstasy. The whins are surely May's ecstasy,' Seanie said.

'The Brits call this place Indian country. They think we're savages,' said Eileen. 'But it's they who are ignorant. When England mired itself in the Dark Ages, Ireland ruled the western world as a seat of learning.'

Seanie wondered if the long history of rebellion in this area had infiltrated the very landscape and bred itself into the inhabitants.

The hamlet of Ballyduff consisted of a row of houses on either side of the through road with a single pub and one mini-supermarket. Just now, an Irish tricolour attached to a telephone pole on what was called the main street fluttered in the breeze. The village also had a ladies hairdressing salon that only opened on Fridays and Saturdays, unless a big local wedding or some other important happening was in the offing. A badly corroded sign for a cobblers shop squeaked in the wind. No boots had been mended there for a long time. At the end of the street, the roof had caved in on an old smithy. Red paint that at one time protected the huge double doors had almost entirely peeled off leaving the bare timber exposed. A pile of rusting horseshoes, metal hoops and bits of iron covered in grass and weeds lay against the gable wall. From amongst the scrap, the horn of an old black anvil was like a finger pointed accusingly at a generation for whom it had lost its relevance. Close by stood the modern-day equivalent of a forge, with balers, hay turners and similar farm machinery parked outside. Perhaps the little community perched on the lee side of a range of hills was settled because of a nearby stream that wriggled its way worm-like towards a more substantial waterway. Now the British Army wouldn't dare cross the bridge that spanned it for fear of it being booby trapped.

The village street was packed with cars, a few Land Rovers and even a couple of tractors. Placing vehicles right up against the door of the premises was not unintended. Occasionally there were people in the bar sought by British security forces, and it gave them time to escape in the event of a raid. The way the cars were parked also hindered drive-by assaults by loyalist gangs, who could lob a bomb or fire a weapon from a moving vehicle.

A security volunteer greeted Seanie as he entered the premises. He had been lounging against a wall just inside the door of the pub. The wall was made of six-inch blocks built on their flat, and was intended to absorb the blast from a bomb. None of these precautions would be particularly noticed by a stranger. Nobody would point them out. This was a society with a long history of rebellion, and talk was instinctively guarded. Informers and those with a loose mouth paid a heavy price.

Seanie and Eileen entered McIver's back lounge. The walls were festooned with blue football jerseys, meant to represent the colours of the Italian national team. McIver had borrowed them from the neighbouring GAA club whose colours, by chance, were also blue. The yellow bunting hanging on the ceiling came courtesy of Mrs Cooney, who looked after the chapel. It had been used to decorate the outside of the building for a confirmation ceremony when the bishop came to the parish. McIver didn't know if the Vatican was part of Italy, but seeing as he had the streamers he thought they couldn't do any harm; and like the jerseys they weren't costing him anything. When Mousey saw them, he said, 'The Bishop's coming to the party.'

'Bishops don't drink,' said Slash.

'They do, and so does the pope.'

'They do not.'

'They drink the wine on the altar,' said Mousey.

'You must be a Paisleyite,' said Slash.

A single ceiling fan did little to dispel the cigarette smoke in the lounge. Couples danced to music played by a two-piece group on the stage. Unoccupied seats were scarce, but Seanie and Eileen found room beside Joey Shine and his sister, Sarah. Seanie ordered a vodka and white for Eileen and a bottle of beer for himself. They settled down, danced a few times and watched the comings and goings.

Ratigan was there with some mates. Every time Alice Bennett went past him, they made a point of ignoring each other.

A rumour spread that the menu would include 'lasagne'. Most people had never seen lasagne. Some had never heard of it. After a while the band called for singers. A commotion coming from Ratigan's table suggested people were encouraging him to perform. After protesting a little, he stood up and took a drink from his glass before marching almost military style to the bandstand. Now the centre of attention, he consulted briefly with the members of the band before launching into 'The Men Behind The Wire'.

When the song ended, everyone applauded loudly and shouts of, '*arís*,' and, 'more,' rang out. He obliged with a stirring rendition of 'The Broad Black Brimmer of the IRA'.

'I can tell by your expression you're not happy with the entertainment,' Joey said to Seanie.

Seanie had a soft spot for Joey, although he was known to be slightly odd. A rebel in a society where the only rebels were political, he was an outsider even to them. Being a free spirit, he didn't recognize normal meal times, or day and night. He ate only when hungry and went to bed only when tired. Sometimes he sported himself in strange outfits as a protest at being told what he could or couldn't wear. Tonight he wore a cowboy outfit complete with brown leather boots, fringed red shirt and a huge white hat. An unkempt brown beard covered all of his lower face.

'Rebel songs are dangerous,' said Seanie, scraping the label of the beer bottle with his thumb nail.

'How so?' asked Joey.

'"The Broad Black Brimmer" is advocating violence.'

'Did you ever listen to the words of the National Anthem?'

'It should be banned also.'

'Jesus!' said Joey. 'People say I'm strange.'

Eileen was listening in on the conversation. She knew that 'The Broad Black Brimmer' caused Seanie particular annoyance because it described a son's admiration for his patriot father. Seanie signalled for the barman. He said he wanted to go in to the back bar for a few minutes, and asked his group what they were having. Eileen had a vodka and white, Sarah had a vodka and red, and Joey had a 7UP. Joey said he never touched alcohol because it distorted reality.

The back bar was the original part of the building. It was separated from the big lounge by a wall with an opening in it so that a single barman could service both places. The cigarette smoke seemed even more dense than in the other room. Blackened roof beams attested to years of assault from nicotine and the open hearth fire. The regulars stayed in their own territory even during a function. Invariably, however, complaints were voiced that the noise coming from the lounge destroyed intelligent conversation.

Seanie greeted everyone in the back bar and said, 'What's the craic?'

'We thought the craic was out in the lounge with the freedom fighters getting youse all patriotic,' said Wee Pat.

'You have to be a non-native to be really patriotic,' said Mousey.

'What are you on about?' said Slash.

'I'm saying that non-Irish patriots are always more militant.'

'Mention one.'

'What about De Valera?'

'You can't count him,' said Slash. 'With a name like that he wasn't Irish to begin with.'

'He kept the Republic out of the war,' said Wee Pat.

'He hung as many IRA people during the war as the British did during the Rising,' said Mousey.

'Why is he so popular with many Northern nationalists then?' asked Slash.

'He's a great Catholic, and his right hand man was a South Armagh man, Frank Aiken, who is still a hero to people of that generation,' said Wee Pat.

'And at every election in the Free State he promised to do away with the border,' said Mousey.

'People will believe anything,' said Slash, eyeing Seanie to see if he would buy a round of drink. 'God, you can't hear your ears with the racket from that band.'

Mousey had a habit of screwing up his nose before he spoke, not unlike a mouse sniffing around. Now he sniffed a couple of times and said to Slash, 'You're talking more gibberish. How can you hear your ears?'

'Your ears are the only part of your body that never stops growing,' said Wee Pat.

'That's wrong,' said Slash. 'The only part of your body that never stops growing is your nails, and they keep growing even after you die.'

'Who told you that?' asked Wee Pat.

'It's true,' said Slash. 'Willie Duggan can tell when he opens a grave how long a corpse has been buried by the length of its nails.'

'That's daft,' said Mousey, shaking his head dismissively. 'What happens when the body decays?'

Slash took a gulp from his glass and twisted the stool so as to be facing the bar customers. Because of a squint in his eyes, everyone got the impression he was looking directly at them. Then, right hand on heart like a Yank standing to attention for the National Anthem, he leaned forward towards them and in a solemn voice said, 'Willie made me swear not to tell anyone, so no one here must ever repeat what I'm going to say.'

Everybody nodded.

'Once, when he was opening a grave that hadn't been used in a very long time, do you know what he discovered? Human nails. No coffin, no body, no anything. Nothing only ten fingernails and ten toenails. And when he measured them, they were thirty-nine inches long.'

There was a hush in the back bar; even the blaring music went unnoticed as everyone tried to comprehend the significance of the story.

Then Wee Pat spoke. 'Slash, you're an eejit of the first order. If you had a cross on your back you'd pass for a donkey.'

Like everyone else, Seanie had been engrossed in Slash's story, but Wee Pat mentioning donkeys brought to his mind the *Exchange and Mart* ad. Here was a bunch of potential customers. When he told them about it, everyone promised to buy one.

Just then the British Army screeched into the village and surrounded the pub. The search operation wasn't unexpected. A new regiment had been stationed in the area. Their commanding officer had said that he would have the entire region free of political unrest within a very short time. Wee Pat thought the guy must be either the greatest British military and political genius in 600 years, or Irish history wasn't his interest in school. McIver made sure his bar licence was up to date.

Everyone, even Sober, was ordered out of the bar. Sober didn't hurry himself, but a burly sergeant helped him along by the scruff of the neck. All were lined up and faced against an outside wall with legs spread.

A British squaddie roared into Slash McMahon's ears, 'Face into the wall and don't move a fuckin' eyelid.' But because of Slash's squint, the squaddie suspected that he might be staring him out. The soldiers dragged him from the line and began to beat him up. 'This will fucking teach you not to look funny at people,' one of them said.

Seanie shouted at them to leave Slash alone. A soldier ordered Seanie to shut up and told him that heroes got the same treatment. The Brits continued to taunt Slash. They made him do press-ups, something that wasn't physically possible on account of his huge belly. Next it was jogging on the spot exercises. An army man stood behind him jeering and prodding his back with the barrel of a rifle, forcing him to lift his knees ever higher. Slash soon collapsed to the ground. Seanie feared the big man might suffer a heart attack. Finally, after taunting and abusing Slash for some time about his lack of fitness, the sergeant in charge said something, and suddenly the soldiers took to their vehicles. They raced off leaving the row of men lined against the wall and their victim lying on the pavement.

When the men went back to the lounge they were told the Brits had taken three women with them: Helen Nugent, Babs Savage and Alice Bennett. The first two were well-known Provo supporters. Why they took Alice was a mystery. Seanie decided it must be because they had no record of her working in the bar. However, an hour later all three emerged from a taxi none the worse for their ordeal.

Dickey Stone came into the bar and arranged for Slash to be taken to a doctor. He said the British Army were the best recruiting sergeant the IRA ever had. Wee Pat argued that many of the soldiers were in fact Irish. If they were from Liverpool then they were almost certainly of Irish descent. 'Very likely, it's your own relatives harassing you,' he said.

'Wouldn't the relations at home be doing the same thing if they got half a chance,' said Mousey Reilly.

8

Seanie found Heathrow Airport scary. The throngs of people from so many different cultures milling around made him think of Ballyduff, where the only coloured person likely to be seen would be a British soldier. Here he felt out of place, and after getting off the plane from Belfast he thought the policemen were looking at him strangely. He told himself he was imagining things, and sat down in a restaurant to wait the two hours for his next flight.

Seanie never noticed the two men until they confronted him. One was very tall with ginger hair and horn-rimmed glasses. The other guy was of medium height and quite ordinary looking. In a tone that clearly meant he expected an immediate response, the tall guy said, 'You're coming with us.'

Seanie jumped up, and in the process knocked against the table next to him, spilling cups of tea. The table's occupants quickly realized that they'd better keep out of whatever was going on.

'Who are you?' said Seanie. 'What's wrong?'

'Please come quietly,' said the ginger-haired man.

Seanie looked around quickly. These guys were scary. Maybe he could run, but to where?

'What's this about?' he asked, hoping his voice wasn't trembling.

'Don't cause a stir. It won't take long,' said the tall man.

'I'm just going about my business.'

'You're making me repeat myself. Follow me, please.'

Seanie had no option but to comply. The man with ginger hair walked in front and the other took up the rear. Airport staff stood to one side. Barriers and access points opened with no questions asked. Finally, they went through a door marked 'Private'.

Seanie surveyed the medium-sized room. There were no windows and no furniture except for a table and three chairs. One wall had a picture of the Queen on it. The opposite wall had a large mirror that seemed somehow out of place.

He said, 'I'm supposed to be catching a flight very shortly.'

'To Malaga I believe,' said ginger hair. He pointed to the single chair, while he and his companion occupied the other two behind the table.

'I'm Roger, and this is Crawford.'

Roger took out a leather-backed notebook from his jacket and placed it on the table. Beside it he laid a silver-plated pen in line with the notebook. The notion of a dentist's chair with the dental tools organized on the tray entered Seanie's mind.

'How do you like married life?' asked Roger.

Seanie wondered how they knew he had been recently married. 'Why have you held me up like this?'

'You will let us ask the questions,' said Roger.

'Why am I being questioned?'

'Please tell us why you're going to Spain?'

Seanie explained that he had arranged to meet a Spanish guy with the intention of buying toy donkeys, importing them to Ireland and selling them at a Spanish party night in the local pub. He got the impression that they already knew this.

'Hmm,' said Roger leaning back in the chair, arms folded

across his chest. He appeared to be looking at some point in space behind Seanie's head. There was silence for a couple of minutes. Seanie hoped they wouldn't hear his heart thumping.

'Have you ever smuggled guns?' said Roger.

'No,' said Seanie.

'Do you know of anyone smuggling guns?'

'No.'

'If a blind eye was turned to some of your activities, would you recompense us with some local gossip?'

Seanie shuffled himself on the seat. 'I don't do anything illegal and I'm not concerned with local gossip.'

'You might be in a position to make a lot of money, depending on the quality of the information.'

'I'm sorry. I lead a very quiet life and don't get involved.'

'Things may become difficult for you. Do you know what I'm saying?'

'Yes.'

'What do you have to say?'

Seanie focused his eyes on the guy's Adam's apple and didn't respond.

'We know you're a smuggler. We know you drink in that Republican den, McIver's. We know your wife Eileen is at home alone now. Let's hope the house doesn't need to be searched and her there alone. Do you want me to continue?'

Seanie stared down at his hands. Where were these guys getting their information? He wanted to say that if they knew so much what did they need him for. But instead he said, 'I'm just going to Spain to buy toy donkeys.'

Roger fiddled with the pen and notebook by placing them at various angles to each other. 'What can you tell us about Seamus Galvin?'

'Nothing,' said Seanie.

'He seems to be a great man for helping the local community.'

'What do you mean?'

'Did he not train the football team?'

Seanie didn't reply.

'What was he getting out of it?'

'I don't know.'

'Might he be involved in smuggling arms?'

'I don't know anything about him.'

Roger leaned across with elbows on the table. He stared Seanie in the eyes. 'Do you realize how many people disappear each year?'

Seanie shook his head.

'Thousands,' said Roger.

Seanie said nothing.

'Never heard of or seen again,' continued Roger in a conspiratorial whisper. 'They just vanish without trace.'

Crawford, who hadn't spoken yet, rose and went over to the looking glass. There came a knock on the door. Crawford answered it and then said to his pal, 'It's for you.'

Roger left the room and Crawford sat down. 'My mother is a Cork woman,' he said.

'Is she?'

'Yeah, so I have sympathy for your position, but my friend here is ruthless. I don't agree with some of the things he does.'

Seanie's hopes lifted. 'I understand. It's not your fault.'

'If you could give us some bit of information, maybe I could get him to go easy on you.'

Seanie's hopes dropped again. 'I don't have any information because I mind my own business.'

'My mother's father had been a member of the old IRA,'

said Crawford.

With the other guy gone, Seanie decided this was his opportunity to ask questions. 'How do you have so much information about me?'

'Roger does all that. I just tag along. But if you could give him a few crumbs it would keep him happy.'

'I'm grateful to you, but I don't have any information. I don't go out much.'

'Sometimes I think Ireland should be all one country. What do you think?'

'I have no interest in politics.'

'If we could get things settled in the North it would help the unification of Ireland.'

'Maybe.'

'But we need all the help and information we can get. Perhaps something about Galvin.'

'I know you're trying to help me and I appreciate it,' said Seanie.

His questioner said nothing for a minute. Then he got out of his seat and went over to the mirror again. The door opened and Roger came back into the room. He stood for a moment caressing a stubble the colour of gingersnap biscuits with his fingers. Seanie thought he looked angry and said a silent prayer that he wouldn't vent it out on him. After sitting down, Roger carefully and methodically removed his horn-rims and extracted a white handkerchief from his pocket. He blew on the lens and then rubbed the glass vigorously with his handkerchief between thumb and forefinger. It reminded Seanie of his old schoolmaster, who on occasion would stand behind some unfortunate pupil and take an ear between thumb and forefinger in order to twist it around. The pain was agonizing.

'Did you consider your position?' asked Roger.

'There isn't anything I can say,' said Seanie.

'Even if you don't go out much you still must hear things.'

Seanie sat up. How did Roger know he'd said that he didn't go out much? He was out of the room at the time. What was going on? As soon as Roger asked the question, Crawford glanced quickly at him and tut-tutted. Then he appeared to smile at some private joke. He began humming 'On the Banks of my Own Lovely Lee'. Roger looked at him, clearly irritated. Then he said to Seanie, 'OK, your code name is Dalai Lama.'

'What's that?'

'It's not a "that" it's a "he", and like you he doesn't say very much,' said Roger.

Crawford stopped humming and started to giggle as if this was very funny. Roger continued, 'If you want to get in touch with us, ring the confidential number, tell the operator it's the Dalai Lama and ask for any member of the World Cup Team.'

Seanie didn't respond. There was a long pause. Then his questioner stood up abruptly, saying, 'There's no point detaining you any longer. There's a constable at the door who will guide you back to the departure area.'

At Torremolinos on the Spanish Costa del Sol the searing heat hit Seanie like a blast from a massive hairdryer. There were lots of people strolling about, either gazing into shop windows or at each other. Some had very tanned skin, presumably burned that way. Some had red skin that was definitely burned. Some had peeling skin, recovering from burns, and some had very white skin, ripe for burning. Little bars emitted strange smells from open doors. Guinness wasn't on sale anywhere. Sangria seemed to be the national drink. On learning it was made from wine and fruit, Seanie decided to buy some cases of cheap wine and let McIver add the other ingredients. It would be a nice touch to serve Sangria on a Spanish theme night.

Seanie hired a car to take him to where he would meet the agent selling the donkeys. As he drove along the coast, with the Mediterranean Sea sparkling blue in the sunlight, he thought of a neighbour woman who regularly spoke in familiar terms about going to the 'Med' on holidays. At times he'd felt a little bit jealous. Now he was looking forward to describing all he had seen to the regulars in McIver's when he got home.

The small factory making the donkeys turned out to be high on the slope of a hillside. His contact, Alonso, waited at the front door wearing a huge straw sombrero with a red ribbon around the crown. He greeted Seanie effusively in broken English, opening his arms wide and displaying two rows of white teeth. Seanie responded in English, while apologizing for not knowing Spanish.

'No problem, signor,' said the Spaniard. 'Come with me.'

The two men entered a display area in the building. The donkeys on show were about a foot high and two feet in length. They came in a variety of colours. Seanie was impressed and could understand how a mother on holiday would be tempted to take one home.

'What about shipment?' Seanie asked the Spaniard.

'No problem, signor. You pay me the money. I give you a receipt. Then I will give you the address of a customs clearance agent here in Torremolinos. Tomorrow you come with him and pick them up. He will document the freight via ship's container to Dublin.'

After handing over the bank draft and exchanging telephone numbers, Seanie left. He would have time to browse around the town and purchase wine for the sangria.

When he returned to his car, Seanie discovered he had a flat tyre. This was a disaster. The factory had been closing for siesta time as he was leaving. He had no Spanish and couldn't make a phone call even if he could find a telephone. As he stood there with the sun beating mercilessly down, a red open-topped sports car roared up and stopped beside him. A man with a west of Ireland accent shouted at him over the windscreen, 'Are you in trouble?'

Seanie couldn't believe his luck. 'Yeah,' he said. 'I have a flat wheel.'

'That's because you left it sitting in the sun. The heat pulls puncture patches off. Hop in and I'll give you a lift to the garage.'

The man turned out to be from Mayo. He told Seanie that he lived here now. He taught English at a local school. Because of the car, Seanie decided there must be a lot of money to be made teaching English. When Seanie told him about wanting to buy wine, the man said that he would take him somewhere he could get it cheaply.

The Titanic Pub had a sign outside with a picture of the legendary ship on it. Inside, it was full of IRA memorabilia. Pictures of famous Irish patriots decorated the walls and a huge tricolour hung from the ceiling. Blown-up photos of Provos on manoeuvres were affixed beside slogans promoting the nationalist movement, Eta. Seanie approached the counter. The barman's face was so badly scarred on one side he seemed to be wearing half of a Halloween mask. Trying not to stare, Seanie asked him if he served Guinness. The man laughed from the good side of his mouth. 'You're from the North,' he said in a strong Belfast accent. 'Try the San Miguel.'

'OK, that'll be fine,' said Seanie.

'Grab a seat,' said the man. 'My name is Reggie. I have a barman coming on shortly and we can talk then. I love to chat with people from home.'

Seanie sat down. The heat was stifling. Before long there were several empty beer bottles in front of him. Reggie still hadn't finished behind the bar. A musician wearing a green T-shirt with *Ireland Abú* written on it prepared to perform on a little makeshift stage. Seanie asked him what he was having and both men drank some more beers. Finally, after much 'helloing' into the mic, the musician strummed his guitar and began to sing 'The Banks of the Ohio'. Then a gang of youths came into the bar. By their accent they were from Dublin, and clearly this wasn't the first bar they had been in that day.

'Off at last,' said Reggie as he appeared beside Seanie, holding a bottle of wine and two glasses. 'This is a house speciality.'

He put down the two sizeable glasses and filled them with red wine. 'Blood of the grape,' the barman remarked as he poured. Both men touched glasses and wished each other good luck. After drinking the toast, Reggie said, 'Tell us all the news. Are you on holidays?'

Seanie didn't want to reveal his mission. Why disclose something that might be built into a lucrative trade and run the risk of competition? He told Reggie that he wanted to buy wine, and the reason why. Reggie said he would sell him whatever he needed, cheaply. He filled up their glasses again. 'Let's drink to the brewing of Irish sangria,' he said.

The Dublin youths were becoming more boisterous. The musician sang 'Follow me up to Carlow'. Seanie didn't know if was the heat or the wine, but his head felt light. Reggie mentioned the importance of taking on board plenty of liquid in a hot climate. He called for more liquor. After another drink or two, Seanie decided Reggie was OK.

The entertainer sang more IRA ballads. Jesus, Seanie thought, there's no getting away from the Troubles. But for some reason it wasn't annoying him as much as usual.

'I was wondering,' he said to Reggie, 'what do the IRA and Eta have in common?'

'I'm surprised at that question,' said Reggie.

'Why is that?'

'They both want freedom from foreign occupation.'

Seanie tried counting the empty bottles on the table but found it difficult to keep his eyes focused. 'To me it seems the opposite,' he said.

'Explain,' said Reggie.

Seanie started to speak. His tongue felt thick. 'The Basque Country is mostly part of the greater Spanish area, and Eta wants to separate from Spain. But in Ireland, the IRA is fighting for Northern Ireland *not* to be separate from the greater Irish area. What's common about that?'

Seanie was pleased with his poser. He sipped away at the wine while waiting for Reggie's response. Just as Reggie was just about to say something, the musician launched into 'The Merry Plough Boy', and instead of answering, the bar owner lay back in his chair. He said, 'Let's drink up and listen to this.'

Seanie was enjoying himself. Nice wine, good company, balmy climate – what more could anyone want? He lifted his glass in a toast and nodded for Reggie to do the same.

'To the blood of the grape.'

'The blood of the grape.'

Both men drank heartily while most of the customers joined in the singing.

'*Some men fight for silver,*
Some men fight for gold,
But the IRA are fighting for,
The land the Saxon hold.'

Seanie went to the toilet. On his way back he got lost and the barman had to show him to his table. Reggie held his glass of wine up to his good eye and swirled the contents around. It crossed Seanie's mind that the scars were not so noticeable when you got used to them. He remembered his granny saying, 'It's what's inside, not what's on the surface that matters.'

When Seanie plopped down on the seat, Reggie was still surveying the wine. He repeated a line from 'The Merry Plough Boy': '*Some men fight for silver, some men fight for gold.*' Then he looked at Seanie. 'What do *you* fight for, Seanie?'

Seanie rubbed his hand over his face. The room seemed to be going around. Eileen said money was his idol, but he'd better act smart and not tell Reggie that.

'I don't know.'

'Are you sure you don't know?'

'What do you fight for?' said Seanie.

'My face is like this because of what I fought for.'

'That's terrible.'

'*C'est la vie, amigo.*'

Seanie made a decision. He leaned closer to Reggie and put an arm around his shoulder. The words seemed strange, as if it wasn't him speaking. 'I know I can tell you. Eileen says I like money.'

'Who the hell is Eileen?' asked Reggie, moving his head to one side in order to get his ear out of Seanie's mouth.

'Eileen is my wife.'

'Oh, right.'

In spite of Reggie's reluctance to rub faces with him, Seanie insisted on pulling his friend closer while confiding in him. 'I want to tell you something very private. I got a great bargain with a guy called Alonso. I'm going to make a lot of money and I would like you to be my partner.'

'Tell me all about it,' said Reggie, signalling to the barman for another bottle.

Seanie's head pounded. He was lying on a bed and about to vomit. A blinding sun shone through an open window. He had to find a toilet. His trousers and T-shirt felt damp. The room started to spin when his feet touched the floor. There was a bathroom a few yards away. He reached it and fell to his knees, throwing up violently into the toilet bowl.

After lying for some time with his head in the WC, intermittingly spewing a mixture of wine and green bile, he became aware of somebody looking down at him.

'What happened to me?' he said.

'*C'est la vie, amigo*,' said Reggie.

'Where am I?'

'God the smell in here is awful.' Reggie went over to the window, which had a long plant on the outside sill with blue and white flowers hanging over the edge. After inhaling a deep breath he said, 'You're in my apartment above the pub. You've had too much vino. But don't worry, I'll get you out to the airport in plenty of time for your flight this evening, and arrange for the lorry that's collecting the rest of your goods to pick up the wine.'

'Will I make it home?' groaned Seanie.

'Of course you will.'

'What did I say last night?'
'What do drunks always say?'

Seanie had to stay in bed for two days. Eileen couldn't understand how one or two wee glasses of wine could cause him to be so sick. She came to the conclusion that it must have been sunstroke. The Irish weren't suited to a hot climate. Seanie consoled himself with the knowledge that he would make a lot of money, and when this shipment was sold he intended going again. He told Eileen he would take her with him the next time, now that he knew his way around.

On his way to the docks to pick up the goods, Seanie counted in his head how much he would make if he got rid of all the donkeys. Eileen's father would be very impressed. When he reached the turn for the shipping office he slowed down. A man materialized out of the shadows in front of the windscreen.

Seanie automatically jammed on the brakes. The driver's door was yanked open and another person pointed a gun at him, shouting at him to stay still. 'Hand over the clearance documents,' said the gunman.

The two men piled into the van and ordered Seanie to proceed towards a huge warehouse on the quayside. After a security guy had inspected the paperwork, the hijackers loaded up the cases of donkeys and wine.

'What's this about?' Seanie said.

'Shut the fuck up and drive,' said the guy who had brandished the gun.

Some thirty miles later the hijackers instructed Seanie to take the next byroad to the left. Half a mile further on they ordered him to pull up in front of a HiAce van parked in a laneway. Only the cases of donkeys were transferred to the

HiAce.

When Seanie told McIver what happened, a shiver went through the bar owner. Seanie knew that he was thinking about what it would be like to lose all that money. But McIver wasn't puzzled by what had happened.

'It's obvious,' he said. 'Somebody who knew about your trip took advantage of the situation. It was guns, not donkeys, that were in those cases.'

The following morning, Seanie was with Cormac and Eileen in the living room when the phone rang.

'That's Alonso now,' he said. 'I have been trying to get through for hours.'

Seanie told the factory owner about having the donkeys stolen. Alonso said that they had been picked up, and after that he knew nothing about them. He expressed sorrow at what had happened. Seanie quizzed him some more, but the Spaniard washed his hands of any responsibility.

'Who knew about you going to Spain?' said Cormac, when Seanie had finished speaking on the phone.

'I talked about it in the pub on the Italian party night,' said Seanie.

'Somebody heard you and set the whole thing up. The guy from Mayo showing up just at the right time is too coincidental. He let down the tyre.'

'I rang Reggie the bar owner,' said Seanie.

'I bet he said he knew nothing about it?'

'Yeah. He must have been involved also.'

Eileen said, 'What did he say exactly?'

'When I told him about losing the donkeys, he said, "*C'est la vie, amigo,*" and hung up.'

'You can be sure Galvin has contacts in Spain,' said Cormac. 'He and Ratigan are behind the whole thing.'

'Is there nothing can be done about it?' said Eileen.

'I can hardly go to the RUC,' said Seanie.

'What about Dickie Stone?'

Seanie thought about it for a moment before shaking his head. 'Dickie probably sanctioned the operation.'

9

Seamus Galvin called to see Seanie. The American said he had materials in storage south of the border that needed moving to Belfast.

'You've a cheek coming to me,' said Seanie, and told the American that he and Ratigan had put him in danger of doing time, not to mention the money he lost. Galvin argued that Seanie now had a chance to recoup his losses and more besides. Seanie was adamant however, and said he would live with what he had lost, but he wanted nothing to do with either of them.

'You would be assisting the cause,' said Galvin, but Seanie told him the cause wasn't any of his concern.

'There's been a shooting close to the village of Ballyduff in South Armagh,' said the newscaster. 'It's reported that a serving member of the RUC has been shot dead in his own home. His name is believed to be Robert Soncroft.'

Seanie had been driving towards the village. He slowed up in order to take in the news. He breathed a little prayer. How can people snuff out a life so casually? His father would have said it was an ignorant question. In wartime a soldier must kill the enemy. But Soncroft was a neighbour. The people who shot the RUC man were almost certainly neighbours also.

He decided to stop at McIver's to hear what was being

said. It was early in the evening, and there were only a few regulars lounging about. Unfortunately, Oul' Wilson, a rabid Republican, was one of them. The atmosphere wasn't any different than usual even though everyone would have heard about Soncroft. Slash sat hunched on a bar stool, two elbows resting on the counter, watching Blue Peter on TV. Beside him, Wee Pat was also engaged in the television. Mousey studied the *Irish News* crossword. Oul' Wilson stood at the counter chatting with Alice behind the bar.

Seanie exchanged pleasantries with everyone and ordered a bottle of Black Label. Wilson turned to Seanie. 'What did you think of the match?' he said, referring to the game on the previous Sunday in which Ballyduff were beaten.

'We were unlucky, but have only ourselves to blame I suppose,' said Seanie.

The two men were talking politely when Slash said, 'Did you hear that?'

'Hear what?' said Mousey, leaving down the newspaper and glancing up at the TV.

'That larrier on the TV says a whale isn't a fish.'

'Will you hush till we hear what's he saying,' said Wee Pat.

'He's right. A whale isn't a fish,' said Mousey.

'Does it live in the sea?' asked Slash.

'Yes, but it's a mammal like a cow,' said Mousey.

'Cows don't live in the sea,' said Slash.

'The young of a whale is called a calf,' said Mousey.

'Does a young whale have four legs?' said Slash. 'The day I see a field full of whales chewing the cud, I'll agree they're cows and not fish.'

'If you'd shut up and listen you might learn something,' said Wee Pat to Slash, before asking Alice to change the station on the television to the 5.45 news on ITN.

As usual, the TV headlines were about incidents in the North of Ireland and included a report on the killing of Soncroft. He had answered a knock on the door and a masked gunman fired two shots at point blank range. Death was instantaneous. Inside the bar everyone watched intently. Nobody spoke. Seanie, observing the customers' reaction, surmised that if Wilson hadn't been present someone would have commented, but then again, perhaps not. Nowadays, when an event took place that didn't meet with popular approval, condemnation was rare. Soncroft would have helped locals get off minor offences, and in reality he was more religious than the majority of his Catholic neighbours, so there should be outrage at his killing. But there wouldn't be. He was an RUC man.

With the news so full of the Troubles, Seanie could feel the tension.

'The Brits had a checkpoint at the stony meadow this morning,' said Wilson.

'They are there regularly,' said Slash.

'Wouldn't it be lovely,' said the veteran Republican, 'to see the bastards' blood running like rain water into the sheughs. If we had the boys of Kilmichael with us now, they would teach them a lesson.'

'God, but you're very blood thirsty,' said Seanie shaking his head.

'Any man who calls himself Irish should be thirsty for British blood,' said Wilson.

'Black Label for me every time instead of blood, no matter whose it is,' said Seanie, holding up his glass of lager.

'Beer was the last thing on the minds of the Kilmichael heroes.'

Alice had left Seanie's bottle of Carling Black Label on the counter. Now Seanie lifted it and poured the remainder into his glass. He set the empty bottle down and then very deliberately said, 'I'm not sure there was anything all that heroic about Kilmichael.'

Wilson's face turned red. 'Jesus,' he said. 'Only for men like Tom Barry, you wouldn't be lying in your warm bed tonight.'

Seanie said, 'Let me tell you something, seeing you insist on going on about it. There are accounts of the ambush which suggest Barry showed no mercy even when the enemy had surrendered.'

Wilson hit the counter with his fist and in the process spilled his pint. 'How dare you say such things. You're not fit to tie their shoelaces,' he shouted.

Behind the bar, Alice pretended to be gazing at the television. She turned to the two men and wiped up the spilled drink. 'Boys, please will you give over, both of you.'

'I'm going now anyway,' said Seanie, draining his glass and setting it on the counter.

'Gimme another one,' demanded Wilson, pushing his empty tumbler towards the barmaid.

As Seanie was leaving, everyone except Wilson said goodbye to him.

A couple of days later, Cormac called to see Seanie. The two friends discussed the Soncroft killing. Then Cormac broached the subject of Galvin's visit with Seanie. 'You refused the run?'

'Yeah, what would you expect?'

'The weapons are badly needed in Belfast.'

'These are the same guns that were shipped in my name and for which I could have done time.'

'Would you change your mind?'

'You know how I feel about all this killing.'

'Guns don't kill people. People kill people,' said Cormac.

'You expect me to be involved with Galvin and Ratigan after what they done on me?'

'For Christ's sake, Seanie, get a grip. You know as well as I do when you're in business your enemy one day is your friend the next. You take the downs and get up and go again, maybe with the one who brought you down. So don't use that as an excuse. They're under siege in the city. This isn't about money.'

Seanie lay back on the sofa and stared at the ceiling. He knew Cormac was correct. In business the only deal that matters is the one in front of you. And he wouldn't have to take money for doing the run.

'I couldn't live with it, Cormac,' said Seanie, 'if I knew some gun I had deliberately smuggled was used to take life.'

'I will have to do the run myself then.'

Seanie closed his eyes as if to shut out what his friend had said. He knew where Cormac's sympathies lay, and he also knew when he decided on something it would be practically impossible to make him change his mind.

'If you must, you must,' he said. 'You know how dangerous it is?'

'I know,' said Cormac.

Seanie spent the next few days in turmoil, his mind preoccupied with the fact that he was letting his friend down. Cormac might pull it off on his own, but he needed him, and if anything went wrong there could be shooting. In that event the best outcome would be a long term inside. He didn't want to contemplate the worst scenario.

Seanie called with his parents on his way home from Soncroft's funeral. As he pulled up in front of the house he could see his father engaged in applying varnish to the outside windows. Holding a tin of varnish in one hand and a paint brush in the other, he asked his son if he had been at the burial.

'Yeah,' replied Seanie. 'You didn't go?'

'It was an RUC man's funeral.'

'He was a decent man.'

'Yes, he was,' said his father, dipping the brush into the tin and then methodically edging the excess varnish off it on the rim. 'But he made a decision, and at the end of the day he was responsible for that decision.'

'What right has anyone to say a person should die because he chooses a particular occupation? Soncroft was a good neighbour.'

'Do you not imagine soldiers in the trenches shooting at one another weren't killing *someone's* good neighbour?' said his father, concentrating on his brush strokes so as not to stain the glass.

'That's war,' said Seanie. 'War that had been declared by democratically elected governments. Where did the Provos get their mandate to kill neighbours?'

Seanie's father paused and set the tin of paint on the window ledge before taking a rag that had been sticking out of his hip pocket and wiping his hands with it. 'They got it before your time.'

'You're going back a long way.'

'We've been subjugated here in the North. The only thing the Brits understand comes from the end of a rifle.'

Seanie watched a sparrowhawk circling high in the sky. 'Soncroft wasn't a Brit. He was an Irishman.'

Seanie's father sighed as he ran his eyes over what he had already painted. 'Yes, that's the real calamity. Soncroft had no say in where he was born, but he did have a choice as to being a policeman.'

'Might he not be defending what he sees as his country?'

'If he's an Irishman,' said his dad, 'he shouldn't be defending the English crown.'

The hawk suddenly swooped down and went out of sight behind a hedge, just as his mother called him from the front door of the house.

'I'll be in now,' he shouted back. 'You missed a bit there,' he told his father, pointing up at a corner of the window.

When he entered the house, he said to his mother, 'You were knitting?'

'Yes,' she said. 'I have to be doing something when I'm watching the box in the corner or I'll feel guilty about wasting time. What do you want? Tea?'

'That'll be fine,' said Seanie, and then after a pause, 'Guilt can be painful.'

His mother, pouring out the tea, looked up sharply. 'Here you are,' she said, handing him a mug of tea and a scone. 'Sit you down in the armchair and take this.'

She made herself comfortable and picked up a newly knitted piece of material. She spread it out on her knees to examine it for flaws. Then, with the long needles between fingers on either hand, and the string of wool looped around her little finger, she began knitting. Seanie wondered why the familiar clicking sound of the needles was strangely comforting. Maybe it reminded him of when he was a child. Back then everything seemed black and white. Now there were shades of grey. After a couple of minutes, his mother settled into a rhythm and said casually, 'I've been wanting to talk you.'

'Oh yeah?'

'Eileen rang me.'

'So?'

'She thinks something has happened between you and Cormac.'

'It's nothing. He wants to do a run I don't like.'

'Is he going to do it without you?'

'Yeah.'

'Then be with him.'

'This particular trip doesn't sit easy with me.'

'Whatever reason you have for not wanting to do it takes second place to being with your friend.'

'It's not that simple.'

Seanie's mother put the knitting down on her knees in order to wind a ball of wool. 'Listen, *amhic*,' she said.

Seanie knew that when his mother called him that, she wasn't asking him to do something, she was telling him.

'I'm your mother. Don't let Cormac down. Are you listening to me?'

Seanie nodded.

'I hope so. Now, help me unravel this wool.'

Later that evening, Seanie rang Cormac. 'About that wee job. Maybe a removal. What do you think?'

Cormac felt no need to ask why Seanie had changed his mind. 'Yeah, I think so.'

'Can we get make-up and everything?' asked Seanie.

'Shouldn't be a problem.'

'Who'll play the dummy's role?'

'I'll tell Ratigan he has to do it.'

'It will serve him right,' said Seanie.

*

Cormac had told Seanie that everything would be ready at the departure point when he arrived, and that he'd not have any contact with either Galvin or Ratigan. He wouldn't see or handle anything on account of his scruples. All would be loaded and ready to go. The materials had been stored in a barn on a lonely out-farm in County Meath. Huge fields of flat pasture surrounded the building. As Seanie approached the store, it was clear that the isolation here arose from being surrounded by prairie ranches, whereas in South Armagh it came from being surrounded by bogs and mountains. But this was hardly a time for musing on notions of inequality, he decided. Total focus was essential. The strategy about to be employed had been successful in the past, but failure on this run would have dire consequences.

'Park inside,' Cormac said to Seanie.

Inside the shed, a man holding a doctor's satchel waited beside a huge black hearse. The hearse contained a coffin. Cormac wore a black suit, black tie and peaked cap. He looked older than usual. 'We're all set and ready to roll,' he said. 'Get stripped and Roddle will do your face.'

Ernest Roddle handed Seanie a black suit and tie, white shirt and black top hat. Then the man sat him on a chair and began to apply stage make-up with materials from the bag. After he had been working for a few minutes, Seanie looked at himself in a little mirror.

'It's amazing what you can do,' he said.

'I can make the living look dead and the dead look alive,' said the make-up artist.

'Is this what I'll be like in another twenty years?' said Seanie, turning and twisting his face to examine it from different angles.

'If you live that long,' said Roddle.

'You never looked so well,' said Cormac. 'Let's get on the road.'

Cormac reversed the huge automobile out of the barn and eased it onto the road. Their route would take them via Dundalk, Newry and Banbridge, eventually picking up the M1, and then on to an address in West Belfast, where the goods were to be deposited. Pedestrians stopped and stared at the hearse as it drove by. Many made a sign of the cross as it passed.

'That's one thing about the Irish,' said Cormac. 'They respect their dead.'

'It's a pity they wouldn't give the living the same respect,' said Seanie.

The hearse and its occupants passed safely through Dundalk. In some instances traffic gave way to them. Anytime this occurred, Seanie politely waved his hand in appreciation. At one junction, a lone Garda gave a formal salute to the hearse as it passed.

'Jesus,' said Seanie.

'That's another thing,' said Cormac. 'Irish people make up their minds about you according to your clothes. If you're dressed like a tinker, you'll be treated like a tinker. If you're dressed like a wealthy guy, you'll be treated different, even if you're as poor as a tinker. Try clothing a millionaire in old duds and see if he'll get into a fancy hotel in Dublin.'

'It's nervousness that has you gabbling so much,' said Seanie.

They crossed the border at Carrickarnon, and once past Newry, the hearse drove at a steady speed. They got through Banbridge, but then a long tailback of traffic appeared, which meant there was a checkpoint ahead.

'What'll we do?' asked Cormac.

'Stay calm,' said Seanie. 'We'll have to bluff it. A hearse can't turn and take a detour. There's a helicopter circling, watching everything.'

Ever so slowly, the hearse edged closer to where the army had set up the checkpoint. Seanie sucked a mint to keep his mouth from being too dry to speak. As the undertaker, he would do the talking. Cormac sat rigid, white knuckles clenching the steering wheel. Just one more vehicle in front. Both of them watched as the police, protected by soldiers, made the driver get out and open the boot. They rummaged through it and then handed him back his driving licence.

It was their turn. The hearse eased up to the stop sign. Cormac rolled down the window, tipped his cap to the policeman and handed him a southern driving licence. Seanie leaned over towards the open window.

'Evening, officer,' he said in his best Dublin accent.

'Evening, sir,' said the policeman in a clipped Ballymena accent that to a stranger would sound Scottish. 'Where are you going?'

'We're conducting a removal to Belfast, 39 Northland Drive, off the Falls Road to be precise. That's if we can find it. We're from Dublin.'

'Who's the remains, sir?'

Dour black orange bastard, Seanie thought to himself, but he had rehearsed his lines. 'A tragic case. Young guy just up from Belfast a week, working on a building site, had an accident, fell off a crane and now we're removing the remains from the morgue to his home. It'll be a sad house tonight.'

The policeman said nothing. He looked at the tax on the windscreen. He looked at the South of Ireland number plates. He looked again at the driving licence and then casually handed it back to Cormac saying, 'Thank you, sir. Move ahead.'

Cormac tipped his cap again and said, 'Thank you, officer.'

He put the vehicle in gear and moved off. Neither of the two men spoke for a few minutes. Then Seanie said, 'You know what saved us?'

'What?'

'He was Irish. He may be a former B-Special for all we know, but being Irish, it was hardly likely he would ask us to open the coffin.'

The hearse picked up the M1 and now had only twelve miles to travel before reaching Belfast. On the left-hand side, the lights of Long Kesh prison camp could be seen. Seanie thought about the inmates inside the compounds. Some of them were people he had gone to school with.

On getting to the end of the motorway, the hearse took a turn at Stockman's Lane for the Falls Road.

'To a stranger there's no difference in the Falls Road and the Shankill Road,' said Cormac.

'Don't you end up on the Shankill driving a motor with a Dublin registration or you'll soon discover the difference,' said Seanie.

'I mean in a way of thinking, except that on both roads they think the opposite.'

'The Falls probably has more in common with the Shankill than it does with Ballyduff,' said Seanie.

Cormac pointed at rows of red-brick dwellings as they were driving by. 'Not too many of the people living in these houses would want to live in our place.'

'Or maybe even want a United Ireland to be ruled from Dublin if it went to that,' said Seanie.

A quarter of a mile further on and suddenly they were on

the fringe of a riot. Gangs of youths had gathered on the roadway and were hijacking vehicles, setting them on fire and using them as barricades. Stones and petrol bombs were being thrown at soldiers who had formed a line behind plastic shields some way ahead. A smell of gas filled the air and every so often the crack of a rubber bullet being discharged could be heard. The rioters were breaking up pavement slabs for missiles. Many of them had scarves or handkerchiefs around their mouths that had probably been soaked in vinegar to dissipate the effect of CS gas. By the numbers involved it obviously wasn't a major disturbance, maybe more of a weekly ritual confrontation between the British Army and locals. It wouldn't even make the newspapers. But at this moment, the hearse would be a prime target. Young rioters wouldn't have much respect for funerals.

Cormac had halted the hearse saying, 'They'll hijack us if we don't get out of here.'

'See if you can get back,' Seanie shouted at him.

Cormac reversed the hearse into a gateway and turned it to face in the opposite direction. Army jeeps had sped in behind them in an attempt to contain the rioters in a pincer movement.

'Jesus God, we're trapped,' said Cormac. 'Which way will I go, forward or back?'

'Keep going forward. We've a better chance with the soldiers.'

Cormac knew that they had a better chance bluffing their way with the soldiers, but the risks involved weren't comparable. The hijackers wouldn't be concerned with them, but if the soldiers discovered their cargo it could mean being shot, and it certainly meant imprisonment. Theirs was the only vehicle moving on the road, and the soldiers setting up the checkpoint could see them slowly approaching. They were running around shouting and clearly all fired up. Cormac ground to a halt and rolled down the window. Two of them stood to the side of the hearse holding rifles across their chests. Before they had a chance to say anything, Cormac tipped his hat and said, 'Evening, officers.'

'What's going on, mate?'

Seanie leaned over. 'We're conducting a removal from a morgue in Dublin, sir.'

'Who's the stiff?'

'A tragic case,' intoned Seanie. 'Young guy just up from Belfast a week, working on a building site, fell off a crane and now we're removing the remains from the morgue to his home. It'll be a sad home tonight.'

Just then a big burly sergeant appeared on the scene pushing the other guys out of the way.

'What's in the box, mate?' he demanded to know of Seanie in a strong London accent.

'A tragic case,' said Seanie repeating his lines. 'Young guy just up from Belfast a week, working on a building site, fell off a crane and now we're removing the remains to his house. It'll be a sad home tonight.'

'OK, open it up mate,' said the Sergeant.

Cormac stared straight ahead, hands gripping the steering wheel. A pal of his, John Homes, had taken off at a checkpoint once and got away with it. But there had been a corner on the road ahead of him which had saved his life. Bullets don't go around corners. There were no corners here. Plus, there would probably be a guy lying by the side of the road with a stinger chain ready to pull it across the path of anyone who attempted this. The chain, studded with nails, would rip the tyres apart.

'I can't open the casket,' said Seanie, hoping they wouldn't hear his heart beating. 'It's against professional ethics.'

'Listen mate, I don't give a fuck for professional ethics.'

'I'm sorry, sir, it's not proper etiquette,' said Seanie.

'Open the fucking coffin or you'll be in one yourself,' bawled the army man pointing the gun at Seanie's head.

'Wait, I'll open it,' said Cormac.

Cormac went around the back of the hearse and lifted up the tailgate. He undid the stays holding the coffin in place. Then he eased the coffin back until it was hanging out a little bit from the rear of the hearse. With black-gloved hands he respectfully unscrewed the lid fasteners and laid them to one side. He paused, bent his head for a couple of seconds and blessed himself. Slowly, he lifted the lid of the coffin. The sergeant stood at his shoulder. Several others jostled each other wanting a peek. They all peered into the open coffin. There was a deathly silence. Seanie sat in the front of the hearse and stared straight ahead. He clasped his hands together in front of his chest, almost reverently, and told himself not to think.

'OK. Get the hell out of here,' he heard the sergeant bellow.

The doors of a large garage beside their destination were wide open, which facilitated the quick disappearance of the hearse from public view. Once inside, both men jumped out and speedily removed the coffin.

'We're clear,' shouted Seanie.

There was a banging from inside the box, and a muffled voice said, 'Get me out of here.'

They lifted the lid. Ratigan sat up wearing a black shroud, his face made-up the colour of death. 'What would have happened if that fucker had stuck a bayonet into me to see if

I was dead?'

'Don't be daft,' said Seanie. 'The Brits don't have bayonets on their rifles.'

'It's lucky you don't have a real corpse on your hands. Those fucking air holes aren't big enough. I thought I would fucking suffocate.'

'Let's get this thing unloaded,' said Cormac. He reached into the side of the hearse and cranked a concealed lever. As he worked the lever, the panel on which the coffin had been resting slowly began to rise, opening up to reveal a hidden storage compartment. It was full of wooden cases.

Ratigan quickly divested himself of his shroud. Underneath he was wearing trousers and a jumper. Hoddle wasn't boasting when he said he could make the living appear like the dead.

Just as the cargo was unloaded, Galvin arrived. Seanie told him and Ratigan that he wanted nothing more to do with either of them. Galvin pointed to the cases on the floor.

'This could be the tip of the iceberg, moneywise,' he said.

Seanie didn't answer him. 'Let's get out of here,' he said to Cormac.

'OK,' said Cormac. 'We shouldn't have any hassle on the way home now that we're legit.'

'I don't think legit is the right word,' said Seanie.

10

Cormac rang Seanie the next morning. 'I'll see you at the pub in a couple of hours,' he said.

Seanie said, 'OK,' and hung up.

Eileen asked who was ringing.

'Somebody who wants to meet me about a run.'

Eileen would never ask questions to do with Seanie's work except in a general way. Not knowing details was in her own interest. She kissed him and said, 'Be careful with all the shooting that's going on.'

Seanie checked his fuel gauge to ensure that he had enough diesel to take him to Dundalk and back. The pub was a local they used in the southern town. If Cormac had meant McIver's, he would have said so.

As he drove towards the border, Seanie fiddled with the radio, but it was on the blink again. He pondered over what had spooked Cormac into arranging a meeting in the south. As a precaution, he decided to take the main Belfast to Dublin highway to Dundalk, and not one of the many unapproved routes. If he was being sought, they wouldn't think of him going the legal route.

Seanie drove into the town of Dundalk, nicknamed 'El Paso' in the English tabloids. It was a reputation not really deserved. That said, one man's tendency to shoot the television screen in whatever bar he happened to be in if his horses fared badly didn't help the town's image. Another enterprising bar owner had a real jail cell door – complete with spy-hole – for a front entrance. His business boomed to the extent that a certain knock was required to gain admission, even though the facilities inside might be judged inferior to a real prison. It was thought some of the clientele felt at home behind the cell door.

Many people on the run did hide out in Dundalk, but those who were active or of interest to the authorities weren't the ones doing the hell-raising. These individuals had an interest in keeping a low profile. The place where Cormac arranged the meeting wouldn't come up on the police radar. Music and sing-songs, Republican or otherwise, weren't tolerated. The owner, a heavy-set lady who wore a lot of lipstick and make-up, kept her political views to herself. Cormac told Seanie he heard an IRA Army Council meeting had been held there recently.

When Seanie arrived, Cormac was chatting with the owner. He motioned Seanie into one of the snugs.

After he sat down, Seanie said, 'What's the story?'

'Didn't you hear the news on the wireless? There was a shoot-out at the garage in Belfast. It said one man believed to be an American had been arrested.'

'Jesus,' said Seanie. 'Galvin! What about Ratigan?'

'It just said others had escaped.'

'What's going on do you think?'

'There has to be a leak,' said Cormac. 'Otherwise how would the Brits have known?'

'Where does that leave us having shifted the stuff?'

The bar owner came into the snug. Gold-rimmed glasses hung from a gold chain around her neck. She held a lit cigarette in fingers that had long nails painted bright red. Her toenails, visible from open slip-ons, were also varnished. 'You're out early for a newly married man,' she said to Seanie.

'Ah, she puts me out,' said Seanie.

'It's increasing the nationalist population up there you should be thinking of,' said the woman.

'I'm doing my best on that front,' said Seanie, laughing. 'Can we have a pot of coffee, please?'

When the woman went out, Cormac said, 'The question is, are we also in danger of being picked up?'

'What do you think?'

'It's hard to know. I'm going to take a holiday, maybe tour the South a bit until things settle down.'

'Running is a sure sign of guilt.'

'I'm not running. It's just a matter of not taking any chances until the dust settles.'

Seanie lay back on the seat and looked around him. They were in an oak timber alcove capable of holding four people at most. The snug had originally been designed for a lady or ladies to have their hot punch away from the company of vulgar men and other more conservative citizens. In practice, it was most useful for being able to get a little tipple without gossipy neighbours knowing. The table was made of solid oak and several ancient-looking scratches attested to its age.

'You're free to roam for a while,' said Seanie. 'I'll have to take my chances and stay put.'

The barmaid arrived with the coffee. 'Now boys, here ye are,' she said, setting the tray down on the table before leaving again. Seanie picked up on the word 'ye'. She must be from the west originally. She certainly wasn't from Belfast.

As Cormac poured out the coffee, Seanie said, 'Let's consider our position in detail. I'm going to suggest something, although it may seem outlandish.'

'What?'

'Ratigan might be working for the Brits.'

'How can you say that?' said Cormac.

'Why did the Heathrow detectives only ask about Galvin?'

'Maybe because Galvin's the international arms dealer. He's the prime target from their perspective.'

'Maybe,' said Seanie. 'But that's another reason why Ratigan, if he were a spy, would be in cahoots with him.'

'What's the evidence for Ratigan being the source of the leak?'

'He's a bully and a braggart.'

'And you don't like him, but that doesn't make him a spy.'

'He escaped and Galvin got caught. It looks too convenient. If Ratigan got out of their clutches, he was either very lucky or they let him go.'

'It would also make him some kind of hero in his own ranks,' said Cormac, 'which would suit his handlers very well.'

'The fact the detectives in London didn't ask about him is damning,' said Seanie.

Cormac pondered this for a few seconds. 'At the time I didn't think that was important.'

'Why would the Brits go to so much trouble setting all this up?' asked Seanie.

'Maybe because Galvin was such a serious threat. After all, he's a trained subversive with international contacts. There are very few people about with a CV to match his.'

'Anyway, the only thing we have to worry about is ourselves,' said Seanie. 'As far as we're concerned, Galvin is not going to turn supergrass for two nonentities like us.'

'And Ratigan? He's the only other one who knows we did the run.'

'If he is the mole, he can hardly blow his cover.'

'I think you're right. We're most likely OK,' said Cormac.

Seanie traced a finger along a scratch on the table. He wondered briefly who made it, and where they were now at this moment in time. Probably long dead.

Seanie took the usual short way home. After going over it all with Cormac, he was convinced that even if the RUC knew he had moved the arms, they couldn't prove it, so what would be the point in them arresting him? He decided to ask Eileen if she would like to go out for a meal that evening.

When he arrived home, the entrance gates to the driveway were shut, which was strange. He got out of the car to open them, thinking maybe Eileen had closed them to keep stray livestock from trampling the garden. As soon as he got out of the van, he was surrounded by hooded figures with guns.

'You can be disabled or come quietly,' one of them said. 'Which will it be?'

'Quietly,' said Seanie, thinking to himself how stupid he was. Neither he nor Cormac thought enough about the fact that the Provos were also going to be very pissed off at losing the guns. They would want to trace the tout.

The kidnappers bundled him into a vehicle. His hands were tied. A headscarf was put over his eyes and another one covered his ears. They asked if they would have to muffle him. He said, 'No.'

As they sped away, Seanie remembered a game he played with his father when he was a child. The idea was to try and tell the car's location on any particular point of the road without looking. His father would ask, 'Where are we now?' Seanie had to keep his eyes closed, and just by listening to the sound of the engine, the swerve of cornering, or the changing of gears, he would try and guess. Perhaps it might be the

Gent's Brae, the Broken Ditch, Mulligan's Corner, and so on. He got very good at it, and now, if it hadn't been for his ears being covered, he might have been able to tell the direction they were going. Counting seconds was his only measuring system on this trip.

After about half an hour the vehicle stopped. Seanie was taken out and led into some kind of building. He recognized the smell of a barnyard. His ears were uncovered and he was ordered to sit down on what he presumed to be a bale of hay. He remembered stories of guys being taken to isolated hay barns, hung up by the ankles and skinned alive to make them talk.

Someone said, 'The interviewer will be along shortly.' It was clear they were wearing mufflers to hide their voices. After that nobody made conversation. Seanie sat there for at least an hour. His bladder felt full. It was all that coffee.

Then a voice, also muffled, said to him, 'OK, O'Rourke, let's begin.' Something about the voice made Seanie think of Dickie Stone.

Seanie said, 'Begin where?'

'For a start, where's Cormac?'

'In Kerry by now I would think,' said Seanie.

'Is he on the gallop?'

'No, letting things settle. I'm dying to take a leak.'

'If I loosen your hands will you behave?'

'Yeah.'

Seanie's hands were untied. He turned his back on where he thought his interrogator stood and relieved himself. He felt a little bit better then, and his hands were left free.

'Are you more comfortable now?' said the voice.

Seanie wasn't sure if he detected a note of sarcasm or not. He had decided to reveal everything that happened as he had nothing to hide, and spent the next hour recounting his adventures in Heathrow and Spain. He told of losing the donkeys, and finally doing the arms run only because Cormac was his friend.

He would have liked to ask his inquisitor if Ratigan's and Galvin's activities were officially sanctioned, but didn't dare. He decided not to reveal his suspicion about the detectives in London not mentioning Ratigan's name. If Cormac and himself were left alone, anything else was no concern of his. This interrogation was obviously an enquiry into where the leak originated, and after that it was none of his business where it led or didn't lead to.

When Seanie finished, he told his questioner of his fear that he'd be lifted by the RUC.

'That won't happen,' said the voice. 'It's the big fish they're after.'

Then the man in the muffler told Seanie he was sorry that he had to abduct him, but he needed to know things. He told Seanie his van was outside and to wait five minutes after they were gone before uncovering his eyes. Seanie sensed the man had turned to leave and he decided to take a chance.

'Do you remember the fumble you made in the final that resulted in the goal?'

'I'll never forget it,' responded the man. Seanie could tell his interrogator had suddenly halted in his tracks. After a pause, Seanie heard him say, 'Jesus, O'Rourke, you're good.'

Seanie was aware that the man had turned around and was coming towards him again. He had caught Dickie Stone out. For a second he feared the worst.

'You know,' Stone said, still in the disguised voice, 'this wee country of ours is going to need people like you in the future. Would you not consider getting involved?'

Seanie tried to hide his relief. 'No,' he said. 'Events like the Soncroft killing sicken me.'

'The killing will end sometime,' Stone said.

Seanie heard him leave, and after a few minutes he removed the scarf. When his eyes adjusted to the light he realized why Stone knew he'd be able to find his way home. They had taken him to Uncle Mick's out-farm. His van wouldn't attract any attention there.

11

Seanie could almost hear the bitterness in the car salesman's voice. Like most big firms, the main Ford dealer was staffed with Protestants. They didn't like having to sell new cars to South Armagh people, and Seanie was after purchasing a new yellow Ford Escort. He felt they had some reason to be bitter. Two more British soldiers had been killed that morning outside Crossmaglen. From a Protestant perspective, these men belonged to their army and were protecting their country from the Catholic terrorists. However, in most cases, the soldiers themselves just wanted their three-month tour of duty to be over. Even though they were supposed to be operating in a part of the UK, it didn't feel like that. This was hostile territory where everybody and everything was suspect. They could trip over a harmless-looking piece of wire that would blow them to pieces, or an innocent-looking farm gate might suddenly explode in their face. Perhaps their biggest fear was a sniper's bullet from the muzzle of an Armalite rifle.

Seanie asked the salesman for a fill of petrol as a luck penny, but he refused saying it wasn't part of the deal. It was a response that lessened Seanie's sympathy for the garage man's political views.

At Seanie's local filling station, the owner, Johnny Martin, wished him well with his new car. Seanie told him one mechanic at the garage said it was the colour of diarrhoea.

Johnny laughed. 'You're lucky they would even sell it to you.'

'Things are bad at the minute,' said Seanie.

'You've no idea,' said Johnny. 'All this talk of a curfew being imposed on certain areas is rubbish. There already is a curfew, a self-imposed one. I wouldn't sell a gallon of petrol after six in the evening.'

'Look at the bright side,' said Seanie. 'You can close up early and have the evenings off.'

'That's not much good if you can't leave the house,' said Johnny.

When he got home, Seanie showed Eileen the new car. She sat inside it, saying, 'It's beautiful, I love it.'

'I like the colour,' said Seanie.

'Don't be using it on any of those night trips and getting it all destroyed.'

'No way.'

'Hmm, I'm not convinced of that.'

'I must go. I have to see Cormac about a run.'

'Be careful. Nobody's out these times.'

'I'll be fine.'

Eileen got out of the car and put her arms around him. 'You're obstinate, pig-headed and stupid, Seanie O'Rourke. Why do I not hate you?'

'Maybe it's because I'm so handsome,' said Seanie, squeezing her tightly to him.

'My father says if you're in love with the cowpat you pass no remarks on the dung.'

'How about I pull the car around the back and we have a quick wee siesta in the back seat just to christen it.'

A big crowd had gathered in McIver's for the Spanish night. The publican had spread the word that Sangria would be served free. Seanie and Cormac were in the lounge having a beer and discussing Cormac's trip down south. The band stopped playing mid-song, and a well know Provo sympathizer took to the bandstand. He asked for quiet and then introduced Frank Ratigan, who emerged from the stage backdrop wearing a huge grin. He was dressed in paramilitary uniform and giving a clenched-fist salute. For a couple seconds there was a stunned silence. Most of those present would suspect Ratigan had been involved with Galvin in the arms escapade.

'Give a big Ballyduff welcome to one of our very own,' said the new master of ceremonies.

Seanie stared. Ratigan was obviously being turned into a hero. Huge applause erupted and shouts of, 'Speech, speech,' were heard.

When the clapping subsided Ratigan took the mic, and after a little hesitation about which end to use, he shouted into it, 'We shall overcome. Up the Provos!'

Almost everyone was applauding and cheering. 'I wonder what genius wrote Ratigan's speech?' said Seanie.

Then the lights went out for a few seconds. After they came on again the IRA man had disappeared.

'I've seen everything now,' said Seanie to Cormac.

'Yeah, it's very strange.'

'Ratigan is leaking,' said Seanie, 'and the Provos are trying to make him into some sort of hero.'

'Ah, you really need to be dead to be a proper hero,' said Cormac.

Seanie noticed Dickie Stone standing at the bar. God, how he couldn't stand Ratigan. He felt like going to Stone and telling him the truth about their new pin-up.

One of the part-time bar staff came over to Seanie's table

and told him he was wanted on the phone.

'Who is it?' Seanie asked.

'I don't know,' said the waitress. 'It's a woman's voice, and she asked if you were in the lounge.'

Seanie told Cormac he'd be back in a minute and went to take the call. McIver had a public phone in the hallway into the pub. He said that it was a convenience for his regulars. Slash maintained the bar owner had the phone installed so that his clients didn't leave to put on a bet and maybe not come back. If there was a band in the lounge it was almost impossible to carry on a conversation.

Seanie lifted the receiver. 'Who is this?'

'Alice. Could you come to my house?'

'What's the matter?'

'Please, I beg you to come now.'

'Can you not say what's wrong, Alice?'

'No.'

A couple leaving the lounge brushed past Seanie. Other people kept going in and out.

Seanie thought for a moment. Alice lived about ten minutes away. 'OK,' he said. 'I'll be there shortly.'

Seanie went back into the lounge and told Cormac he had to see someone. 'Don't be taking on any dicey runs with the way things are,' said Cormac.

When Seanie arrived at Mrs Bennett's home, he could see that the house and its surroundings had vastly improved since the night of Screwy's kneecapping. The roof and fascia boards of the widows had been repaired and the entire house repainted. Even the outhouses had been whitewashed. Alice was putting the extra money to good use. He noticed the window curtain being disturbed. She must have heard him drive into the yard, but she wouldn't have recognized the new car. He knocked on the door. There was no answer. He knocked harder and then still harder. She must have thought it was somebody else. He shouted in through the key hole, 'Alice, this is Seanie O'Rourke.'

There was a pause. A voice said, 'Who is there?'

'It's me, Seanie.'

'Where's your van?'

'I have a new car. Open the door.'

Seanie saw the curtain move again. Screwy's shooting had clearly made her ultra-cautious. She shouted, 'Stand away from the door.'

The clematis growing around the entrance was blocking her view of him. Seanie stood back. He saw her face at the window. Then he heard locks being turned and bolts being drawn back. The kitchen was almost in darkness, but even in the gloom of a single candle, Seanie could see Alice looked no better than after the attack on her son. Her face was gaunt and drawn. Her hair was a mess. Her clothes were unkempt. Her eyes were full of fear.

'Oh my God, thank you, thank you for coming,' she said to Seanie with her face buried in her hands.

'What's going on Alice? Have you no electricity?'

'They're going to shoot me.'

'Don't be daft. No one's going to shoot you.'

Seanie looked around for the light switch. The woman was clearly terrified.

'Where's Screwy?' he asked.

'Don't turn on the light. He's with his uncle. Will you help me?'

'Of course I'll help you.'

'They're coming for me tonight.'

'Who's coming?'

'The IRA.'

'Don't worry. They won't be back. Anyway Screwy's not here.'

'It's me they want. They're saying I'm an informer.'

The word made Seanie start.

'Say that again.'

'If I'm not out of the country by midnight tonight they are going to shoot me.'

'Jesus, Alice, what are you on about?'

'They have accused me of giving information to the RUC.'

Seanie glanced around the kitchen. Unwashed cups and mugs were scattered about. Some still had coffee in them that hadn't been touched. The floor was covered in crumbs, and bed blankets were bundled up on the settee in an untidy heap. A little table had a vase of withered flowers sitting on it.

Seanie took her by the hand and led her over to the settee. 'Now sit down and start at the beginning,' he said.

'Will you talk to them?'

'If the IRA ordered you out of the country by midnight, then me talking to them will not save you. Why aren't you gone by now for Christ's sake?'

'Gone where?'

'The Free State, England, anywhere.'

'They said out of the country. They would get me in the Free State, and I'm not going to England. I would rather die.'

'You can't mean that.'

'How would I survive in England. I'm fifty-four. I have no money and no schooling and would have no friends there. I'd be better off dead.'

The widow laid her forehead on the arm of the settee and began to sob.

'Are you an informer, Alice?' said Seanie.

She didn't answer for a few seconds. 'I had to get my own back on Ratigan. He shot my son. He's ruined my life.'

'How did you find out who shot Screwy?'

'You hear things in the bar.'

Seanie could understand her wanting revenge. He thought of the money he lost on the donkeys, and the risk he and Cormac took transporting the arms to Belfast.

'We'll have to get you out of here.'

'I'm not going to England. They can shoot me if they want to.'

'What can I do then?'

'Will you talk to them? They'll listen to you.'

Seanie tried to think. Alice was right. She wouldn't survive in England. She would be forced to return very quickly, and that was assuming she would even make it back. But she was naive to think he could do anything. He looked at his watch and jumped up. The bar would be closing shortly. 'I'll be back before long. Keep the door locked.'

Just before he went out the door, Seanie turned and asked Alice how the Provos knew it was her. Alice said that on the night the bar was raided and she was arrested along with the other girls, she was the only one taken for interrogation inside the barracks. The other two must have told this to the Provos, which made them suspicious.

'What about McIver?' said Seanie. 'Does he know about any of this?'

'No. He wouldn't do anything about it. The Provos are his customers.'

'Put the bar on the door. Keep the lights out and pretend no one's here until I get back.'

When Seanie came back into the lounge, a fat woman was squealing into the microphone, '*Country Roads Take Me Home.*'

Most people weren't listening to the singer. Part-time bar staff were going around handing out plates of ham sandwiches, cocktail sausages and bits of cheese. McIver had instructed them to explain to his customers that the food was called 'Tapas'.

Annie Mooney grabbed Seanie by the jacket as he passed. She liked to know everyone's business. 'How is your father, Seanie? The last time I saw him he was very flushed looking.'

'He's fine thanks,' said Seanie.

'My poor Aloysius, Lord have mercy on him, had a very flushed face just before he died.'

'Excuse me please. I have to talk to someone,' said Seanie.

Seanie went over to where Dickie Stone was standing at the bar. 'Dickie, I've just been talking to Alice Bennett.'

'You're a fucking busybody, O'Rourke, do you know that?'

'Can you stop what's going on?'

'With your background, you know better than most the rules of the game.'

'Jesus Christ, Dickie, this isn't a game.'

'I wish it were.'

'She had good reasons.'

'There's never a good reason for being a tout.'

'Maybe not, but still,' Seanie started to say. However, before he could finish, Stone had turned his back on him. The Provo sat on the edge of a bar stool and clasped a glass of Club Orange with both hands. He gazed at it saying nothing.

'Will you not hear me out?' said Seanie.

Stone didn't answer for a moment. Then he said, 'You know that people have been arrested and arms lost.'

Seanie stood silent for a few seconds. 'She's a widow woman, Dickie. I don't have to tell you her story.'

'I'm sorry,' said Stone.

Seanie knew in his heart that the man was correct. Informers weren't tolerated in any conflict, and in this area especially touts never received mercy.

'She won't go to England. She'll die first.'

'She got a choice,' said Stone.

'Ratigan was the only one she was after.'

Stone didn't reply.

'Please, Dickie, it won't do the cause any damage if she isn't disappeared.'

The Provo shook his head.

'Is the IRA's struggle not for the right of self-determination?' said Seanie. 'Has a widow woman not the right to fight back against an injustice?'

Still Stone didn't answer. Seanie stared at him. It seemed hopeless. 'Can I take her to the Free State? You won't hear of her again.'

Stone sipped at his orange without lifting his head.

'Has the IRA lost all humanity?' Seanie pleaded. Then he had a sudden inspiration. 'If it was my father's decision to make I know what it would be . . . and so do you.'

The IRA man concentrated on the glass of orange in his hands. Seanie wasn't conscious of the hubbub around him. Finally, after what seemed an eternity, Stone said, 'The Free State is a big area. It might be possible for someone to live there unnoticed until the war is over, if they kept their head down.'

Even before the last word had been uttered Seanie was moving away. Stone looked up at the clock behind the bar. 'It's probably too late.'

Seanie knew McIver always kept that clock fast for getting customers out at closing time. He rushed over to Cormac.

'Let's go,' he said.

On his way out he opened the door into the back bar and peeked in quickly. He wanted to check if the usual Republicans were present. They weren't. The other regulars were there. Slash had a mug of Sangria in his hand. There were wine stains around his mouth and he had a pint of stout on the counter. He was holding forth on the way McIver should be congratulated for his efforts in bringing nations together in friendship. 'When we have a United Ireland, McIver should be granted a knighthood,' he said.

'My God,' Seanie said to himself and closed the door again.

On the way back to the widow's house, Seanie explained to Cormac what was happening.

'Christ, Seanie,' said Cormac. 'The last thing I said to you was not to be taking on any dangerous runs. Now we'll have the Brits *and* the IRA after our blood.'

'It's not that bad,' said Seanie. 'Stone as much as said if we got Alice holed up somewhere in the Free State that would be the end of the matter until things settled down.'

'Holed up. Like where?' said Cormac.

Seanie didn't look at Cormac when he said, 'Haven't you an aunt living in Virginia?'

Where do you get these schemes?' said Cormac. 'Anyway, she might be the wrong person. Her father was a blue shirt.'

'You're aunt's father was a blue shirt. That's some skeleton to have in the family cupboard.'

Cormac didn't reply. Seanie pulled the car into the Bennett's yard. He saw the curtain move. Alice was still there. She opened the door for them.

'Let's get you out of here fast,' Seanie said to her. 'There's no time to pack. We're taking you to the Free State.'

Alice insisted on putting some clothes into a plastic jumbo bag while Seanie urged her to hurry up. Eventually they got her and her bag bundled into the car, and were just about to take off when the lights of another vehicle came into view.

'That's them,' said Cormac. 'What'll we do?'

Seanie reversed his car into a barn out of sight. There were a heap of five-gallon oil drums lying around. Seanie jumped out of the car and after giving a couple of them a shake tossed one onto the back seat. 'What's that for?' asked Cormac.

'I don't know yet. It might come in handy,' said Seanie.

The vehicle coming up the lane was a Land Rover. There were at least two occupants in it along with the driver. As soon as it wheeled into the yard, Seanie sped out of the barn and out onto the road.

'Could we not have told them you got permission for me to go to the Free State,' said Alice.

'They're on active service,' said Seanie, 'with orders that haven't been countermanded. Plus they won't recognize this car. They'll think we're enemy agents in an unmarked car ferreting you away.'

He drove as fast as he could. It wouldn't take the IRA unit long to turn around and give chase. Seanie knew these guys were not like young McCracken. They were highly trained assassins. It would be a massive coup for them to kill British undercover people.

'We'll head for Carrickmacross,' he said, 'and try to get into our lock-up without being seen.'

Cormac kept his eyes on the road behind them. Soon he could see the lights of their pursuers. 'They'll see us going into the garage unless we can get enough distance between us,' he said.

'I can't go any quicker,' said Seanie.

There was no other traffic. The Troubles put an end to people straying far from home. The Land Rover didn't make up any distance, but it was still there after ten miles. Nobody inside the car spoke. Seanie and Cormac both knew those behind them would be puzzled at their quarry heading towards the border instead of away from it. The Escort crossed the frontier line. They were now in the Free State. This would make the Provos even more determined to overtake them. Why would British agents risk entering the Irish Republic? Five miles from Carrick, Seanie told Cormac to take off his coat and jumper and Alice likewise. He directed them to stuff them into the black plastic bag. He got Cormac to empty some of the oil from the drum into it. On a deserted stretch of roadway a mile from the town, he stopped abruptly and jumped out of the car, taking the bag with him. While Cormac poured the reminder of the oil across the road from verge to verge, Seanie put a lit match to the bag and tossed it on top of the spilt liquid. In seconds, an inferno raged. 'That'll slow them up,' he said to himself. Very soon they were in a garage belonging to an unoccupied house in the centre of the town.

Two hours later Seanie drove cautiously out of the garage. In forty minutes they were in the little Cavan town of Virginia. Cormac's aunt had to be awakened. Seanie didn't know whether he should mention the fact that Alice had informed on the IRA. If Cormac's aunt was anti-IRA, she might be more inclined to help. In the end, Seanie decided to tell the whole story. The Cavan woman was full of sympathy and delighted to be able to help out. Alice could stay there as long as she wished. She had plenty of room and would welcome the company.

Seanie and Cormac spoke very little on the way back. There was always a chance their pursuers were still looking for them. After turning onto yet another rarely used side road, Cormac said, 'Besides the customs and the Brits, you have managed to add what is supposed to be our own side to the list of people we have to avoid.'

12

'Oh no,' said Seanie to himself when he entered McIver's. Big Hen Ramsey was holding court. The Hen was hard to listen to. He had been abroad, up in the wilds of Canada working in the mines. Now he was back on holidays boasting about his travels. He was never the brightest at school. Seanie remembered on one occasion during sums class the teacher explained that if a farmer had only one cow then that was 100 per cent of his animals. He asked the class if everyone understood this. Big Hen as usual piped up and said it was easy, and then went on to explain that if the cow had a calf the farmer would have 150 per cent-worth of animals because a calf was half the size of a cow.

Seanie went over to where Cormac was sitting along with Wee Pat and Slash. He took Cormac aside and explained to him that the Covered Wagon pub in Castleblaney was under new management and opening at the weekend. He had only heard about it today. They needed to get there as soon as possible if they were to be first in with an offer to supply cheap drink.

'Is it wise to be going tonight?' said Cormac.

'There's plenty of other smugglers willing to run the risk of being out. If we take the Lough Ross route we'll be all right.'

Then the Hen interrupted them. He put his arm around

Seanie saying, 'Ah, my old school mate. Do you know what's the most exciting thing happening in Ballyduff?'

'No,' said Seanie, trying to extricate himself from Big Hen's embrace without causing insult.

'It's watching Oul' Lynch behind the counter slicing bacon,' said the returned emigrant, followed by a big guffaw.

'I suppose there's more excitement in Canada,' said Seanie.

'The cold! You people have no idea what it's like. One week and most of you would be dead. I've learned to withstand temperatures that nobody here could tolerate.'

'Oh yeah?'

'Would you like a demonstration?'

'I'm just heading off.'

'Hold on for a minute. Bar Keep,' shouted Hen at McIver, a way of addressing the barman he must have learned in Canada. 'Fill two dishes of water and bring them here to me.'

McIver, keen to please a customer who obviously did well and had money to spend, produced two basins of water while the rest of the patrons waited expectantly to see what was coming next. Big Hen instructed the barman to get a container of ice. Then Hen put his hand in his pocket and took out what looked like pebbles. 'These are gold nuggets,' he proclaimed, holding them in the palm of his hand.

They didn't look like gold nuggets. They weren't shiny and only faintly the colour of gold. But after everybody had inspected them, Big Hen took one of them and held it aloft. 'I will bet one of these against twenty pounds that I will keep my bare foot in one of these dishes of water longer than any man here. The barman holds the bet.'

Hen picked up the container of ice and poured half of it into one basin and half of it into the other one. 'Who will take me on?'

Nobody was keen to accept the challenge for two reasons: one because they thought they wouldn't win, and secondly because very few of them had twenty pounds.

'Is there no one among you who is not a coward?' taunted Big Hen. 'This piece of gold is worth maybe forty pounds, but any man, if he's good enough, doesn't have to go through what I suffered to get it.'

Eventually, Seanie stood up. 'OK, somebody has to accept the bet,' he said.

Cormac tugged urgently at Seanie's jacket and pulled him down to whisper in his ear. 'Are you mad? Don't do it.'

Seanie looked at him. 'I'm not doing it. You are.'

Cormac turned his back to Seanie and made himself comfortable where he sat, 'No way,' he said.

'Get up there and I'll cover the bet,' said Seanie. 'Maybe the cold water will stop you thinking about women for a while.'

Cormac protested vigorously, but when Seanie announced that Cormac would compete on the terms agreed, he couldn't back down. Cormac warned Seanie he'd lose as Big Hen would never give in. Seanie told his friend to trust him, a response that made his friend roll his eyes up to heaven. Big Hen and Cormac each removed one shoe and sock, rolled up their trouser leg and placed a foot in the icy water.

Both men winced when the cold water touched their bare skin. But Seanie knew that behind his laid-back exterior, Cormac had ferocious mental strength.

'More ice,' shouted Hen.

Seanie hoped that Cormac realized Big Hen's bravado was more to do with psychology than being oblivious to the cold. Another container of ice was evenly distributed between the dishes. The expression on the competitors' faces revealed the torment they were going through. There wasn't a sound in the bar. Even Mousey Reilly and Slash had stopped baiting each other. Minutes passed as the two men stood with one foot each in a dish of icy water. Both of them had their eyes tightly closed and fists clenched. At the beginning, Seanie felt sympathy for Cormac because he knew that for him to withdraw first would be very difficult. But after a few more minutes, he had sympathy for Big Hen also. On and on it went. Everybody knew one of them had to surrender.

Seanie was standing beside Dickie Stone. Another couple of minutes passed, then Seanie whispered to Stone, 'A draw would be a fair result.'

Stone nodded and stepped in front of the two competitors. 'I think we've seen enough. I will declare the test evens if both of you agree?'

Either Cormac had transported himself to somewhere else or he wasn't able to answer. He just nodded his head. Big Hen also gave his assent. Each man removed his foot from the water with difficulty, and McIver gave them a towel with instructions to rub the frozen limb vigorously. The contestants received a big round of applause.

When the men had recovered sufficiently, Seanie told Big Hen he would collect his winnings now from McIver.

'What winnings?' Big Hen demanded to know. 'It was a draw.'

'The bet was you would keep your foot in longer than anyone.'

'That's cheating,' said Big Hen.

Seanie shrugged. 'You drew up the rules.'

Big Hen was cornered. To lose face in front of everyone by trying to get out of the bet would be worse than losing the nugget. 'Take it,' he said. 'There's plenty more where that came from.'

With the buzz in the bar returning to normal, Seanie said to Cormac, 'Are you ready?'

Wee Pat overhearing him said, 'It's risky to be travelling.'

'There's others who'll take the risk,' said Seanie. 'Anyway it can't be that bad.'

Cormac sounded as if Seanie had a gun at his head. 'I suppose I'll have to go with you.'

Seanie never doubted that his friend would accompany him. Before leaving he went over to the counter. He was telling McIver to put up a drink for Hen when he felt Slash at his shoulder. 'Seanie O'Rourke,' said Slash, 'I bet you're just as rich as Big Hen.'

'Do you think so?' said Seanie.

'And you're one brave man, as was your father before you. Just like yourself, he never let the enemy dictate where and when he could travel.'

'Give Slash a pint also,' said Seanie to the barman.

The roads were almost empty of traffic. For a half an hour they travelled and met only one vehicle. Seanie thought about Slash saying he made as much money staying at home as Big Hen got by emigrating. But if he went abroad, he would be away from all the awful stuff going on around him. Every day was now getting worse and worse with random shootings, and families being wiped out in their homes by sectarian loyalists. McIver had argued one night that there was so much collusion going on between undercover agents, the army, the police, and loyalist gangs that it would be fifty years before the truth came out, if ever.

'What scheme are you planning now?' said Cormac.

'Slash was blowing me up about how well I did without

going to Canada.'

'Slash would chat Paisley up if he thought he would get a drink.'

Seanie said nothing. It was lovely to be driving a new car with hardly a sound from the engine, unlike the old HiAce van. Cormac stared at the road ahead and every so often slipped off a shoe to massage his foot. 'I could lose my foot yet over that last escapade,' he said.

'If you had an artificial foot we could make a fortune. God! What's that about?'

An oncoming car had flashed its lights furiously at them. Clearly the driver was telling them to get out of there. At the next lane Seanie wheeled the car around and headed back the way he had just come. It was dark now. 'We're not going to make Blaney tonight it seems.'

'We should have took everyone's advice,' said Cormac.

'We'll just have to try again in the morning.'

'We still have to get home.'

'Relax,' said Seanie.

Ahead of them they could see a light moving around in a circle. When they got closer a man with a torch flagged them down. Seanie stopped the car and rolled down the window. The man hurried over, obviously scared. He told them he saw their lights from his bungalow and thought they belonged to a neighbour. There had been a huge explosion a few minutes previously and he wanted to warn him about it. Seanie asked where the explosion had been.

'I would say about a mile down this road,' said the man pointing in the direction Seanie and Cormac were now travelling.

'We are just after coming that way,' said Cormac.

The farmer pointed his torch into both their faces. 'I don't know you?'

'We're from Ballyduff.'

'What are you doing driving around these roads?'

'We had a wee bit of business to do in Blaney.'

'Oh yeah?' said the man.

'If there's some commotion going on both behind us and ahead of us, we can't go back nor forward,' said Seanie.

He got out of the car to get his bearings. The countryside looked dark and foreboding. There were neither stars nor moon in the sky. One lonely looking light, signifying a house, shone away in the distance. A breeze caused the leaves on the trees arching over the road to rustle. Other than that there was silence. For some reason Seanie remembered his granny's words: 'Even the birds of the air go to their nests at night.'

'Would it be possible for us to hole up in that barn for the night,' Seanie asked, pointing to a hay barn beside the man's house.

'No way! If they find you I'd be in serious trouble, and I have a wife and a house full of children.'

Cormac asked him about the little boreen up ahead. The farmer said it would lead to just outside Crossmaglen, but he wouldn't advise going there. Cormac asked, 'Why?'

The man said, 'You know yourself.'

Crossmaglen, right on the border with the Irish Republic, was the unofficial capital of South Armagh, and some would say South Armagh's reputation for being lawless wasn't undeserved. The British Army had a base in Crossmaglen that was so heavily fortified it had become a tourist attraction for foreign journalists, not that they would be allowed to take photographs; undoubtedly, they were being filmed when gaping at it. To further secure the modern-day fort, in what British politicians called 'Indian territory', the adjacent GAA playing fields had also been commandeered. Because of the fear of ambush, all goods and services to supply the base had to be ferried in by helicopters. These were rumoured to be equipped with anti-missile defence capability.

'We don't have much choice,' said Seanie.

'There's another little road that bypasses Cross,' said the farmer.

'That's the road for us,' said Cormac.

'Maybe,' said the farmer.

'What's wrong with it?'

'It's one of those roads the British Army watch all the time. They could be anywhere, either undercover or lying in ditches.'

'What's your advice?' said Seanie.

'My advice would be to get somewhere safe for the night. This new regiment have lost a lot of men. There will be a price to be paid by someone.'

'I say we go to Crossmaglen,' said Seanie.

'And what then?' said Cormac.

'If we could get to Mickey Reilly's, he would let us stay the night.'

Mickey Reilly owned a pub in the town. Since the start of the Troubles it had become a favourite watering hole for journalists. Because there was nearly always a reporter hanging about it, the British Army didn't give Mickey much hassle. They would usually try to avoid bad publicity.

'What about the other road,' said Cormac.

'If we were stopped on it, it would be a disaster,' said Seanie.

'What if we're stopped in Crossmaglen?'

'It's a built-up area and there'll be people around, so we wouldn't be so isolated.'

'Maybe,' said Cormac.

'OK, Crossmaglen it is,' said Seanie. 'Thanks,' he said as an afterthought to the man through the window. They were just pulling away when he ran after them, rapping the roof with his torch and shouting at them, 'Keep your lights off.'

Cormac waved his hand to him in acknowledgement. Seanie turned into the extremely narrow road. There was grass growing in the centre of it.

'Just pray God we've picked the right road,' said Cormac.

The bushes on the hedgerows brushed the side of the car. Seanie drove cautiously with only sidelights switched on. The farmer was right. Headlights would be more easily spotted from the air. Away in the distance, a bright glare in the sky coming from Crossmaglen Army barracks could be seen. The fortifications included huge searchlights that shone out from the top of watchtowers, both to dazzle and illuminate would-be attackers.

It was on the tip of Seanie's tongue to say they would soon be in Crossmaglen, when the unmistakable whirring sound of a helicopter could be heard. Seanie immediately pulled in and stopped beneath a tree.

The helicopter flew overhead and touched down a couple of fields away and then quickly sped away again. The chopper could be putting down personnel, or collecting them after they had been on patrol. If they were picking up people it might be OK, but if this was a drop-off the soldiers could now be at their rear or ahead of them; there was no way of knowing.

'We should have went the other road,' said Cormac.

'There's no other option now but to keep going forward,' said Seanie.

He took off again, slowly. Cormac kept glancing up into

the sky, the unspoken fear being that the helicopter had seen them but was biding its time. Perhaps it might be playing a waiting game in order to monitor their movements. If so, it would suddenly appear and swoop down on them. They couldn't outrun it.

Another couple of miles and still all was clear when abruptly, almost ahead of them, a main road came into view. They were coming out at Crossmaglen. At the T-junction Seanie turned towards the town and switched on dipped headlights. He drove cautiously. Everywhere looked to be deserted. Not a living thing could be seen. A tattered tricolour hung limply from a lamp post. On the window sill of a boarded-up pub someone had discarded a half-full glass of beer. A white football lay abandoned in the footpath gutter. Even inside the car the two men could sense the eerie silence. They were entering a ghost town.

'Jesus, where is everyone?' murmured Cormac to himself.

Just as he spoke, a helicopter rose from the general area of the barracks. In a second it was hovering over the car. The draught from its blades caused a whirlwind of dust, cigarette ends and empty crisp bags. Seanie could feel a drag on the car from the aircraft's tailwind. He'd have to make a dash for it, but it was too late. From the cover of buildings, living shadows silently materialized. The soldiers' faces were blackened, the whites of their eyes shining. In seconds they had surrounded the car with pointed guns.

'We're dead,' Seanie breathed.

13

The soldiers cursed and yelled. They bashed in the roof of the car and battered the bonnet with rifle butts. They shattered the windscreen and rear window. They ripped the doors almost off their hinges. Then they yanked Seanie and Cormac from the vehicle and flung them against a signpost by the side of the town square. The sign pointing towards Newry gave Seanie a strange, fleeting sense of hope. For an instant, familiarity with the name Newry caused him to feel he was at home and safe. His feet were spread wide and his face jammed against the bollard. He could taste the metallic paint. They were kicking him between the legs. His trousers ripped at the seams. He felt himself being knocked to the ground. Someone was standing on his head. He prayed feverishly that he wouldn't be seriously injured. Then they were dragging him back to the car. He was ordered to start the engine. Cormac lay unconscious in the front seat.

Soldiers walked on either side of the vehicle with their rifles poked through the broken windows at Seanie and Cormac, pointing at their heads.

'Drive slowly you bastard,' one of them said to Seanie.

Someone shouted, 'Up above.'

Seanie's escort swung his rifle and pointed it at the rooftops along the street. The same English voice roared, 'Fire fucking first.'

Seanie tried to keep a constant pressure on the accelerator pedal. These guys were scared. Any sudden movement, even a bump on the road, and he'd be dead. Had anyone seen what the soldiers were doing to them? Almost certainly not. Ahead of them loomed the heavily fortified barracks. A cat darted across the road. For a second Seanie envied it. Cormac groaned a couple of times. He'd got a worse doing than himself. His escort jabbed the rifle into Seanie's ear and said, 'Tell your mate to keep his fucking mouth closed.'

Seanie tried to say something. No words came out. The huge steel doors of the barracks opened up. They were entering a yard. Concrete blocks, bags of cement, coils of barbed wire, and other building materials were strewn about it. Strings of lighted electric blubs between upright poles swayed in the wind and cast ghostly shadows on the ground. Alsatian dogs barked madly behind a wired enclosure and sprang against the fence, crazy to attack. White foam spittle from their fangs spewed onto the wire mesh and dripped to the ground. Seanie didn't notice Cormac being hauled from the car.

'Let the dogs free,' he heard someone shout.

They put him against a wall and pushed a revolver down his throat. He had to escape. The Gaelic field must be on the other side of the yard. He had played there once in a schoolboy final. They played across it instead of up and down. He had twisted his ankle and his daddy had carried him off in his arms. A barrage of bodies descended on top of him. He was being kicked all over the yard. As youngsters being taught football skills, the coach would shout incessantly, 'Don't everyone go for the same ball.' These people were like kids with a ball who had never been coached. Far away, like an echo, dogs were barking and someone was saying, 'He'll soon be fucking dead.'

He was on his back. His arms had been stretched out wide. Concrete blocks were being placed on his hands to secure him in position. The soldiers were tying a stone to the end of a piece of rope but it kept falling off. They had to redo it several times. The stone glinted in the light of the swaying bulbs. It was bigger than the Hen's gold nugget. Why were they pulling his legs apart and putting blocks on them? Once he saw the hen lift a six inch block with one hand. They were going to whip him between the legs.

Two rows of soldiers stood facing each other. 'We're giving you a guard of honour,' someone bawled into Seanie's ear. He was meant to walk between the lines. Several other soldiers were holding him up. They threw him towards the first person in the line. He was caught and flung towards the opposite side. There seemed to be a lot of laughing and shouting. Some of the soldiers battered him with rifles. Others tried to kick him across to their colleagues. His legs wouldn't hold him up. A black boot loomed in front of his face. The sole had dried clay and bits of grass stuck to it. The blades of grass were very green. He was at the end of the line. His face had no feeling. A voice was saying, 'They're not ready for him yet. Take him back to the yard.'

If he could get up and run they'd shoot him. Better to die than what they would do to him back in the yard.

Seanie came to, lying on a stairway. He realized he was still alive. A soldier peered into his face. Another soldier had a can of coke in his hand, 'Drink this,' he said.

He reached it over to Seanie's lips. Seanie was about to try and drink when the soldier hit the bottom of the can with the flat of his hand and jammed it into Seanie's face.

'OK, you fucking bastard, it's talk time,' said the first soldier. He seemed to have some authority.

Seanie tried to lift his hand to feel what had happened to his face. Maybe he would survive.

'What's this for?' asked the officer.

He was holding a small plastic bag in front of Seanie containing something that looked like marzipan. Seanie didn't know what it was. He tried to shake his head.

'What were you going to do with it?' asked the soldier again, waving the bag in front of Seanie's eyes.

Seanie mumbled, 'I don't know what it is.' He couldn't hear his words. Maybe there were no sounds coming out.

'It was found under the fucking seat of your car.'

'I know nothing about it.' Had he a hole in his face where his mouth was?

'Do you know what it is?'

Seanie shook his head.

'It's nitrobenzene.'

Again, Seanie shook his head.

'Are you in the IRA?'

Seanie started to cry.

'Do you know any IRA men?' asked his questioner.

Seanie nodded.

'What are their names?'

'Joe Lennon.'

'Who else?'

'Flint Garvey.'

'Are you trying to be smart?'

Seanie shook his head as hard as he could.

'Those two bastards are already in jail,' said the interrogator. 'Do you know any others?'

Seanie shook his head. His questioner glanced at the second soldier. Seanie felt himself being hauled up the stairs. A smell of disinfectant filled his nostrils. There was a room at the head of the stairs. The grey concrete floor looked scrubbed. He felt cold. The room felt cold. The bare white walls seemed cold. A wooden table had been placed in the centre of the floor. A lighted electric bulb on a length of wire hung from the ceiling. Soldiers were removing the bulb and attaching something into the socket. He felt himself being hoisted onto the table, face up. There were people standing behind his head. They were holding his shoulders. He could tell they were still working on the electric fitting. Something sharp, like a knife, touched his skin.

Seanie lay whimpering on a stairwell. His knees were huddled up to his chin. Soldiers walking by peered curiously at him for a minute or two and then moved on. They laughed and talked and drank from cans and bottles. But mainly they swore and cursed. One of them approached Seanie and prodded him with his toe. Seanie started, and pressed himself tighter against the wall. The soldier walked away shaking his head.

After some time, a couple of soldiers came. One of them said, 'On your feet, bastard,' and hauled him upright.

He couldn't stand, but they dragged him through a doorway. It led outside. An army personnel carrier was parked there. When the air hit Seanie his awareness recovered a little. He was manoeuvred around the back of the vehicle and loaded into it. After a while he noticed Cormac lying motionless under the bench seat opposite. An argument was going on between the soldiers. Cormac seemed to be alive.

'I'm not driving,' someone said.

'What's your fucking problem?' a different voice asked.

'What you're doing to those fucking guys is my problem.'

'Listen mate, if you're not happy with what's going on we'll get another driver.'

Seanie prayed silently that the objecting soldier would drive. Eventually, after a fierce argument, the reluctant soldier agreed to do the journey, and several army personnel piled into the carrier. They crushed Seanie up against the rear door. The lighting inside was dim. A soldier sitting opposite made him open his mouth. He shoved the rifle down Seanie's throat. The cold steel choked him. He could see the trigger finger tighten.

'Within a week they'll have a fucking song made about you,' said the soldier.

There was a clicking sound. The gun either jammed or there was no round in the breech. As the vehicle moved off they tried to make Cormac sing, 'We do like to be beside the seaside.'

Seanie couldn't see what they were doing to Cormac, but it didn't matter. He knew Cormac wouldn't sing for them. He wouldn't either. There was no point. But maybe he would? Then a soldier with red hair, who looked to be little more than a teenager, lit a cigarette. His face was covered in pimples and he'd a habit of baring his teeth like a dog. He put the lighted end over to the side of Seanie's face. Seanie tried to move his head. Why was the soldier enjoying doing this?

'You'll put the fucking wagon on fire,' an army colleague said.

'I'll send the bastard to hell.'

'He'll be there when you arrive,' said his companion and gave a big guffaw.

Seanie discovered the more he moved his face away from the cigarette, the more a sharp object sticking out of the rear door burrowed into the back of his head, but this wasn't as bad as being burned by a cigarette. He didn't realize he had been screaming, but must have been because the driver shouted out, 'What the fuck are you doing to those guys back there?'

The red head shouted back, 'Shut the fuck up and drive.'

Seanie had picked up in the conversation among his captors that they were being taken to Bessbrook. The village's redundant linen mill was now the headquarters of the British Army for the entire region. Because the compound was out of bounds for inspection, people maintained the British government had stored nuclear warheads underground there. Even before they reached the complex the constant sound of helicopters could be heard. Huge barricades and security fencing surrounded the outer perimeter. As the personnel carrier penetrated deeper and deeper into the heart of the compound, it stopped at various checkpoints. When the vehicle halted for the last time, Seanie and Cormac were taken inside a building. The place seemed to be a maze of dark, gloomy corridors with huge rooms leading off them. Some of the rooms were filled with abandoned machinery once used for spinning linen. Derelict cables and wires protruded from walls and ceilings. A dank, musty smell, like hay that had been baled wet, pervaded the place. Seanie tried to concentrate on what was happening. From the chatter amongst their captors, they were to be processed. He didn't know what this meant. He was flung against a wall. A photographer took pictures. One soldier kissed him on the mouth as the images were being recorded. He could get the taste of stale beer. Everyone laughed and jeered.

Seanie was propped against a wall in a search position. He knew the crazy red-headed youth was beside him.

'You're a fucking glory hunter,' someone said, probably to Red Head.

'There'll be one less of the bastards,' was the reply.

There was the sound of feet running, and then quiet. Seanie tried to turn his head. The others had disappeared. The mad boy soldier was going to kill him. They'd say there had been an accident. An excruciating pain in his side overwhelmed Seanie. Everything went dark.

When he came to, his body felt on fire. He couldn't breathe and was gasping for air. Someone was pumping his chest. Soldiers stood looking down at him. One of them said, 'Vomit on that floor, mate, and I'll kick your guts in.'

Seanie was still lying on his side in a foetal position when Cormac emerged from the medic's room. His facial injuries had been stitched up. The treatment didn't look professional. Seanie was dragged along the floor into the room.

'You're still alive?' said the medic in a surprised tone. 'It's my job to prepare you for handing over to the RUC, and I have to make you handsome looking or they won't accept you. Those fucking Irish cops are all fucking queers.'

The medic laughed at his own wit, and after giving Seanie a superficial examination said, 'I'm only a tailor. No stitches. Get out to fuck.'

The two of them were again loaded into the personnel carrier. Cormac kept passing in and out of consciousness. He maintained a low guttural groaning when awake. On reaching the RUC barracks in Newry, the two men were left sitting in the carrier guarded by one soldier. After some time an RUC man appeared. He looked in at them. Seanie heard the policeman say, 'Jesus, what happened to these pair?'

Seanie felt tears of relief on his face when he heard the

Irish accent. 'They fell getting into the wagon,' was the answer.

'We want nothing to do with them,' said the policeman in an adamant tone.

'Why not?' asked the soldier.

'We're not taking responsibility for their condition.'

'They were carrying explosives.'

'How can we explain the injuries?' said the Irish voice.

'Can you not charge them?'

'We'd have to arrest them first.'

'Arrest the bastards.'

'What if one of them dies?'

'They won't die.'

'Even if they don't, they're hospital cases.'

'What can we do with them?' asked the soldier.

'There's a bottomless bog a couple of miles out the road,' said the Irish voice.

The same soldiers returned, accompanied by another man in civilian clothes. He seemed to be an officer of some kind. As soon as he got into the vehicle he said, 'OK you two bastards, it's my job to sort out this fucking mess and I'm pissed off, so make the slightest move and you'll be sorry you were ever born.'

Red Head laughed at this. The new man looked at him and Red Head stopped laughing immediately. Seanie tried to assess his injuries. Most of his body was numb. The pain in his chest was agonizing. Maybe he would die. His face felt strange, like it had been frozen at the dentist. Suddenly, the jeep swerved and the officer began to verbally abuse the driver. 'I'll have you fucking skinned alive if you hit that dog,' he said.

Seanie figured out there was a dog on the road and the

officer wanted the driver to go around it. During the commotion, Seanie moved just a faction to ease his discomfort. But the officer caught him doing so and hit him a rabbit punch on the back of the neck. Seanie thought his neck had been broken. Then the officer turned his attention back to the driver saying, 'Be very, very fucking careful soldier.'

Seanie tried to stay still. This guy was even scarier than Red Head.

After maybe two hours the officer said, 'We'll soon be there. Time for some R and R.'

Seanie tried to catch Cormac's eye. Where was 'there'? Because of the travelling time he would guess Belfast. Then the vehicle see-sawed over high ramps before stopping.

'Hi mate,' Seanie could hear the driver say to someone. 'We have some people on board for documentation.'

The back door of the carrier swung open and a solider looked in. 'Welcome,' he said, addressing the two prisoners. 'We hope you enjoy your stay.'

Then, laughing, he banged the door closed and Seanie heard him say, 'OK, move on.'

The carrier drove a short distance before coming to a halt. Soldiers prodded and jabbed their prisoners to get out, but finally had to assist them. Cormac collapsed on the ground. They were in a courtyard of some kind. Grim-looking structures enclosed the area. They entered a small door that led to a large empty room. The room had been painted white a long time ago. There was graffiti all over the place. Someone had scrawled on the wall with a black marker, 'Holding Sty for IRA Pigs.'

A wooden bench had been placed against one wall. Seanie sat down where someone had doodled a naked woman. Two soldiers were left guarding them.

After some time the officer returned with a matronly female. She was dressed in a white nurse's uniform with red army sergeant stripes. Seanie felt himself swaying and darkness closing in. When his sight started to return he was lying on the floor and the officer and nurse were looking down at him. She was saying to the officer, 'It's just a little prissy fainting fit.'

'They maintain they didn't do anything,' said the officer.

'They all say that,' said the nurse.

When Seanie saw the stripes on the nurse's uniform he knew they were in the military wing of Musgrave Park Hospital. The British Army had opened a section in the complex dedicated to treating their own causalities. This part became known as the Military Wing. Fortified like a barracks in a war zone, it was also used as a treatment centre for IRA prisoners who needed hospitalization. Some time back, Brose Rafferty, a friend of Seanie's, was picked up by the Brits and subjected to horrendous treatment, including being shot. He was admitted to the Military Wing. When released, he refused to talk about his experiences in it.

Cormac was in severe distress and moaning about going to the toilet. Two orderlies helped him and Seanie to a toilet area. Cormac wasn't able to urinate. His belly looked to be distended. The same two orderlies then led Seanie through a hospital ward containing about twelve beds. Two of the beds had occupants. Other young men, either in dressing gowns or pyjamas, watched television in a corner of the room. Seanie straightened himself up as best he could. These patients were British soldiers. One of them, his leg encased in plaster of Paris, tried to block their path saying, 'You'll go out of here in a box, you fucker.'

The orderlies brushed Seanie past the man and led him into a room. A doctor wearing a white coat over a soldier's uniform sat at a desk. Another person with a stethoscope around his neck came in. 'We've two terrorist patients who appear to be in limbo,' the first doctor said to his colleague in an upper-class English accent.

'What's their status?' asked the second doctor, who also had an English accent.

'The arresting soldiers report that while resisting capture they sustained injuries, but because of the injuries, the Northern Ireland police are not willing to accept them.'

'Perhaps if you officially record what occurred the RUC will be satisfied?'

The first doctor turned to Seanie. 'OK. What happened to you?'

Seanie wondered at the question. Wasn't it apparent what had happened to him? The doctor was trying to scare him. 'The soldiers did this to me.'

The doctor took a note of his reply. Seanie realized a different response would have meant there were no allegations made about what caused his condition. There was no examination.

After leaving the surgery, Seanie was taken back out to the hospital ward. Cormac was already there lying hunched on the floor. Two chairs were placed in the centre of the room. Seanie and Cormac were made to sit on them facing one another. They were told not to blink. A soldier stood behind each of them. If one of them blinked then the other got struck on the base of the neck with the butt of a rifle and vice versa. A patient in a wheelchair came close to Seanie. He had a pair of crutches resting where his legs ended, and his long hair was tied in a pony-tail. Seanie concentrated on the tip of

Cormac's chin. The rest of the hospital inmates had short crew cuts. The legless man must have been in hospital a long time. He jabbed Seanie in the testicles with one of the crutches. He waved it in front of Seanie's eyes. He tickled his nose with its tip. He asked him to suck it. Seanie kept his mouth closed and his eyes open wide trying hard not to blink. The nurse with the sergeant's stripes stood by a patient's bedside. She smiled at Seanie's facial contortions. On the television screen, John Wayne led a cavalcade of soldiers out of a fort to the music of 'She Wore a Yellow Ribbon'. No one was watching it. A doctor passing through the ward stopped for a minute to observe the cripple amusing himself.

They were back in the army truck. Seanie had been made lie face down on the seat. He felt he was smothering. When forced to move, the thump of a rifle butt caused his head to shift a fraction, which allowed him to breathe. At one point they must have been going by a UDR camp because one of the soldiers suggested dumping them in it. The Ulster Defence Regiment had evolved out of an armed militia known as the B-Specials. The B-Specials had a reputation among nationalists for being beyond the law. Due to political pressure it had been disbanded and renamed, but only the title had changed.

The threat passed, and two hours later the lorry appeared to be pulling into a yard somewhere. 'I'll be glad to see the fucking last of you two,' said the officer.

Seanie and Cormac were unloaded from the personnel carrier. They were back at the RUC police station in Newry.

Half dragged and half carried, they were taken to separate rooms. Seanie tried to understand what was going on. He remembered hearing somewhere that deep breathing helps clear the brain if concussed. Even though it gave him agonizing chest pain he tried to take some deep breaths. Maybe being documented in the military wing had persuaded the police to accept them. But they were still reluctant to be involved.

'They dump their dirty work on us,' he heard one of them say.

Seanie was fingerprinted and forensic swabs were taken from his hands and fingernails. Before being placed in a cell, he was told someone would be taking a statement from him. There was no bed, no toilet facilities, and nowhere to sit in the cell. Some inmates had scraped their names and the date they were there on the walls. The stench of urine was overpowering. Seanie lay shivering on the bare concrete floor and thought of his father and stories he told about the times he spent in various barracks.

'Never make a statement when arrested,' he would warn Seanie when he was a boy. Making a statement meant giving an account, in writing, of the incident that had resulted in one being questioned by the police. He always used the expression, 'when arrested'. At that time he saw his son's arrest as almost inevitable.

A policeman arrived. 'You need to be in hospital,' he said to Seanie in a concerned tone. 'The people who left you in that condition should be jailed.'

He said he'd be back in a few minutes to take a statement. Although glad to see someone not intent on hurting him, Seanie didn't have the energy to reply. Shortly afterwards, a different policeman came into the cell. His face was so red with rage it could have been burned by the sun. He called Seanie a murdering terrorist and Republican scum. 'You're a rat,' he said, 'only fit to be poisoned.'

Seanie could hear the howling and squealing of people being questioned somewhere else in the building. He cowered in the corner of the cell thinking he couldn't take any more.

Another few minutes passed before the friendly RUC man came back. 'Are you ready to confess and get it all off your chest,' he said. 'You'll feel better.'

The policeman wrote Seanie's name, age, and a couple of other details on top of a page. He asked him what he wanted to confess. Seanie tried to clear his mind. Then conjuring up all his resolve, he said, 'The soldiers beat me up. I had no explosives in my car and know nothing about them.' Then he stopped.

'Is that all you want to say?' asked the policeman, surprised.

Seanie nodded.

'Are you sure?'

Seanie nodded again.

'Oh well,' said the cop.

When signing the statement, Seanie thought again of his father and the doctrine he preached: not to incriminate oneself further by signing something without a lawyer present. But he wasn't guilty of anything.

He was placed back in the cell, and was there just a few minutes when the angry policeman unlocked the door and entered.

'I've seen the statement you lying bastard,' he bawled into Seanie's face. 'Do you see this?' He waved a bullet in front of Seanie's eyes. 'It's for you.'

14

Seanie was in a bath. A man in a white coat sponged his face. When he had cleaned off some of the dried blood, the man exclaimed, 'Jesus, it's Seanie O'Rourke.'

After a few minutes, Seanie recognized him. It was an old school friend called Eric. 'Where am I?' he asked, having only a hazy recollection of being taken from the police station.

'You're in Newry General Hospital.'

'What's happening to me?'

'You're being held for having explosives.'

'Where's Cormac?'

'He's OK. There are police guards outside the door.'

Seanie was taken to a room in which there were two beds facing each other end to end. Cormac was in one of them. A policeman in uniform sat beside it. A nurse with the name Sister McGahon pinned to her uniform helped Seanie into bed. As she leaned over to fix the pillows he could feel the softness of her breasts on his chest. She smelled of Lifebuoy soap. He was safe here. She gave Seanie some tablets. A haze of jumbled images appeared inside his head. He was in a strange yard playing football but couldn't get to the ball. At the same time he was under water gasping for air, and a woman with sergeant stripes on her bare arm was laughing at him. Cormac was singing a funny song.

When Seanie awoke the next day, Cormac was already

awake. Two policemen were sitting chatting to each other. Nurse McGahon came into the ward, and after asking Seanie how he was feeling, she leaned across him as if to fix the pillows. She still smelled of Lifebuoy soap.

'I can get you out of here,' she whispered into Seanie's ear.

'How?' mumbled Seanie.

'I'll send out word. You'll be across the border in an hour.'

'What about the police guards?'

'They'll be taken care of. What do you want to do?'

'Ask Cormac.'

The nurse returned in a couple of minutes. 'He said yes.'

Seanie struggled to lift himself up. 'If we escape, we'll look guilty. We didn't do anything, and we'd be on the run.'

Nurse McGahon didn't try to persuade him.

Medical procedures and tests on Seanie and Cormac occupied the next two days. Other than a cracked jawbone, Seanie had sustained no permanent injuries. Cormac had internal damage that would take much longer to heal. During the madness in the prison yard when the soldiers were focused on Seanie, Cormac had tried to escape by crawling under army trucks. In the darkness he managed to elude his captors for some time and made it to the perimeter wall. Recaptured, the futile attempt only served to increase his ill-treatment.

Being guarded by the armed police restricted their conversation. However, Seanie could make his way over to Cormac's bed, and they talked in whispers. Then on the third day, a detective named Gordon appeared. He was a middle-aged man with a serious face and a nervous tic that caused his head to move involuntarily, reminding Seanie of a robin on the branch of a tree. He informed them that he would be formally charging them with having explosives, and a hearing would be held in the ward later that evening. Their relatives had been told to organize a solicitor. After the hearing they would be remanded in custody. A helicopter was standing by to transfer them to the military wing of Musgrave Park Hospital. When they had recovered sufficiently they would go to Crumlin Road Gaol while awaiting trial. He said from a policing perspective this hospital was not a secure environment. When Seanie asked could they not get bail, the detective's tic became more pronounced. He explained that on such a serious charge bail would be opposed and automatically refused by the Justice.

Then he charged each of them in turn with having explosives substances in their possession with intent to endanger life. He asked Seanie if he wished to say anything. Seanie said, 'I'm not guilty.' The policeman wrote this down. After being charged, Cormac was asked if he wished to say anything. 'Nothing,' said Cormac in disgust. The policeman also wrote this down.

Once he had gone, Seanie went over to Cormac's bedside.

'No way am I going back to the military wing,' said Cormac.

'We'll have to make a break for it,' said Seanie.

'We should have been gone when we'd the chance.'

'I know.'

'Why don't you ever listen?' said Cormac.

'Now's not the time to be arguing about that. We need to get hold of Sister McGahon. Can you walk?'

'I'll crawl on my belly sooner than return to that military wing hellhole.'

It was Sister McGahon's day off. Seanie asked the ward nurse to ring her. He told her to tell the Sister that he and Cormac had changed their minds about the trip and needed to go immediately. While they waited, the captives couldn't discuss how their rescuers might set about freeing them because of the police guards who were constantly coming in and out of the ward. One of them, a religious zealot, had tried to approach the subject of repentance a couple of times with his captives, but when rebuffed by silence he decided the devil had them in his grip. But now the boot was on the other foot. The intending escapees didn't want the policemen to suspect anything. Seanie asked the man who wanted to save their souls for a cigarette. The request pleased the policeman immensely. Maybe the Lord was answering his prayers. He told them he didn't smoke, or agree with such self-indulgence, but would send out for some. While they waited, Seanie had Cormac out of the bed trying to get him to walk, which helped pass the time and calm their nerves.

The ward nurse came back. She told them she had eventually managed to get in touch with Sister McGahon's mother who said her daughter wasn't at her own home but she would try and contact her. Seanie got up, lay down, and got up again. He tried to visualize how a getaway would be mounted. What if it wasn't successful? What if he or Cormac got shot?

A man came into the room. He said his job was to prepare the ward to be used as a courtroom. Just then, the ward nurse returned to say Sister McGahon had gone to Dublin for the day.

Cormac was distraught. He blamed Seanie. 'Due to you thinking you know everything,' he said, not caring now if the guards heard him or not, 'we're back in yon place with the nurse wearing sergeant's stripes. Then if we survive that, it's Crumlin Road Gaol.'

'I'm sorry,' said Seanie.

'Sorry?' said Cormac, firing a book at the wall in anger. 'What good is that?'

'What can I say?' said Seanie.

'If you weren't so pig-headed stubborn we never would have went out that night to begin with, and then me as big a dummy as yourself followed everything you said.'

Cormac lay down on the bed and pulled the blankets over his head. 'God, but I'm one idiot.'

The hospital ward was now a temporary courtroom. The court attendant placed a battered-looking Bible on the table that would suffice for a judge's bench. The man told Seanie he never had to set up a courtroom in hospital before, so he took the Bible just in case. He said it was supposed to be the same one Thomas Russell took the oath on during his trial.

'Thomas Russell had this actual Bible in his hands,' said Seanie to Cormac, trying to mollify his friend.

'They hung him,' said Cormac from under the blankets.

Shortly afterwards, Seanie's father and his Uncle Gerry were ushered into the room. Seanie's heart sank even further. Gerry was a lawyer, and by common consent, had one of the most brilliant legal minds in the country. 'It's a pity about the drink,' people would often say.

Gerry was a chronic alcoholic. Always broke, he only managed to survive by pulling strokes, which he loved to boast about when inebriated. Though totally boring after hearing them a few times, one of Seanie's favourites involved a drunk driving charge. Gerry's client was guilty and had no hope of winning the case, which is maybe why he asked Gerry to represent him. He was also wealthy, so there would be a nice fee if Gerry could swing it. The case opened just before lunch and then adjourned for the break. During the interval, while having lunch in a pub restaurant, Gerry noticed the prosecution officer going to the toilet. Gerry was a good customer in the bar. He gave the barman a handsome tip to lock the prosecution officer in the toilet and to pretend there was a problem with the lock. Other customers were diverted to a different toilet. When the court resumed, the judge enquired about the missing prosecutor. Gerry informed him that the last time he saw the prosecutor he was in a bar having refreshments. The judge – a cranky master in his own house type – waited and waited. Eventually, when the missing man failed to turn up, he angrily ridiculed the lack of an explanation for his absence and dismissed the case.

Seanie's uncle said they hadn't much time to prepare. He wanted to hear all that happened. The smell of drink off him was overpowering.

Just before the case commenced, Eileen and Cormac's mother were allowed in to visit the two men. As soon as she entered the room, Eileen rushed towards Seanie and began to hug him.

'I'm sorry ma'am,' said the policeman standing beside the bed. 'There must be no physical contact with the prisoner.'

Eileen didn't heed him and kept her arms around Seanie. Seeing the fury on Cormac's mother's face, Cormac's guard said nothing when she embraced her son. Then she turned to the two policemen and began to call them names. 'Torturers, murderers, English scum,' she screamed at them.

Both RUC men took up positions away from the beds and stayed silent. They didn't interfere any more in the emotional reunions. When Uncle Gerry heard about the commotion he made Cormac's mother promise to stay quiet during the trial, saying it would only make things worse for the two men if she caused any disturbance. He reminded them that Seanie and Cormac were at this moment more worried about their immediate future than their recent past.

The Justice's table was centred in the space between the bottom of each bed. In front of it sat the prosecuting police chief, Inspector Goodboy, and the accused men's solicitor, Uncle Gerry. Because of space restrictions, only Eileen and Cormac's mother were allowed to be present. They sat on chairs against the far wall. Seanie's father had wanted to be present, but Gerry told him that it would be better if he wasn't seen. His background might have a negative impact in this situation.

Goodboy and Uncle Gerry studied documents. The court attendant stood just inside the door. The room was stuffy. The windows had reinforced steel shutters. There was a smell of alcohol. Everyone waited. A wasp took off from somewhere and broke the stillness, before setting down again.

At last there came a little rap on the door. The attendant shouted, 'Everyone stand.'

This instruction caused Seanie, who was propped up with pillows, to smile thinly. He caught Cormac's eye, who was also sitting up, obviously in discomfort. They were both wearing the same navy blue hospital pyjamas. Seanie tried to make himself more comfortable. He was angry. Everyone stand? They weren't able to stand. Was that guy an idiot?

The attendant opened the door. A small, delicate man with receding grey hair, dressed in a brown suit, entered the room. Seanie wondered about the little man's background. He remembered Uncle Gerry explaining to him when he was a child that judges were solicitors before being appointed judges. He had asked his uncle would he become a judge? Gerry had smiled and said it was unlikely. On being pressed why, Gerry said he dug with the wrong foot. At the time

Seanie didn't know what this meant, but he had no doubt as to which foot this person who would decide their future dug with.

Justice Finn allowed himself a brief glance at his surroundings and then focused on where he would be seated. He sat down and quickly scrutinized the charge sheet before peering over his half-moon glasses to address Gerry. 'Do you wish to say anything in respect to the charges levied against the two accused before I decide on a course of action?'

Seanie thought he sounded impatient, almost as if he wanted an unpleasant chore over and done with. 'I wish to point out,' continued the judge, 'this is likely to be a decision which I understand the defendants were made aware of when being charged.'

Seanie shook his head. The outcome was settled. Almost hesitantly, Uncle Gerry rose to his feet. The solicitor was wearing a blue pinstriped suit. A purple handkerchief protruded from the top pocket. The matching waistcoat had buttons missing due to pressure from a distended belly. The heels of his shoes had a forty-five degree angle to them. Seanie had never seen him dressed any other way. His mother often told a story that once when Seanie was a child and she was putting on his pyjamas, he asked her if Uncle Gerry wore pyjamas or his suit in bed. Now his face was fleshy and unhealthy looking; little remained of his once handsome features.

He just stood there. Then very slowly he began to survey the room, as if trying think of something to say. He looked at Eileen and Cormac's mother sitting nervously on chairs against the wall. He looked at the steel-shuttered windows blocking out any chink of daylight. He looked at the court attendant standing almost to attention. He looked at Seanie propped up in bed. He looked at Cormac. Finally, turning towards the judge he focused his eyes on him. 'May it please Your Honour to spend a couple of moments taking note of our surroundings.'

Seanie had forgotten how much he loved listening to his uncle's voice. When he spoke he could turn words into poetry. Sentences were not said as much as performed. At college he had been involved in amateur dramatics, and he once had a small part in an Abbey Theatre production in Dublin. This was at a time when he could carouse all night and be fine the following day. Nevertheless, although it wasn't spoken about in the family, rumours had reached home that the high hopes for him becoming a famous actor were not helped by his sometimes turning up for performances under the influence. He eventually graduated as a solicitor. A courtroom is just another stage, he would say. 'Words,' he liked to pronounce grandly, hands waving in the air as if he were performing Shakespeare, 'are the tools of the actor, and words are the tools of the advocate.'

Now he paused as everyone, including the Justice, instinctively looked around the ward. Then Gerry spoke. His voice rose as he articulated the words. 'When you, Your Honour, my valued friend beside me, and myself, were learning how to practice our noble profession, a profession that seeks justice for the guilty *and* the innocent, did any of us envisage it would be conducted in environments such as we find ourselves this evening?'

When he finished the sentence he waved his hand theatrically, indicating the room, and then paused to let the words sink in. In sharp contrast his voice went low. 'What's of importance here is not the guilt or innocence of these two men. It's not the false charge levelled against them. It's not the fact that they have been set up to lessen the culpability of people guilty of a much more heinous crime. No. What's of importance here is something much more fundamental. It's something that goes to the heart of our way of life. Regardless of the guilt or innocence of these victims, I ask, should this hearing have to be conducted in these surroundings and in these circumstances?'

Again he paused. 'Because if the answer is yes, then I do not wish any more to be involved in such a travesty. When I make representations to so-called higher authorities as to what has happened to victims such as these two men, I'm met with,' he shouted the word, '*silence.*'

'*Silence,*' he cried out, 'is the noise that was heard from the Nazi camps in Germany. *Silence*, is the noise that was heard from the Stalinist gulags in Russia. *Silence*, is the noise being heard from the army generals in Northern Ireland.'

Then his voice became almost a whisper. 'This court must not stay silent. It must not stay silent when confronted with a defendant who has been subjected to a mock crucifixion. It must not stay silent when confronted with a defendant that has been subjected to live entombment.'

Seanie realized that Gerry was referring to his own whipping in a crucifixion position, and to Cormac being buried under concrete blocks. Once more Gerry paused, straightened his shoulders, and again his voice kept rising as he spoke. 'This court *must* take account of the environment we find ourselves in. This court *must*,' he paused, 'this court *must* take into account the condition of these men. This court *must* allow these victims time to recover in an atmosphere which is not just another arm of the organization whose actions were responsible for them ending up as patients in this hospital.'

Again he stopped for several moments. Then in a normal professional voice, he said, 'I am asking that it may please the court to remand the accused on bail until such a time as they can be vindicated at trial.'

Gerry plonked down on his seat. He pulled the purple handkerchief from his top pocket and dabbed the perspiration on his brow. Justice Finn cleared his throat politely and loosened the front collar of his shirt with his little finger. He kept looking at the papers in front of him. Then, glancing up, he nodded almost imperceptibly towards the police inspector.

Inspector Goodboy stood up. He was middle-aged, tall and good-looking, the way Protestants are good-looking. He wore an inspector's uniform with three gold stars on the shoulders. Seanie wondered if he had got much ridicule when growing up because of his name. Maybe if he had, it would have made him more sensitive to other people; but, maybe it would have made him more resentful. 'Your Honour,' said the Inspector, 'I am constrained to oppose the granting of bail to the accused.'

He spoke with a clipped, slightly Scottish accent indicating he was raised in North Antrim, and almost certainly descended from solid, Presbyterian planter stock. They weren't always the worst, thought Seanie. Then Goodboy stopped before continuing. 'However, I wish to say something more. My colleague, whom I hold in the highest regard, has made an impassioned plea for justice to be done. These are sentiments I cannot disagree with. It's in all our interests that righteousness be achieved. It would be self-defeating if people who quite obviously have been treated in an abominable fashion were not to be given every chance to recover in an environment that fully facilitates that recuperation. My impression is that the medical attention being provided in this present location is most suitable.'

At that point the wasp that had been periodically flitting about the room started to buzz around the judge. He tried to brush it away but it kept encircling his head until he eventually called a halt to the prosecutor's speech, and asked the court attendant to do something about it. The prosecutor sat down and everybody watched while the court attendant followed the wasp, waiting for it to land. After it alighted, he struck at it with a sheaf of documents that he got from Gerry. The wasp escaped every strike, and after a few more misses, the judge ordered the court attendant to desist. 'Never mind,' he said. 'The case will soon be concluded.'

The prosecutor stood up again and continued. 'I began by saying that it is my duty in cases such as the present one to oppose bail. But, may it please Your Honour, I recognize when you are making your learned decision that you may wish to take account of wider considerations in this instance. Judicial requirements, with their bare legal strictures, are not always the only or sometimes even the best option. I have listened carefully to the words of the defendants' solicitor and respectfully state that I will have no issue if you were to decide upon an alternative course to the one that may have been envisaged.'

The inspector sat down. There was quiet in the room. The wasp had stopped buzzing. All eyes were on the little man in a brown suit, peering at sheaves of papers. Outside, the noise of a passing helicopter made a swishing sound. The judge cleared his throat again. Then lifting his head and speaking into the distance, he said, 'On the following conditions I will grant bail to the two defendants.'

Nobody heard the rest of his judgment. Eileen and

Cormac's mother started clapping. Even the court attendant seemed delighted. Bail was set at £10,000 each, but when the hubbub had died down there was concern at such an enormous amount. This was until Gerry explained it wasn't necessary to lodge the actual money in court. Getting someone to sign a bond, which was forfeited in event of the accused not turning up, was all that was necessary.

Gerry told them that what swayed the judge was the fact that they were in hospital, and that the prosecutor was agreeable to them getting bail. Neither of these things would apply when the case came to trial. But in the meantime, they were free men. 'God, I could do with a drink,' he said. 'Where did Goodboy go? I had arranged to meet up with him after the hearing.'

At last Seanie and Cormac could talk openly together about what had happened. Cormac said there was no point in them arguing over whether they should ever have gone out that night as they couldn't change what happened.

'Where do we go from here?' asked Seanie.

'Let's get out of this place first before we start making any plans,' said Cormac.

Sister McGahon visited them that night, and when told about the wasp incident, she said it was an IRA wasp. Seanie said it was Thomas Russell's spirit. When the nurse hugged them both on leaving, Seanie decided she always used the same Lifebuoy soap. Later, he heard a chopper take off. He fell asleep figuring out how a transport helicopter full of soldiers might be brought down.

15

Seanie sat in the hotel car park. He was early. This was the hotel in which he had his wedding reception. The weather had been beautiful then; today, it was mizzling rain. He felt he should be more excited about what he intended to do. He looked around to check for strangers coming and going, but there were very few cars about. It was too early in the evening for much to be happening in the hotel. His mind kept drifting back to his wedding day and the excitement of his love for Eileen, and how beautiful she looked. A jeep pulled up alongside his car. Seanie got out of his car and into the passenger side of the Land Rover.

Dickie Stone was putting on weight and getting a middle-aged look about him. The Northern Ireland security forces were well aware of his status in the Provos' chain of command, but at this stage of his life he wouldn't be involved in active service. Even though the police regularly arrested him they could do little about his activities. However, nothing went on in the IRA locally without his approval. The two men chatted for a minute about a young couple they could see entering the hotel, and decided they must be there to book their wedding.

'What about Ratigan?' said Seanie. 'He's become some kind of legend.'

Stone smiled. 'Legends are often built on falsehoods and

yarns. Ratigan's only a fifty per cent man as regard the struggle. The other half has to do with greed. He's holed up across the border, around Monaghan somewhere.'

'I agree with you about his commitment to the cause,' said Seanie.

'I'm going to take a little look around,' said Stone. 'The enemy have all kinds of surveillance equipment nowadays that you only find out about when it's too late.'

Seanie watched him stroll casually around the car park. Nobody would be suspicious about what he was doing. On his return he said to Seanie, 'What's on your mind?'

'I want to join up,' said Seanie. He had been looking forward to this moment and seeing Stone's expression. He knew Stone had despaired of ever getting him involved.

The IRA man didn't reply for a minute or two. Then he said, 'Seanie, I know you want revenge. While ideally this should not be the reason for wanting to be a member of the IRA, it's usually possible to tell if a man's suitable material. I've known you for a long time, Seanie. You're not suitable material.'

'What do you mean?'

'You don't have what it takes to do what has to be done.'

'That's bullshit.'

'It requires a certain kind of person, Seanie.'

'Didn't you always want me to follow in my father's footsteps?'

'Your talents are at a political level.'

'My father always wanted me to play my part, and now so do I, but not going around distributing pamphlets.'

'You've given me two reasons for wanting to shoot British soldiers. One, for revenge, and two, because your father wants you to. Irish patriots are not driven by a desire for revenge or because their parents would like them to die for Ireland. However, this isn't why I'm not going to recommend you.'

'Why then?'

'Because you'd baulk at certain tasks.'

'You're wrong,' said Seanie.

'I'm sorry,' said Stone. 'And I have to go now. We've sat here long enough.'

Stone started up the Land Rover. 'Join Sinn Féin, Seanie. That's where you'll make the biggest impact.'

Seanie went back to his own vehicle. How could he get revenge without help? Was Stone right about him?

Seanie was reading the newspaper when Eileen came in carrying the shopping. He jumped up to help her. She set the bags down on the table. 'I've news to tell you.'

'Oh yeah?' said Seanie.

'I'm pregnant.'

'What?'

'I'm pregnant.'

Seanie stared at her. 'Jesus! How do you know?'

Eileen burst out laughing. 'I was at the doctor.'

Seanie threw his arms around her. 'God, that's unbelievable.'

'Why?'

'It just is.'

'Other people have had babies, you know.'

'Wait until Cormac hears about this,' said Seanie.

'The doctor wants to monitor me very closely.'

Seanie held her at arm's length to look into her face. 'Why? What's wrong?'

'There's nothing wrong. It's just all the trouble you've

been in, and the trial and everything. He thinks I'm under a lot of stress.'

'God forbid, if anything were to happen the baby, it would be the fault of those English bastards.'

'Don't be daft, Seanie. That's not going to happen.'

'You sit down and rest. From now on I'm doing the shopping and everything.'

'That great,' said Eileen. 'I wish I'd have got pregnant sooner.'

'Just leave everything to me,' said Seanie.

'Seanie,' said Eileen, extracting herself from his arms and sitting down on the sofa, 'would you think of moving somewhere else?'

'Why?'

'Because this isn't the best place to be bringing up a child.'

'Maybe the Troubles will soon end.'

'They haven't ended around here for these last three hundred years.'

'This is our home, where we were born and reared.'

'It's a war zone, that's what it is.'

'We didn't start the war.'

'No, and look what happened to you.'

'I'm still alive,' said Seanie.

'Alive!' said Eileen angrily. 'I'm not bringing a child into this world just to be alive. And I'm not bringing a child into the world to be shot, or to be jailed . . . or to die for Ireland.'

Seanie sat down beside Eileen and put his arms around her. 'It'll be all right, darling. No one's going to die for Ireland, be shot for Ireland, go to jail for Ireland, or let anything else happen to them for Ireland.'

The balmy ripeness of a late summer evening had settled over the fields. Rank smells of fresh silage in pits and slurry being spread on newly mown meadows filled the air. Crows were circling and busily cawing their goodnights to each other above the tree tops. Seanie meandered casually by the side of the ditch. The doctor had told him to exercise. He had put it from his mind that he should really be doing a brisk walk. Away in the distance he could see Eileen working in the back garden, probably weeding the shrub beds. He wished she would heed the doctor and rest more. Would the baby be a boy or a girl, he wondered. He picked up a stone and lobbed it ahead of him towards a clump of briars. Where it landed, something stirred. It was most likely a pheasant, or a hare's nest he had disturbed. Maybe, if he was lucky, a hen pheasant's nest. That would be interesting. He could check on it every day and watch the progression of the chicks or the eggs, if there were any. When he reached the spot where the stone landed Seanie couldn't see any sign of life, but there was a mass of tangled shrubs and undergrowth. Determined to find the nest, he hacked at the tangled bushes with a tree branch. After just a few swipes he found a space that had been fashioned out in the drain of the ditch. There were empty bully beef cans and cigarette packets lying around. He had stumbled upon an SAS hide. These soldiers were the elite of the British armed services. From this position they had a clear view of his house. They had been watching his comings and goings, who knows for how long. Worst of all, Eileen had a habit of not pulling the blinds on these long, summer evenings. Everything going on inside the house would have been clearly visible. He looked around him. Maybe they had him in their sights at this minute. They could even have their binoculars trained on Eileen in the garden. Seanie walked home much faster. He couldn't her tell about his discovery, it would only scare her.

The evening football match ended all square. Ballyduff was hard hit by losing team members to emigration, to prison cells, and to others being on the run. Two of their best players in years now lay in the cemetery's Republican plot. So a draw against an opposition that headed the league table wasn't a bad result. Seanie said so to Dickie Stone on the way out. He had manoeuvred his exit to be accidently walking beside him. Stone agreed. When they came to Stone's jeep, Seanie asked could he avail of this chance meeting to have a word with him. 'No problem,' said Stone. 'Jump in.'

Seanie got into the passenger seat. Most of the spectators had drifted away by now and it was almost dark. A street light illuminated the inside of the vehicle with an orange glare.

'Dickie,' said Seanie coming straight to the point. 'What did you mean by saying I was too cowardly to be accepted.'

Stone shook his head in a gesture of mild frustration. 'I didn't say you were too cowardly to be accepted. I said you would baulk at certain tasks.'

'I will hold my own and face the enemy in any situation,' said Seanie.

'You don't understand, Seanie, the nature of the enemy you might be called on to face.'

'So I'm cowardly?'

'No.'

'What am I then?'

Stone stared out through the windscreen and thought for a few moments. Then he said, 'You're lucky.'

'I don't understand,' said Seanie.

'You probably don't,' said Stone. 'But I better be getting home.'

'Please wait,' said Seanie. 'Don't leave me like this. You said last time about how long we've known each other. Surely you owe me something. What do you mean by the nature of the enemy?'

Again Stone didn't answer immediately, and it seemed to Seanie that the IRA man had made up his mind to elaborate. Seanie pressed home his opportunity. 'I won't back down under fire.'

A thin smile appeared on Stone's mouth. 'The enemy may not be firing at you,' he said.

Seanie knew there was more coming so he said nothing. 'This war Seanie, like most guerrilla wars, is not conducted in the manner of two armies facing each other in battle, or even very seldom in an actual firefight. That's the heroic bit.'

Stone stopped talking and watched a car drive into the car park, turn and drive out again. Satisfied it wasn't anyone interested in himself, he continued, 'In this type of war the most dangerous enemy, the one that inflicts the most damage, never confronts you face to face in battle.'

Seanie waited to hear more. 'Think of this, Seanie. You're in a cold, isolated tin shed somewhere. Maybe the rain is leaking through the roof. It's dark outside. The wind is howling. In front of you is someone who might have sat beside you at school. He is tied to a chair, blindfolded and gagged. You think of Eileen at home. She is wondering where you are and what you are doing at this minute. But you put thoughts of her out of your mind because you are on active service and have a job to do. The man in the chair is an informer, Seanie. He is the most dangerous enemy of all, and as in any army when confronted by the enemy, it is your job to eliminate him. You point the gun in your hand at the back of his head. You know that underneath the blindfold, his eyes are wide open. You know they are mad with terror. You know that if you remove the gag he will promise you anything in the world if you let him live. Anything in the world in his power to give. You know he will screech and sob. He will beg, plead, and beseech you. He will kiss your feet if you want. Perhaps you will remember that he once let you play with his champion conker. At that moment, Seanie, you will hesitate. You will hesitate because you know that the spark that is life in front of you will be extinguished in an instant. In the blink of an eye you will have turned a pulsating, living force into something as lifeless as an old mattress on a rubbish dump. The eyes underneath the blindfold will still be wide open, but now they are frozen and glassy. You will know all this, so you will baulk at doing what has to be done.'

Stone paused. His voice changed to a whisper. He seemed to be speaking to himself now. 'What you will not know about is the dreams, Seanie.'

Seanie glanced over at Stone. The IRA veteran's face had a strange expression. Maybe it was the orange glare from the street lamp playing tricks. The Provo took a deep breath and turned to him. 'Go home, Seanie,' he said.

Seanie hesitated for a few moments before getting out of the vehicle. Then, just as he was about to close the door and move away, Stone said, 'Seanie.'

'Yeah?'

'You're not a coward.'

Seanie didn't reply.

The football committee had organized the party in McIver's as a gesture of solidarity after what had happened to two of their members. Cormac had taken his own car and he met with Seanie and Eileen outside the pub. It wouldn't be safe for two men on remand to travel together. When they entered at the bar, people clapped. Seanie found it all a bit embarrassing. They didn't really do anything to merit a celebration. But McIver would get a little business on a quiet night, and it would also be good for the club's morale. The most surprising thing was that everyone seemed to think he and Cormac had been on an IRA mission when arrested. There wasn't any point in arguing otherwise. Slash upgraded him from being as good a man as his father to being an even better man than his father. Seanie told them about coming upon the soldier's nest. 'Those guys,' said Slash, 'have binoculars so powerful they can see every bad tooth in your mouth from five miles away.'

The craic was good. Cormac was pressed to say something about what the soldiers did to him. He described how concrete blocks had been built on his shoulders while he was in a search position against a wall. He dared not move and they kept building still more blocks on top of each other. He felt his back was about to snap. But then one of the soldiers kicked him between the legs, knocking him, blocks and all, to the ground. 'It was such a relief,' he said, 'I almost thanked him.'

Eileen complained of being tired after a couple of hours, so Seanie made his excuses and they left. On their way home they were stopped at a checkpoint. Eileen was driving in the hope that if held up, Seanie's identity wouldn't be checked. At first the soldiers were pleasant enough. This was before they radioed the details of her licence to Central Control. Once word came back, it became clear by their changed attitude that the soldiers had recognized who the couple were. As far as they were concerned, Seanie was a terrorist out on bail. After some chat among themselves, one of the soldiers

A Fight For Freedom

pointed towards a group of his comrades about a quarter of a mile further up the road. He told Eileen to move ahead slowly and stop at an old derelict house alongside the road. She was to await permission before advancing any further. Eileen drove cautiously to the deserted dwelling and halted. She was now parked halfway between the two checkpoints. Seanie noticed a rope leading from the checkpoint up ahead running into the house. Then it struck him. A roadside bomb had been discovered in the building and a disposal team had attached a rope to it. The explosive device was being hauled out of the house, yards from where they were made to park the car. If it detonated, the report would be that he and Eileen were transporting a bomb and it exploded prematurely, or it had gone off as they were driving past.

Eileen also spotted the rope and realized the danger they were in. 'What'll we do?' she asked, terrified.

Seanie said nothing for a moment. The soldiers were scared and trigger-happy. If they tried to drive away they would probably be shot. If they stayed still and the bomb exploded they would likely die. He looked at Eileen and thought of the baby growing inside her. A bomb blast can travel in any direction. It might take the opposite course away from them. There may not be a bomb. Even if there was, it may not go off. Better to stay where they were and hope.

'It's a false alarm,' Seanie said to Eileen. 'But just to be sure bend over and cover your head with your arms.'

Eileen didn't speak. She did as Seanie instructed. He also covered his face, but watched through his fingers as the rope slowly pulled whatever it was fastened to out of the house. The object turned out to be a plastic farm fertilizer bag with something inside it. Bit by bit the suspect bomb was edged out. Seanie prayed it wouldn't snag on anything. Eventually it was clear of the building. It inched ever closer to where they were parked. Finally, after what seemed an eternity, the bag lay on the roadside. The attached rope gave a few sharp jerks. Nothing happened.

Seanie felt himself beginning to breathe again when he saw the soldiers up ahead coming towards the car. On reaching it, one of them glanced into the bag. He gave it a kick and said to Seanie, 'You have as many fucking lives as a cat, mate.'

Seanie looked at him without reply. Maybe they suspected all along there was no bomb in the bag. Maybe they thought there was and were now disappointed. He would never know. They were told they could go. No words were spoken until they reached home. Once there, Eileen jumped out of the car and rushed into the house. Seanie sat for a moment collecting his thoughts. Enough was enough. In spite of what Stone said, he was entitled to fight back. When he went into the house he found Eileen lying on the bed sobbing into the pillows. She kept saying she couldn't take any more. Seanie hugged her and said, 'We'll get even with the bastards.'

Eileen put her two hands over her ears and screeched, 'I don't want to get even. I want to get away.'

There were about a dozen people in the bar when he walked in. One guy who had been down on the pool cue about to strike hesitated and straightened himself up to look at the stranger. The rest of the customers, mostly young fellas, also stared. Seanie acted casually. The bar wouldn't be this quiet if he hadn't entered. At the counter the barman feigned disinterest in him when he asked for a bottle of Harp. The clicking of pool balls began again. That didn't mean the players had lost their curiosity. In a strong Belfast accent the barman said, 'It's a dull night.'

For a moment Seanie pondered why there were so many Belfast barmen working pubs in the border region. But he knew the man's statement had nothing to do with friendliness or about increasing business. Least of all was it about the weather. Seanie just nodded agreement.

He surveyed the room. It had practically none of the trappings of a Provo haunt, except perhaps for a huge picture of Fergal O'Hanlon on the back wall, which was to be expected. He had passed a memorial to him on the way into town. O'Hanlon had been shot dead along with Sean South in an attack on Brookeborough RUC barracks. That was during the Fifties Border Campaign. He remembered his father's distress when the news came through about the deaths of the two men. He had wanted to put his arms around his daddy's neck and console him, but couldn't.

'The white ball is stuck, Billy,' one of the pool players shouted to the barman.

'Drop a few balls into the same pocket,' he replied. 'That should release it.'

Seanie sipped his beer and glanced at the details of O'Hanlon's life printed beneath the picture. Dickie Stone had been active then. Would he have been a member of the unit that attacked the police station? He always spoke with great affection for O'Hanlon. Perhaps with Stone being from South Armagh and the dead hero being a Monaghan man, they had a lot in common.

Seanie turned to Billy the barman and asked him if Frank Ratigan often came in.

'I don't know the name,' was the reply.

Seanie leaned forward, and in a low voice said, 'Will you see to it that he gets a message that Seanie O'Rourke wants to meet with him in the Oasis on Friday evening at nine.'

Billy just looked at Seanie. He didn't reply. Seanie took another swallow of his drink. As he turned to leave he pulled a pound note from his pocket and placed the tip under his glass. It was still half-full of beer.

On Friday evening, as Seanie sat in the bar lounge of the Oasis, he reflected on the hotel's strange name. It was located in an isolated part of Patrick Kavanagh's 'Stony grey soil of Monaghan', only a few miles from where the poet was born. He decided it was well named. Its remoteness suited his requirements just now.

Ratigan's scout wasn't very professional. It would be obvious to anyone watching what he was at. Seanie was going to wave to him but decided not to. It might be an insult to let the man know he had been uncovered. Ratigan didn't introduce him to Seanie. The scout moved away to keep a lookout while the meeting took place. The Provo was taking no chances. Set-ups were not uncommon, and the SAS had recently taken to entering the Republic in attempts to kidnap leading Provos. As he shook Seanie's hand, Ratigan said, 'I heard about your adventures.'

Seanie ordered a drink for them both.

'You have become a bit of a Michael Collins,' said Seanie, deciding a bit of flattery wouldn't do any harm.

'Fuck Michael Collins,' said Ratigan.

Seanie was about to take a sip from his beer. 'Why do you say that?'

'He was swanning around like some kind of Irish General Custer.'

'Oh yeah?'

'And like Custer, he was in places he shouldn't have been.'

'Perhaps.'

'Because of that he came to the same sticky end. Anyway, let's get down to business.'

'It's my adventures, as you call them, that has me here.'

'How I can help?'

'I need a weapon, an assault rifle. One with the capacity to inflict serious casualties.'

Ratigan didn't speak for a few moments. He opened and closed his fist, seemingly studying the mechanics of his hand. Then he said, 'I can see where you're coming from, but what about talking to Stone and joining up?'

'Stone's no help. He thinks I'm too soft.'

Seanie could see it didn't take much to make Ratigan animated about the IRA leader. 'He's only a bollocks,' said Ratigan. 'It's a nursery he should be running,'

'Yeah.'

'It's only natural you should want to get your own back, but it may not be easy to access what you're looking for.'

'You can't do it?'

'I didn't say that. However, there's a strict check kept on materials; the quartermaster is a stickler. Usually he won't release weapons unless he's satisfied the operation has been officially sanctioned. It will cost you.'

Seanie put his hand in his pocket and took out two fifty pound notes. 'Will this cover it?'

He could see the greed in the IRA man's eyes. 'Who's Stone to say you can or cannot get revenge on the bastards who abused you?' said Ratigan.

'That's what I think,' said Seanie.

'We go back a long way. I always knew you had the right breeding in you.'

Seanie said nothing.

'Leave it with me and I'll be in touch. Pass the leaves

under the table. I'll need them to sweeten certain people.'

Seanie knew that Ratigan wouldn't require bribes to get what he wanted, but still he handed him the money.

16

Each time Seanie and Cormac appeared in court, the prosecution said they hadn't completed their enquiries and the case was adjourned. Most times, Uncle Gerry turned up for the hearing. On this occasion, he was nowhere to be seen. His assistant, Phonsie, gave them a wave when they came into the court room. When their case was called, the young solicitor stood up and said that he represented the two men, and that he was seeking a renewal of their bail on the same terms. As the prosecution had no objections, the Justice duly granted the request. Afterwards, Phonsie said Gerry wanted to see them in his office.

Gerry's office was located at the top of a staircase in a building adjacent to the courthouse. The carpet on the stairs was dirty and frayed. He didn't have a receptionist. Inside the small smoky office, old land maps rested on their end in a corner beside a huge filing cabinet. Three kitchen chairs were piled on top of each other against a wall, and a desk littered with documents filled the centre of the room. It was covered with cigarette burns and the rim marks of coffee cups. On top of the documents, an ashtray overflowed with cigarette butts. Gerry, who had been drinking, sat behind the desk.

Seanie decided not to say anything about the solicitor's failure to attend the court, knowing he would make the excuse that the bail renewal was only a formality.

'Grab a chair,' said his uncle, who seemed cheery and keen to engage in small talk. He asked how they were doing.

'OK,' said Seanie.

'Fully recovered?'

'Almost.'

'What about Eileen?'

'She's fine.'

'And your mother, Cormac?'

'Fine also,' said Cormac.

Seanie began to suspect something was wrong.

'Will either of you have a drink?' Gerry asked.

Both of them said no.

'You don't mind if I have one?'

Without waiting for an answer, Gerry got up and went over to a filing cabinet. He pulled open a drawer and from among a jumble of files he extracted a half-empty bottle of Powers whiskey. On top of the filing cabinet were two mugs covered in coffee stains. One still had some foul-looking stuff in it. Gerry slid up the window sash and tossed the contents through the opening. Seanie wondered what was underneath the window. The solicitor, pouring some whiskey into one of the mugs, said, '*Sláinte.*'

The raw liquor made him choke. 'You sure you won't have one?' he said hoarsely.

Both men nodded.

'Did you ever hear about the time I got McIver off for serving after hours?'

'Gerry, we heard about that. Can you please concentrate on *our* case,' said Seanie.

Gerry took another gulp from the cup. 'Yeah, I guess I should,' he said, and then paused for a few moments.

'Well?' said Seanie.

Gerry lowered his eyes to some papers lying on his desk. 'The frenzy results are not good,' he muttered.

'What are you saying?' asked Seanie.

Gerry looked up and cleared his throat. 'I have the evidence from the forensic people in front of me.'

'And so?' said Seanie.

'You know when the RUC took those swabs in Newry Police Station?'

'What about them?'

'They came back positive.'

'What does that mean?'

'It means you had been handling explosives.'

'That can't be right.'

'There were traces found on your hands and under your fingernails.'

'What about me?' said Cormac.

'Clear,' said Gerry.

'I don't understand. Why Seanie and not me?'

Gerry shrugged his shoulders.

'What does it mean for us?' said Seanie.

The solicitor pushed aside the documents littering the desk and leaned forward. 'Let me lay it on the line to you, Seanie.'

Seanie recoiled from the blast of whiskey breath that hit him in the face.

'One, you have been charged with having explosives in your possession. Two, the name O'Rourke, and the fact you're from South Armagh, on its own is almost enough to convict you. Three, the explosives existed because you were shown them. Four, there will be any amount of witnesses prepared to swear on oath they found them in your car. Five, you were arrested in a border area not a mile from where two soldiers were killed by bomb explosions on that day. Six, the results of the forensics prove you had handled explosives. What it all boils down to is that you've no chance of convincing a judge or jury you're innocent.'

Gerry lit a cigarette, inhaled deeply, and then continued with the smoke coming from his mouth. 'In your case, it's different, Cormac. You were only a passenger in the car and can claim you just went along for the ride, unaware of Seanie's involvement.'

At the mention of involvement, Seanie protested angrily, 'What do you mean involvement? I had *no* involvement.'

'Be that as it may,' said Gerry. 'Cormac can, I am sure, come up with witnesses that will say he tried to persuade you not to be out late at night. It wasn't his car *and*, crucially, he didn't have positive results from the forensics.'

'What can I do?' asked Seanie.

'I'm not sure if there's anything you can do.'

'I want to take a lie detector test.'

'Maybe you should consider that carefully. I don't know if it's your best course of action,' said the solicitor.

'*You* don't believe me,' said Seanie.

'Whether or not I believe you is irrelevant. It's what the jury believes that counts.'

'How can you convince a jury if you're not convinced yourself?'

'It won't be me. You'll have a barrister fighting your case.'

'What about the lie detector test?'

'If you insist, but most judges have no belief in it, so what's the point? If it goes well it isn't taken into account, and if it doesn't . . .' Gerry shrugged his shoulders.

'I know Seanie didn't have explosives in the car, but how can the forensic results be accounted for?' asked Cormac.

'Either the soldiers put the substance on my hands when I

was unconscious, or the tests are wrong,' said Seanie.

'What length of sentence are we talking about?' said Cormac.

'At a guess, seven to ten,' replied Gerry. 'Are you sure you won't have a drink?'

They both said no. The solicitor shook his head as he poured himself another whiskey. 'It's going to be very difficult.'

'How difficult?' Seanie wanted to know.

'Seanie, you don't need legal training to appreciate what you're faced with.'

Seanie headed towards home, but before reaching it he branched off onto a side road. The road was a little used boreen, but he knew every inch of it. He drove slowly. The Brits might be able to stop you because they had guns, but it wasn't their country. It wasn't their home, and he knew things about this landscape they didn't know. It was one of these features he was looking for now. He hoped it was still there. On entering the side road he pulled in to the verge and peered through the hedge. He could see a clump of bushes in front of him. They hadn't been disturbed in years by the look of them. Carrying a torch, he climbed over the ditch, got down on his hands and knees and crept under them as best he could. The briars tore his skin. Nettles stung him everywhere. By the time he was a couple of yards into the clump, his hands were bloody and his face scratched. But it was still there – the entrance to the cave.

It wasn't really a cave. It was a souterrain, and there were many in this area, although the vast majority were now filled in. He had been taught the history of them at school. Some experts thought they were perhaps thousands of years old, but weren't sure what they were used for. Perhaps they were used for storing food or hiding in during times of trouble. From playing in it as a boy, Seanie knew this one like the back of his hand. He knew about the three chambers. He knew about the spyhole in one of the chambers that convinced the archaeologists the tunnel must have been used for hiding in. He knew it had an exit almost half a mile away. Now he wanted to see if he could still traverse it from end to end.

Seanie made his way along the burrow. The passageway was dank and littered with fallen stones. A bat almost hit him in the face as it whooshed past. He ignored the pain from the knocks as a result of hitting his head and body against the rocky sides and stone roof. In the largest chamber he searched for his name. It was still visible where he had scrawled it on a stone. There was no sign of the candles or of the packet of cigarettes he had hidden on a ledge just above it.

Seanie stopped to rest for a moment. When playing there he had imagined himself to be a Rapparee alongside Redmond O'Hanlon. Three hundred years on from the time of the Rapparees, and it was still the same enemy.

On he went, crouched and stumbling, his route lit by the powerful torch beam. Then, short of breath and badly scraped, he could hear water flowing. It was the river which he expected to find at the exit. In front of him, all grown in, were huge clumps of shrubs closing off the outlet. He disturbed a water hen's nest, and the two inhabitants ran off squawking. They would never have expected humans to be in there.

Seanie clawed his way through the shrubs and emerged into the daylight. He was standing in a little stream, and in front of him he had a clear view of the main road. He could wait here for days for a patrol to pass, or perhaps lure them in. With a rapid-fire rifle he would wreak havoc before they knew what hit them. Then all he would need was a getaway car at the other end of the tunnel. It might be hours before the enemy advanced towards his firing position, and perhaps days before they chanced entering the tunnel. After the gun attack he'd be safely across the border in thirty minutes.

Seanie arrived home dusty, dirty and covered in scratches and bruises. Eileen was in bed. She looked at him in amazement when he entered the room.

'Are you not feeling well?' said Seanie.

'The doctor was here this morning. He ordered complete bed rest for me. What in the name of God were you at?'

'McAdam had a heifer stuck in a sheugh full of briars. We had an awful job getting it out.'

Seanie sat down on the bed. 'Darling,' he said, 'tomorrow, if you're well enough, we're going house-hunting. I can't have you living here and me in the South. I would never get to see you.'

'What are you saying, Seanie?'

Seanie reached over and took his wife by the hand. He explained to her about the forensic results, and how he had little chance of getting off when the case came to trial. He said it was better now, while he had freedom of movement North and South, to get his affairs sorted out because he didn't intend to turn up at the trial. 'It would be daft to go like a lamb to slaughter.'

'I desperately want to get away from all the shooting and killing,' said Eileen, 'but you'll be a wanted man. You, who is always helping people and could never hurt anyone.'

Seanie stood up. 'I'll make you a cup of tea.'

*

Eileen wanted their new house to be close to her parents' home. Clogherhead, a popular seaside resort, would be within easy reach. It had become a place of sanctuary for Northerners escaping the Troubles. Eileen found what she wanted, a holiday home chalet in a nice residential estate, so close to the sea the waves could be heard lapping the shore. They could rent it for the present. A Garda squad car came into the estate while they were there. This suggested to Seanie that there might be another guy on the run staying in the area. He asked the auctioneer if he knew anything about the people who would be their neighbours. The estate agent thought someone from the North, with an Irish name he couldn't pronounce, had a house beside them.

The plan was to move the following week and get settled in while Seanie was still legitimately at large. Eileen was having difficulties with her pregnancy, which was another reason to move as soon as possible. Her doctor told her to avoid stress and to get away from the Troubles if she possibly could. Everything seemed sorted, until Seanie's mother rang to say his father had been taken ill.

17

Seanie went immediately to Daisy Hill Hospital, where his father had been admitted. As he walked down the corridor leading to his father's ward he met his old school friend Eric. 'It's great to see you,' Eric said. 'I've been reading about the court case.'

Seanie thanked him for his kindness during his time in Newry General Hospital.

'I suppose,' said Eric, 'when you go down that road you are prepared for this type of thing to happen. Anyway, now you can get your own back on the bastards.'

'It would take a lot of getting back,' said Seanie.

'Yeah, I would think that's right. Anyway, good luck.'

Before going into his father's ward, Seanie stopped at the nurse's station. He asked about his father's condition. The nurse said he was conscious but had suffered a severe heart attack. The next forty-eight hours would be critical. Close relatives could visit, but they were not to stay too long.

Seanie entered the ward. His first reaction was a mixture of shock and sadness. His father looked old and frail. His face was ashen, his hair whiter than ever, and his eyes seemed lifeless.

Once Seanie remembered his mother saying to her husband that his eyes were runny, and he had jokingly replied, 'It's the first sign of death, *a chuisle.*'

Now his eyes really were watery. A plastic bag fastened upside down to a frame beside the bed dripped colourless liquid into his father's thin white arm. The old man's eyes lit up when he saw Seanie. '*Dia dhuit, a mhic*, hello my son,' he said, weakly.

'Hello Dad, how are you?'

'It's coming to my time,' said his father in a hoarse whisper. He put out his free arm to grasp Seanie's hand.

'Nonsense, you'll soon be up and about.'

'Everyone dies,' said his father. 'It's only a matter of how and when.' After a pause to catch his breath, he continued. 'Autumn is a natural time to go, when so many other living things are returning to the soil.'

'I wish you wouldn't talk like that.'

'There's only one thing more I would have wanted.'

'To see your country united,' said Seanie.

'Yes.'

'It will happen.'

'Not in our lifetime is what the old people used to say.'

'You did all you could, even if I didn't.'

'What do you mean, son?'

'I've never lived up to your expectations, Dad. But I intend to change all that.'

His father asked Seanie for a drink of water. There was a half-full tumbler on the locker. Seanie held him up and let him sip from the glass. Then he laid him back against the pillows. It seemed to Seanie as if he was trying to gather his strength.

'Seanie, I want to say something to you.'

'You can say it when you're better. Save your energy.' Seanie smoothed the hair back on his father's forehead, and said, 'I can see now you were right all along. I just want you to know I intend to play my part in the struggle.'

'What has changed your mind?'

'What the Brits did to Cormac and myself convinced me.'

His father lay back and stayed quiet for a few moments. Then clearly mustering up his energy, he said, 'Come closer to me, *a mhic*.'

Seanie pulled his chair up against the edge of the bed and put his face nearer to the old man.

'Do you know, Seanie, what a soldier does?'

'He kills the enemy.'

'Why does he kill the enemy?'

'To win the war.'

'Why do you want to kill the enemy?'

Seanie didn't reply. The old man coughed a couple of times, rested for a moment and then said, 'A soldier doesn't hate his enemy. A soldier hates what he represents.'

His father stopped and took deep breaths. Then he said, 'Patriots are not motivated by revenge.'

Seanie recalled Dickie Stone saying something similar. 'But you've always wanted me to be part of the struggle.'

His father turned his head on the pillow. As if talking to himself, he said, 'It's not that simple. I've made many mistakes in my life.'

'Everyone makes mistakes, Dad.'

Again his father sighed and seemed to drift off.

'Some can only be seen when it's too late,' he said. 'Everyone should be allowed to have their own hopes.'

The nurse came into the ward and told Seanie he would have to go now and let the patient get some sleep. Seanie was about to leave when his father abruptly reached out and grabbed his arm, surprising him with the fierceness of the grip. 'You're going to have a son of your own soon.'

'It might be a girl,' said Seanie, attempting to be light-hearted.

'It'll be a boy.'

Seanie's father inhaled deeply, the rattle in his throat clearly audible. 'My son,' he said, drawing on all his strength, 'I always wanted what was right for you.'

'I know that, Dad.'

'I won't live to see my grandson.'

'You will live to see him, Dad.'

'Let him follow his own path.'

Exhausted by the effort, the old man's eyelids drooped and he took a fit of coughing. Seanie felt the grip loosen.

'Your father has to rest now,' insisted the nurse.

Seanie stood up and gazed down at his father for a few moments. The old man lay still, his eyes closed. Where was he in his mind, Seanie wondered. Training a band of volunteers? Playing in a football match? Perhaps he was back to the time when he first got married. His mother often talked about how happy they were then. Seanie bent over and kissed his father lightly on the forehead. It was impossible to know. Maybe he was just sleeping.

The next day the family was sent for. When Seanie got there the rosary was being said by family members. Seanie sat at the side of the bed and held his father's hand. Watching him he knew he would also die. Before this, it was something that would never happen. Now, seeing his parent breathing his last, it struck him that the person in the bed was, in a sense, himself.

The old man's breathing got ever more shallow. Finally, it stopped altogether. His eyes became glazed. There was no drama. It was over. Seanie held the limp hand not wanting to let go. He placed it across the dead man's chest and breathed,

'Thanks, Dad.'

It would be a Republican funeral. Many times during his later years Seanie's father talked about the emotional and historical significance of Republican funerals, and had said if he didn't get to die for Ireland then he would be buried for Ireland.

Dickie Stone, in discussion with Seanie and his mother, told them that he would look after the political side of things. In practice this meant the IRA took almost total control. Two members of Na Fianna Éireann, the Republican youth wing, stood guard beside the corpse throughout the two days and two nights of the waking. The most common remarks Seanie noticed people make, either to one of the family or whispered to each other as they gazed affectionately at the dead man's face, was, 'Doesn't he look himself,' or, 'There's not a bit of change on him.'

All of those who attended the wake and funeral were aware of Seanie's upcoming trial, and many of them wished him luck when shaking his hand. Mrs Reel, Seanie's old teacher in infants class said, 'That was a terrible thing them soldiers did on you, Seanie.'

'Yes it was.'

'They're bad people.'

'Indeed they are.'

'They shouldn't be here anyway.'

'You're right.'

'I bet you don't want to have anything more to do with them.'

'You can say that again.'

What did she expect him to say? He could hardly disagree with her. But it was not very satisfactory to the woman. Sympathizers wanted more insight, maybe about what he was going to do about it, or how it affected him, or perhaps more likely, to hear something new that could be relayed on in gossip. He detected a change in people's attitude towards him since his arrest. Some looked at him slightly in awe, some kept more distance than would normally be the case, and some openly encouraged him to get his own back. All of them were, or at least pretended to be, on his side.

Gerry, being a brother of the deceased, stayed the whole time. He amazed Seanie with his capacity for alcohol and his lack of need for sleep. He kept the conversation going with tales and yarns relating to court cases, most of them to do with strokes and fast ones he pulled. One of these involved Red McGee. 'Red McGee,' he said, 'was charged with smuggling grain. But at the time of the seizure he had escaped, only to be arrested later. My defence was that the wrong person had been charged. I argued it was a case of mistaken identity, which could easily happen in the poor light when the seizure had been effected. However, the prosecution had managed to get a photo of Red which proved it was him. I put Red into the witness box, but as soon as he took the oath I made an excuse to the judge that I had come away without some important documents, and asked for a thirty minute recess. When the court resumed, and the witness took the stand again, I asked him whether he was involved in smuggling on the night in question. The answer was no. Then I produced a whole range of witnesses and asked each of them the same question, pointing to the defendant. Where was that man on the night of the offence? All of them swore he was with them or they had seen him and he couldn't therefore be somewhere else. I won my case. No one present knew that Red had an identical twin. It was the Red's twin I put into the witness box after the thirty minute recess.'

When Gerry paused for admiration, Seanie decided to slip off for a rest in an adjacent bedroom. A few hours later, when he awoke, Gerry was still telling the story of Red McGee, and repeating the yarn to a different audience.

On the second evening, perhaps at the busiest time of the entire proceedings, Stone told Seanie that plans had been made for an important visitor, a certain Frank Ratigan. 'Like myself,' he said, 'you may not be a fan of the guy, but it's what your father would want. He was as conscious as the rest of us that whoever wins the propaganda war wins the war.'

Seanie knew Stone was right about his father. He often said, 'Heroes don't come to be because of heroic acts. They are created by people who require heroes.'

The Provos needed all the heroes they could get.

Stone cleared the front drive of traffic. Shortly afterwards a convoy of four large cars wheeled up to the front door. Young men, mostly strangers, got out of them and entered the wake house. They were followed by Big Frank Ratigan. He was dressed casually and hadn't shaved. Seanie quickly realized the convoy was a decoy. Ratigan may have been in an adjacent neighbour's house these past couple of days. He could have been ordered to go there once the news that Seanie's father was seriously ill became known. Stone was demonstrating that the British writ didn't run here. This was South Armagh, and a local man, no matter how much he was sought by the British Army, could appear at will. Stories would later be leaked for the attention of the Northern Ireland security forces, as well as for local gossip. These would be yarns exaggerating Ratigan's activities during the funeral – perhaps his making a speech or leading a parade of volunteers. With the passing of time the tales would create their own momentum. Stone knew it wasn't what actually happened that had significance, but rather what was said to have happened.

Now Ratigan stood in front of the coffin and addressed everyone in the room. 'With the memory of men such as Paddy O'Rourke to inspire us, how can we lose?' He shook hands with all the family, but didn't stop there. Acting like a celebrity, he reached out to all the neighbours and shook their hands, whether they wanted to or not. Later Seanie sat beside him. They chatted about the dead man, and then Ratigan, leaning close, whispered, 'Those goods are being sorted. I'll be in touch with you as soon as the funeral is over. I may need some more money but we can sort that out on delivery.'

Seanie acknowledged this with a slight nod.

The wanted man left almost immediately after with the young Sinn Féin activists. While British soldiers on checkpoint duty were focusing on the convoy, he would be whisked into a local safe house, and make his escape across the border when things settled.

After Ratigan had left, Stone said to Seanie, 'I was watching you and the hero. I didn't know the two of you were so friendly.'

'He put himself into great danger being here,' said Seanie. 'I have to be sociable.'

Stone grunted something unintelligible.

On the morning of the burial, the remains were placed in a casket. Before the lid was put on the coffin, Seanie's mother gave her husband a last kiss on the forehead. She bent down and Seanie heard her whisper, '*Slán go fóill, a chuisle,*' into his ear.

The Rosary was then recited, and a tricolour draped over

the coffin. A pair of black leather gloves and a black beret were placed on top of the tricolour. When he was a child, Seanie had asked his father why he kept the black gloves, seeing as he never used them. 'Someday you will have your answer,' was the reply.

Seanie and male relatives of the deceased family carried the coffin for the first five hundred yards, preceded by a hearse. In front of the hearse a lone piper marched in full regalia playing funeral airs. Following Mass, the coffin was carried to the Republican plot in the cemetery and lowered into the grave, accompanied by a lament on the bagpipes. Local men filled back the soil, and when finished, placed the shovels over the newly closed grave in the shape of a cross. A decade of the Rosary was said in Irish and an oration was given by a leading member of Sinn Féin. Then three masked and uniformed IRA men stepped out from the crowd. On command, they fired a volley of shots over the grave before retreating to mingle with the mourners. There was loud applause. Seanie remembered the first time he had seen this. It was very exciting and he wanted to be part of a firing party when he grew up. There had been applause then too. Parents had children at today's funeral; maybe, in some cases, brought to see the spectacle as he had been. Their feelings were surely no different from his at that age. Would these children's thinking change? Some would keep their ambition. Eileen was adamant their child would not be exposed to violent republicanism until it was old enough to decide for itself. Finally, the piper played 'Danny Boy'. As the sounds of the haunting melody filled the still air there wasn't a stir among the mourners. Seanie let his gaze sweep over the scene. The IRA definitely knew how to organize a funeral.

*

The family spent that evening at home. Eileen, who had managed to make it to the ceremonies, said, 'Everyone had a good word to say about him.'

Seanie's mother said, 'Paddy, God love him, always said, "*Más mian leat do mholadh, faigh bás.*"'

'What does that mean?' asked Eileen.

'In English,' said Seanie, 'it's, "If you want to be praised, die."'

'Everything was very nice anyway,' said Eileen. 'Although I'm not sure if firing shots over the grave is to be welcomed.'

'Why do you say that?' said Seanie's mother.

'Would you want shots fired over your grave, Seanie?' asked Eileen.

'Maybe . . . if I had been involved in active service,' he said.

18

Seanie put on his best suit and tie for the bail renewal hearing. 'His law suit', Eileen had started to call it. Cormac met him outside the courthouse. The courtroom had the old furniture smell of an antique store, and the hushed sombre atmosphere reminded Seanie of his father's wake. While they waited, he wondered if the bleak white walls ever heard the sound of a hearty laugh.

Theirs was the first case called. Uncle Gerry again failed to put in an appearance.

Phonsie stood up and requested a renewal of bail on the same terms as before. Phonsie was thirty-two but would pass for seventeen. He always gave the impression of looking for somewhere to hide. Seanie wondered if he stayed with Gerry from lack of ambition, or if he was just too kind-hearted to abandon his uncle.

The Justice's face was the colour of beetroot. He looked to be suffering from a severe hangover. Impatiently shaking his head following Phonsie's application, he lifted a document in pudgy white fingers and pointed it at the solicitor, saying, 'It appears you're not aware that Lord Diplock's recommendations are being enforced from today. The Minster signed the order last Friday. I don't have the authority to grant bail to the defendants.'

Seanie and Cormac were confused about what was

happening. Phonsie didn't seem to know either. He was on his feet now. 'Your honour,' he started to say, when he was interrupted by the Justice.

'Am I not making myself clear? The defendants will be remanded in custody. Next application please.'

Phonsie was standing again. 'I beg you, Your Honour, before you make an order, can I have just a few minutes to explain to my clients what's involved? This has come as a complete shock.'

The Justice put up his hands in a gesture of resignation. 'It shouldn't have. However, you may approach the prisoners.'

Phonsie came over to where they were seated. He explained that Lord Diplock had been chairing a committee to change aspects of the law in the North of Ireland, and they had decided on a range of recommendations. 'I wasn't aware they would be implemented so soon.'

'What the hell does it mean for us?' asked Seanie.

'It means you cannot get bail at a lower court, which this is. You have to apply to the High Court. It also means, if all the recommendations are accepted, you won't have a jury at your trial. Just a single judge on his own will decide the case.'

'Forget about the trial, when can you apply to the High Court?' said Cormac.

'I'm afraid that will take some time, and meanwhile you will be taken to Crumlin Road jail.'

'No way,' said Cormac.

At that, the Justice said his patience had been exhausted, and would the solicitor resume his seat. Phonsie moved away from the two men, saying, 'Thanks, Your Honour.'

Cormac turned to Seanie and said, 'I'm going.'

'What?'

'I'm going out through yon door this minute.'

Seanie glanced at their surroundings. There was only one exit with just a single policeman guarding it. A few more RUC men, probably witnesses in other cases, sat on the benches opposite. Surprise would get them to the door and perhaps outside. But what then? Soldiers were stationed all around the building.

'Are you coming?' asked Cormac.

Seanie thought of Eileen and the baby. 'No. Good luck.'

Cormac vaulted over the side of the box seating to the floor below. In a flash he was at the door. He gave the police officer a shoulder tackle and was gone. Other policemen jumped on top of Seanie and knocked him to the floor, even though he hadn't moved. Handcuffs were clapped on his wrists. He was hauled to his feet.

'Just in case you get any smart ideas also,' a burly policeman said to him.

When the handcuffs were snapped on Seanie, a piece of skin got caught in the lock. The entire incident had taken less than a minute. The Justice called a recess. Seanie was loaded onto an armoured Land Rover and left sitting in it. His wrist stung where the skin was snagged. Some policemen got into the vehicle and it moved off. In about ten minutes he was back at the same RUC barracks he had been in twice before. His granny always said that if you visit a place once you will be back three times. As he was being led from the barracks yard he noticed his yellow Ford Escort. The police had said they wouldn't return it until after the trial. The front of the car was bashed in as if someone had driven it into a wall. Seeing it now made him think of Eileen. 'That's my car,' he said to his police escort, nodding towards it. The policeman neither looked at the car nor replied.

Seanie's handcuffs were removed. He was shoved into a

cell. Cormac sat there hunched in the corner with his back to the wall. He seemed badly shaken.

'Jesus! Are you OK?' said Seanie.

'I gave the bastards a run for their money.'

'I was afraid you'd be shot.'

'How come we didn't know about this Diplock thing?'

'I don't know if it's Gerry's fault or not.'

'What are we going to do?'

'I hope Phonsie gets word to Eileen,' said Seanie.

Cormac started pacing the cramped space. 'Seanie, I can't do time,' he said.

'It'll only be for a couple of weeks.'

'A couple of hours is too much.'

'Sit down, you're making me as bad as yourself.'

Cormac sat down. He drew his knees up to his chest and hugged his legs. Seanie looked at him. The expression on his friend's face was one he had never seen before.

'I've always had a horror of being confined.'

'You're far braver than me,' said Seanie.

'Brave my arse.'

The smell of urine was as overpowering as before. With no furniture of any kind, Seanie and Cormac had to sit on the bare concrete floor. For a moment, Seanie thought of suggesting to Cormac that they scratch their names beside the other graffiti on the walls. A policeman appeared with two portions of stew in tin bowls. Each mouthful was like eating a spoonful of salt.

Seanie also had fears about jail. Neither of them were members of the IRA, and he was wondering how those inside would react to them. Cormac suddenly jumped up saying he wanted to go the jacks. He began to bang madly on the cell door. A policeman came and opened it. Cormac immediately dashed past him and down the corridor. Before the door was shut in Seanie's face, he saw Cormac disappear around the corner. A short while later, the cell door opened again and Cormac was bundled back in. His clothes were in disarray and blood poured from a cut over one eye.

Seanie and Cormac were transported in an armoured police van to Crumlin Road Gaol. On arrival, they were taken through a maze of corridors to a reception area manned by two prison officers. Their handcuffs were removed and the policemen departed. The prison officers began to make fun of the way they were dressed. They concentrated on Seanie in his dark blue suit and tie.

'What have we here?' one of the wardens asked him.

'A male model,' said the other one.

'He can't be a model, he's a terrorist.'

'I know what he is,' said the second guy. 'He's the terrorists' accountant.'

All their belongings were confiscated and itemized. Then, one at a time, they were taken to a huge bathroom to be washed. Seanie was stripped and ordered to get into a bath. Steam rose from the water.

'Get in or be fucking thrown in,' he was told.

Seanie placed one foot into the tub. Jesus! It would peel the skin off him. He remembered seeing butchered pigs being doused with boiling water to soften the bristles. The wardens got him by the arms and tried to force him into the bath. Just then, another man in uniform came in to the room saying, 'What the hell's going on?' in a London accent. The newcomer ordered his colleagues to stop the messing.

After that, Seanie and Cormac were put into a cell for the night. There were two single beds with mattresses and blankets, also two chamber pots. The salty stew had made

Seanie thirsty. Not knowing how long they would be kept there, he banged on the solid black door to get someone's attention. A voice asked what he wanted.

'Can I have a drink of water please?' said Seanie.

The man on the other side laughed. Seanie lay down and tried to forget his thirst. Cormac kept jumping out of the bunk to pace the cell back and forth for a couple of minutes before lying down again. Each time he got back into the bunk, Seanie hoped that this time his pal would stay still. Seanie recalled his father saying that prison for certain people, especially if they were used to being outdoors all the time, was torture.

A warden sat behind a table to interview the prisoners. He asked if they wanted to align themselves to the Provos, the Officials, or the ODCs. Following a split in the IRA in 1969, two separate groupings emerged. They became known as the Official IRA and the Provisional IRA. To associate themselves with the Officials or the Provos would entitle them to political status if either of the factions were agreeable to having them on their wing of the prison. The prison officers were against political status being granted to anyone. They said it would be like the inmates running the asylum. However, it had been a government decision, so they had to work the system. In response, they christened people who weren't entitled to political status 'ODCs': ordinary decent criminals. Replying to the man's question, Cormac said, 'We're from South Armagh.'

'Fucking Apaches,' said the warden. 'Which one of you is Sitting Bull?' Without waiting for an answer, he wrote down, 'B Wing, the Provos.'

Seanie would have liked to inform him that Sitting Bull

was a Sioux.

They were taken to B Wing of the jail and handed over to the IRA officer in charge of the prisoners, known as the OC. He made arrangements for them to be interrogated. New prisoners were always debriefed. In the vast majority of cases, these people had been arrested either on active service or picked up at some other location. It was imperative for their comrades to know if they had talked, and what the Brits knew. The result of the interview would be passed on to the command structure on the outside.

The meeting was conducted by the OC and two other men. The OC's name was Bertie, his second in command's name was Connie. The third man was called Brian. Brian was quartermaster on the landing. The first two were from Belfast, as were almost all those on B Wing. Brian came from Tyrone. The commanding officer was a pleasant-looking, middle-aged man. He walked with a limp. As he sat down he said, 'The oul' leg is playing up again, but there's no point in having a war wound if no one knows about it.'

He nudged his second in command and said, 'What do you say, Connie?'

Connie's right hand consisted of a stump with a thumb and finger on either side of it. He was nicknamed 'the Crab'. The OC let the Crab do the questioning.

'Are you army members?' he wanted to know.

Seanie stared at him. By his demeanour the guy was definitely a fanatic. 'Which army?' said Seanie. There were at least half a dozen armies in the North of Ireland. He knew this answer wouldn't endear him to his inquisitor.

'The Irish Republican Army,' shouted the Crab into Seanie's face.

'No,' said Seanie.

'What happened you?' the OC asked Cormac. Cormac's eye was black and blue and had swollen up.

Cormac shrugged his shoulders. 'I thought I might relieve the RUC of my company, but they didn't want me to go.'

The OC seemed impressed, but the Crab was more dismissive. 'It's our duty as prisoners of war to avail of every opportunity to escape,' he said.

Seanie wondered about himself being described as a prisoner of war. However, both he and Cormac agreed to accept Irish Republican Army discipline, which included not taking orders from the screws. Orders must come from an IRA officer. The screw would tell the officer and he'd relay it on.

Because Cormac and Seanie had more in common with Brian than the city folk, the trio became friendly. The Belfast prisoners were critical of rural volunteers and were convinced Belfast produced the best and smartest fighters. Some of the younger ones would practice mock ambushes along the landing. Their antics reminded Seanie of children playing cowboys and Indians. But the Crab told Seanie it was likely he would piss himself if he had to go on a mission. Cormac remarked privately to Seanie, 'If they're so good, why are so many of them locked up?'

'Yeah, and none from our locality,' said Seanie.

'You're forgetting about us,' said Cormac.

Seanie just looked at him.

The prison had multiple floors enclosing an atrium. Each landing had a row of cells on both sides of the chasm with a huge wire mesh net strung across the divide like a trampoline, which prevented objects being thrown below. People sometimes jumped onto the net but they weren't going anywhere. Each cell had a wooden door with a peek-hole, which the occupants invariably stuffed up. Taking out the light bulb also prevented anyone from observing what was going on inside. The most watched programme on television in the common room was the six o'clock Ulster Television News. Reports of a successful IRA operation always got a huge cheer. There were news snippets about Cormac's escape exploits which gained him respect with the prisoners. Brian suggested to Seanie that he could say he was also involved in the getaway attempt. Then he could taunt Crab by asking him if *he* had put up any fight when being arrested.

When Brian took them on a tour of the workshop, Cormac's eyes lit up on seeing the facilities. He loved working with his hands. Brian said that lots of people who found confinement difficult would immerse themselves in creating artefacts. Books were plentiful and Seanie read a lot. Other times he would lie in his bunk for hours staring at the ceiling, which caused Cormac to ask what he was watching so intently.

'I'm waiting to see if it appears,' said Seanie.

Immediately, Cormac was up on one elbow staring at Seanie. 'What appears?'

'There's a small cobweb up there. I wonder where the spider is?'

'Good God Almighty,' said Cormac.

Cormac became totally preoccupied in constructing a sailing ship and began to sleep better. Seanie asked Brian what had happened to Crab's hand.

'He likes people to think,' said Brian, 'that he lost it in action, but everyone knows he got it caught in a lawnmower when he was a child. That's what the OC was slagging him about earlier when he talked about his war wound.'

The Crab didn't like Seanie. Brian thought his antagonism

might have to do with Seanie not being a member of the IRA. 'Maybe the Crab,' said the quartermaster, 'wants people to know how much of a true-blue he is.'

The conversation turned to Cormac and Seanie's possible future. Brian maintained Diplock's proposals were the thin end of the wedge. 'We'll all be criminalized,' he said. 'The new rules were mostly to do with getting rid of political status and introducing legal internment.'

'How will that work?' said Seanie.

'By keeping people locked up indefinitely without trial.'

'Can they do that?'

'They're already at it. I'm here eighteen months and I've had no trial. Many others are here just as long.' Brian shook his head. 'I don't think you will get bail. And when a trial does happen, it will be a hanging court. With juries abolished, the system is designed with one aim in mind: to obtain convictions.'

'You're not giving us much hope,' said Seanie.

'The big idea behind all this is doing away with political status. That's their ultimate goal. And mark my words, if they attempt that, the prisoners won't accept it.'

Seanie's mother and Cormac's sister came on a visit. They brought fresh clothes and news of home. Eileen was fine but confined to bed much of the time. Gerry was preparing an application for the High Court. Hopefully it would be heard within three weeks. Neither of the prisoners mentioned the gossip about their situation. Seanie told his mother to make sure Eileen was OK, and on no account should she visit him and put herself under stress. The only important thing was the baby. Eileen sent a letter with Seanie's mother. She was getting on well and loved the house. She could feel the baby kicking away like mad. He would be a great footballer. The neighbours were friendly, and the man that Seanie thought might be a Provo was very nice. He didn't talk about himself either, so she felt under no pressure to explain her situation, but he definitely wasn't an IRA man.

Lying on their bunks following the visit, Seanie and Cormac were depressed. They always knew when one inmate a few doors away had a visit. When he returned to his cell he would cry for hours. After listening to the sobbing prisoner for some time, Cormac said, 'Do you think we'll *ever* get out of here?'

'My granny used to say talking is the best medicine for taking you out of yourself,' said Seanie.

Cormac didn't respond, and again neither of the men said anything for a long while. Then Seanie said, 'Did you ever hear how Slash got the name Slash?'

Cormac mumbled something into the pillow.

'McIver told me about it,' said Seanie. 'It seems when he was a young fellow, Slash got drunk around the town one day. This was before the Troubles. Anyway, he was walking up the street when he decided he needed to take a piss. Being Slash, he didn't care much where he did it. So he stood at an entry in full few of everyone and was doing the job when two policemen came on him. He was summonsed for urinating in a public space. In court the case had only started when Slash jumped up and said, "Your Honour, I was only having a slash." The Justice said, "If you'd have spent a penny it would have saved you two pounds." A headline in the local *Frontier Sentinel* the following week said, "Two Pounds a Slash," and the name stuck.'

There was no response from Cormac. Seanie closed his eyes and thought of Eileen and the baby. Now and again he glanced up to see if there was any sign of the spider.

19

Seanie read Eileen's letters again and again. The correspondence was mostly about the new baby. If it was a boy, they might call him Patrick after Seanie's father; and if a girl, maybe Sarah after Eileen's mother. No matter how much she wanted to see him, the doctor was adamant that with the pregnancy stabilized and going fine, she shouldn't take any chances. Her mother would come and stay with her for a couple of days at a time. They had picked a great place to settle. The sea was wonderful and the air healthy. But best of all, no bombs or house raids, and no checkpoints if she went shopping. It was almost as if the Troubles in the North were in some country on the other side of the world. In fact, many people either didn't really know much about what was going on 'up there', or didn't want to know. She thought they were frightened of it spreading to their patch. Her Northern neighbour was usually there at the weekend and they had got friendly with each other. Enclosed in a letter was a little piece of seaweed. It was for Seanie to smell and to remind him he would soon be free to walk the beach with her and the baby. It was due in only ten weeks. She had everyone praying he'd be home for the birth.

Seanie told Eileen about the prison routine. Each morning everyone would stand to attention in the mess room while the national anthem was sung in Irish.

'Copy me,' Brian the quartermaster told Seanie and Cormac on their first morning. He stood with his feet apart, shoulders back, head up, both arms behind his back slightly bent, and one hand gripping the other wrist.

After breakfast, wrote Seanie, cells were inspected and beds checked that they were made properly. There was freedom of movement on the wing until lock-up at eight. He would rise in the morning at seven, slop out, and take a shower in the communal wash room. The toilets had doors similar to those in saloon bars in cowboy films. He was lucky to have political status, for he would have found the constant surveillance and lack of privacy very difficult. During the day he lay on his bunk reading until the words on the pages were coming out of his ears. Cormac had become totally occupied with constructing his sailing ship. He used guitar strings for ropes. Art canvas functioned as a sail and a modified tin top became a steering wheel on the bridge. Seanie kept the seaweed on his pillow, and it was very apt because Cormac intended putting it across the bow of his boat.

Seanie told Eileen how much he missed the smell of her lying next to him, and of waking sometimes in the night thinking she was beside him. He mentioned missing other smells. Freshly mown grass was one; another was his mother's baking. For some reason he could also recall the smell of a leather football and of tar melting on the road in summer.

Seanie didn't tell Eileen of the conflict between the Crab and himself. It began on his first morning. He and Cormac were standing to attention as instructed by Brian. The Crab paused for a second and gave them a scathing look. Seanie just stared straight ahead, but he said to Cormac and Brian afterwards, 'I'm going to have to take that guy on at some point.'

After that, Crab was constantly complaining to Seanie. Maybe his bed wasn't made up correctly, or the cell wasn't tidy. One time he accused him of not having shaved that day. On another occasion Crab lifted a book that Seanie had been reading and tossed it contemptuously aside, saying, 'You're no good with your hands either.'

Seanie felt like saying that at least he managed not to get his caught in a lawnmower.

'It would suit you better to go to the history lessons,' said the Crab. 'But you think you know more than anyone else.'

Seanie had gone to one lecture, but found it boring and left after twenty minutes. He decided he had better make an effort to attend again. It turned out to be the Crab who was giving the talk. There were about twenty-five people present. Seanie sat down and listened to the Crab ramble on for half an hour about the way Oliver Cromwell slaughtered the Irish and what the English did to his fellow countrymen. Finally, Seanie could stick it no longer. He stood up and said, 'Mr Speaker, would it not be more useful to try and put the Cromwellian period into the context of the time, and see what could be learned about it from that perspective?'

The Crab didn't know what to say. 'What are you on about?' he spluttered.

'We all know about the atrocities Cromwell carried out, but his motives might be interesting to explore,' said Seanie.

'His motives were to kill and butcher as many Irish as he could,' said the Crab. His face was the colour of a Royal Mail letter box.

'My granny told me,' said Seanie, 'that Ireland was the only country in the world where the losers rather than the winners wrote the history, and that's part of the reason why the Irish narrative is such a tale of woe.'

'Fuck your granny,' someone shouted from the back of the room.

The Crab was on his feet. 'Have you not an ounce of respect in you for your ancestors?'

'Did you know,' said Seanie, 'Cromwell was a Republican?'

'You're disrupting everything with your bullshit.'

'Maybe he was just as sincere a Republican as yourself,' said Seanie.

The Crab's resentment boiled over. He was being compared to Cromwell. He jumped down from the platform and made for Seanie as if to launch an attack. Seanie stood up to him.

The Crab stuck his face right against Seanie's and said, 'You have a nerve. Men laid down their lives for political status and you sneer at them while taking advantage of their sacrifice. What have you ever done to be allowed onto this wing, never mind make a laugh of us?'

Seanie hardly noticed the ripple of agreement that spread among the attendees. Stung by the ring of truth, he lashed back. 'What about yourself, running around with two fingers stuck in the air pretending you're the greatest thing since Padraig Pearse, when everyone knows you're just a Belfast bowsie who wouldn't know his arse from his elbow. Any army that has you in it isn't much of an army.'

At that the Crab caught Seanie by the throat with his two fingers and forced him down onto the floor. A mini-riot broke out, as if it was just waiting for a spark to set it off. People began shouting and breaking up chairs. Teacups and mugs were smashed against walls. One teenager climbed up onto a low beam that straddled the room. He kept bouncing up and down on his hunkers and making ape-like sounds.

The Crab had Seanie on the ground and was squeezing the breath out of him with a vice-like grip. Nobody interfered with them except Brian who eventually managed to pull the Crab off Seanie.

'We have to get you out of here,' he shouted into Seanie's ear.

Just then the OC strode into the room. He grabbed a chair and stood on it. 'Volunteers,' he roared. 'Stand to attention.'

The young fellow on the beam stopped his ape noises. There was silence for a second. Then an inmate threw down the chair he was holding and stood to attention. Everyone followed suit except Seanie who was on his hands and knees gasping to get his breath back.

'Confine that prisoner to his cell,' the OC ordered Brian. 'The rest of you rabble get this place cleared up immediately.'

Brian escorted Seanie back to his cell. Cormac had just returned from the workshop.

'Your pal is some genius,' Brian said to Cormac. 'He's managed to start a prison riot, which in here is tantamount to an army mutiny, unless officially sanctioned, and at the same time succeeded in turning almost all of the prisoners against him.'

'What did he do?' asked Cormac.

'He called Crab a Belfast bowsie and more besides,' said Brian.

Seanie rubbed his throat. It was red and bruised. 'What will happen?' he croaked.

'I think you'll be thrown off the wing,' said Brian.

'And what then?' said Cormac.

'The Stickies won't have him after he's claimed Provo status, so he'll be clapped in with the Crims.'

Cormac threw his arms in the air. 'Jesus,' he said to Seanie.

'Could you not keep your mouth closed?'

By morning Seanie's throat had worsened. He couldn't go to breakfast. Cormac notified Crab, as second in command, that Seanie was sick, but didn't say anything more.

Then after breakfast, Brian rushed into Seanie's cell saying, 'Maybe this is your lucky day. The OC has been informed your bail application is being heard tomorrow. No decision will be taken about you before that.'

Seanie lay staring at the ceiling. He didn't know which was more painful, his throat or the anger he felt at himself. 'What'll they do to me if I don't get bail?' he said.

Brian sat on the edge of Cormac's bunk, his face serious. 'You're not an army member so there can't be a court martial. Maybe you will just be ejected from the wing. Pray that you get bail is my advice.'

At the courthouse where the bail hearing would take place, Seanie and Cormac were directed into a side room. Gerry was there waiting. 'How are you boys?' he asked, looking grave.

'Are you getting us out of here?' said Cormac.

'There's rumours of a huge riot in the jail,' said Gerry. 'What happened?'

'Jails are always full of rumours,' said Cormac.

'Why are you wearing a scarf around your neck?' Gerry asked Seanie.

'Tonsillitis,' mumbled Seanie. 'Now can we talk about getting home.'

'Sit down,' said his uncle.

'We're sitting this past month,' said Cormac.

'It's not all good news,' said Gerry.

Seanie put his hand on Cormac's shoulder. The way he was feeling he couldn't cope with Cormac doing another runner. 'For Christ's sake, Gerry, will you tell us what's going on?' he said.

Gerry tossed the documents he had been holding onto the table. 'They're dropping the charges against Cormac and will oppose you getting bail, Seanie.'

There was a hush in the room for several seconds, then Gerry spoke again. 'Everything has changed since Diplock. It's going to be a single judge hearing the case. That means no jury, and no jury means the verdict will be decided on the evidence alone. Where a jury might say you're bound to be both guilty, a judge will rely simply on the evidence, and there is absolutely none against Cormac. He can produce witnesses to prove he didn't want you to go out that night. It wasn't his car. There are no forensics. So there's no evidence for the judge to convict. On the other hand, the prosecution *does* believe you're both guilty, and they want to get one of you at least. They're afraid it might piss the judge off if they bring Cormac to trial with nothing to show, and he might let the two of you off. That's why they're concentrating on you, Seanie, and will oppose bail to make sure they get you. They are not going to take the chance of you not turning up for the trial. Oh, and by the way, it wouldn't have mattered if I'd been at the bail renewal. Nobody except the judges knew Diplock was going to be enforced then. In fact, some of them put all their cases back until the directive was circulated. You were just unlucky.'

'What can we do?' said Seanie, almost in a whisper.

'I will look for bail, that's the most I can promise you.'

'I can't go back to that place.'

'If they don't give us bail,' said Gerry, 'I will argue that the trial should happen as soon as possible, and I want to do the case myself. Normally you would have a barrister, but cases like yours are run of the mill at the moment. The barrister will assume you're guilty. There isn't much kudos in it for him. He won't have much interest in you. At least I will do everything possible.'

When the bail application was called, Seanie sat alone and tried not to show any fear of being by himself. He had said to Cormac, 'One out, just one more to go.' The judge, wearing a horsehair wig, peered down at everybody. Seanie glanced up at him. God on his throne.

Gerry asked that his client's bail terms be renewed. He had kept to the terms as previously set out and would continue to do so. The prosecution solicitor was young, and dressed immaculately in a grey suit and tie. Addressing the judge, he said, 'There is a strong *prima facie* case against the accused. New evidence has come to light since bail was first granted that proves the accused had been handling explosive substances. The charges are serious, and the accused should be remanded in custody.'

Gerry was on his feet. 'Your Honour, being remanded in custody is equivalent to being interned without trial. People must be presumed innocent until found guilty. My client is having his fundamental rights denied if not granted bail.'

Then it was the turn of the prosecution. 'I beg leave to differ, Your Honour. Society has a duty to protect its citizens, and most especially those people whose job it is to enforce laws passed by the democratically elected parliament. The accused is charged with activities detrimental to these imperatives.'

Gerry, who had only half sat down, was upright again. 'May it please the court, society is composed of individuals, and if the individual's rights are not respected, how can society's rights be upheld?'

The judge nodded towards the prosecutor for a response.

He said, 'The rights of society as a whole must always be greater than the rights of one individual. The most basic right of all is the right to life. The charge sheet in this case delineates offences that would deny that right.'

Gerry's face was red with indignation. In spite of his anxiety, Seanie recognized his uncle's commitment. Waving the charge sheet like a tic-tac man at a race meeting, the lawyer declared, 'A charge sheet is just that; a piece of paper. Yet my young learned friend wants to deprive my client of his liberty because of some text on a piece of paper – text that will be vigorously challenged when the case comes to trial. Nothing has been proven. Nothing has been tested. No evidence has been considered by any court of justice. To remand my client in custody is equivalent to finding him guilty without even the most basic trial. M'lord, we will have regressed to the law of the jungle.'

'Your Honour,' replied the prosecutor, 'I respectfully suggest to you that just as a mother is sometimes forced to do distasteful things to keep her child from possible danger, and here I'm not suggesting *proven* danger, yet I am saying *possible* danger, so must the state act likewise. In this instance, to protect those whose function it is to protect us all.'

'I've heard enough,' said the judge curtly. 'Bail application refused. The accused will be remanded in custody.' He looked around the room. 'Next case.'

20

Seanie stayed in his cell for the next couple of days pleading illness. The bail refusal and the Crab affair had left him in a state of despair. He couldn't settle his mind to read. For hours he'd watch the web to see if a spider would appear. He knew now how a cat could sit waiting on a mouse for so long. Just concentrate hard enough and time begins to lose meaning. There was a smudge on the ceiling that looked like the letter B, and he tried to think of how many words began with B. There were obvious ones like bastard, bitch, bad, banjaxed, and so on. He reached forty words at one stage, but would need to write them down so as not to use the same one twice.

On the third day Brian came into his cell. 'Listen Seanie, it's time you quit lying there feeling sorry for yourself.'

'I didn't do anything to be in this dump.'

'Lots of people on this wing didn't do anything, but they're here and they get on with it.'

'Have any of them as much reason to feel as hard done by as me?'

'What about Shorty Shields?'

'What about him?'

'The Brits raided his house. Before they left, one of them produced a revolver and told him they could tell by matching the ballistics it had been used on a job where a man had been shot dead. They wanted to know if it belonged to him. Shorty had never even seen it before. The guy holding the gun threw it at him. Shorty instinctively caught it. The following week he was arrested and charged with murder. They had the murder weapon with his fingerprints on it. He's been in here now nine months.'

'I'm sorry about that,' said Seanie, 'but not knowing what's going to happen is driving me nuts. Am I going to be put off the wing?'

Brian said that the OC was a fair man, but tough when it came to discipline. He didn't know what would happen. In the meantime, Seanie could finish Cormac's boat. It would keep him occupied.

Seanie didn't answer.

'What do you say?' said Brian.

'I'll think about it.'

Brian looked around the cell. Seanie was lying on his bunk wearing a vest with a blue serge blanket pulled over him. Cormac's bunk on the other side of the cell had a pile of books and magazines lying on it. On a steel locker beside Seanie's bed were two photos of Eileen, his father's memoriam card, two rotten bananas, and a slice of brown bread with jam on it. A dirty cup, half-full of cold tea, obscured the pictures.

'What's there to fucking think about?' said Brian, indicating the cell. 'If you could see yourself you'd cry.'

'I feel like crying.'

'You're having a fucking pity party.'

Seanie stared at the wall for a few seconds. 'All right then. Stand over in that corner for a moment.'

'What the hell?' said Brian, but he did as requested.

Seanie got a tiny piece of bread and then climbed up on

Brian's shoulders. He placed the bread in the spider's web. 'If the bread disappears,' he said, 'I'll know it's in there.'

Brian said nothing.

That evening Brian informed Seanie that a hearing had been arranged for the following morning to discuss the row. It would be held in the OC's cell. Both he and the Crab as staff officers would be in attendance. When Seanie asked Brian what was likely to happen, Brian said he didn't know, but warned Seanie that although they were friends, he was not to expect any favours.

Next morning when he entered the OC's cell, Seanie felt as if he was in a library. Shelves of books covered the walls. All of the well-known poets were represented, and dozens of titles to do with Irish history. Che Guevara's *Guerrilla Warfare* lay beside Plato's *Symposium* on the solitary bunk.

Brian and the Crab were seated behind a table with the OC in the middle. 'Sit down, please,' said the senior officer to Seanie, indicating a chair in front of the table. Neither Brian nor the Crab spoke. 'You were refused bail,' said the OC to Seanie.

'Yes, sir,' said Seanie.

The OC shook his head resignedly. 'That's the way things are going. OK,' he said. 'I have here a detailed account of what happened between you and my junior officer. Before anything is decided, you're being granted an opportunity to state your case.'

'I realize now,' said Seanie, 'that I was totally in the wrong. I agreed to accept army discipline and I didn't keep my word. I am sorry, and if I get a second chance it won't happen again.'

Nobody spoke for a few seconds after Seanie had finished. Then the OC asked him why he said Cromwell was a

Republican. Seanie shifted nervously in his seat, and didn't reply.

'This claim of yours has caused a lot of resentment. I'm wondering why you haven't referred to it in your admission of guilt?'

Brian had advised him that if he was stuck, to kick to touch. 'There's very little more to say about it.'

'So Cromwell was a Republican then?' said the OC.

Seanie squirmed and turned. His interrogator wasn't going to let up. 'I suppose so,' he said.

'Hmm,' said the OC. Then he turned to his two companions. 'Do either of you want to comment?'

Brian shook his head.

'Maybe Trevelyan,' said the Crab, 'was a Republican also, and made sure our forebears got their dinner every day?'

Seanie felt he didn't have to answer and said nothing. But the OC said, 'Have you nothing to say? One so full of opinions would surely have thoughts about the Englishman blamed for causing the Irish Famine.'

Seanie felt trapped. The OC was pushing him. He had to say something. 'I think perhaps society still operates in a way not dissimilar to Trevelyan's strategy.'

The Crab turned to his commanding officer in frustration. 'Do we have to listen to this?'

'Have you somewhere to go?' asked the OC.

Brian smiled. The Crab didn't answer.

'Maybe you will explain what you mean,' the OC said to Seanie.

'It's not important . . . I'm prepared to apologize to the staff officer for not obeying the conditions.'

'Will you share your thinking on Trevelyan with us?'

'It's only silly.'

'Do I have to make it an order?'

Seanie decided if he was going to be thrown off the wing anyway, he had nothing to lose. 'Can I ask the staff officer a couple of questions?' he said, pointing to the Crab.

'I'm not in the witness box and you are not a barrister,' said the Crab.

'OK. Maybe I can ask the quartermaster instead.'

'No, ask me,' said the Crab. 'I'm not afraid of your questions.'

'If you brought out a big mortgage on your home, then lost your job and couldn't repay the loan, what would happen?'

Crab appealed to his OC again. 'Sir, what has this got to do with anything?'

The OC looked at the Crab. 'Didn't you agree to answer his questions?'

The Crab shook his head impatiently. 'I would lose my house.'

'But that wouldn't be fair. You weren't responsible for your bad luck.'

'That's the way it is.'

'Could the government not pay your mortgage for you?'

'The government's money comes from the people, so it's they who would be paying my mortgage, which wouldn't be fair on them.'

'Why not?'

'Because they have to pay their own mortgage and can't be expected to pay mine also.'

'Again, why not?'

'Because if that was the case everyone would be at it.'

'What would be wrong with that?'

'People have to be taught things or they never learn. You

have to take responsibility for yourself and not expect others to do it for you. That way leads to chaos. Nobody would act responsibly.'

Seanie turned his gaze to the OC and said, 'Sir, you've just heard Trevelyan's fundamental argument for letting the Irish starve.'

The Crab protested, 'You're using trick questions.'

Seanie didn't answer. Brian sat pondering. The OC rested his elbows on the table with his chin in the palms of his hands. Then, as if he had decided something, he took a deep breath and said to Seanie, 'If nobody has anything else to say perhaps you will wait outside. We will call you.' Seanie stepped out of the cell, but he wasn't kept for more than a couple of minutes. When he went in again, the OC said, 'A meeting of all volunteers is being arranged for this afternoon. Please attend.'

All the prisoners were crowded into the common room. Visits, as well as appointments with legal advisers, had to be put on hold. The OC's summons took precedence over everything else. Seanie sat at the edge of a row beside an inmate he had become friendly with. The Crab and Brian were behind a table on a makeshift stage. There was an empty chair for the OC who hadn't arrived yet. A hush descended when he marched into the room and up onto the stage, precisely at the arranged time. His limp was pronounced. He didn't sit down, but took up a position at the centre of the platform and let his gaze wander over the crowd. It included a few teenagers, some with acne on their faces. Those with ages ranging from twenty to forty were in the majority. There were two older men in the room. One stood out because of his bald head.

Then the OC began. '*A Fhianna Éireann, a chairde,* during the confrontation which preceded disgraceful scenes a few days ago, reference had been made to war wounds. I want to begin what I have to say by revealing something that only very few know. As a young recruit, many years ago, maybe before some of you here were even born, I was selected to go on a mission. It involved attacking an RUC barracks. The details are not necessary, but everything that could go wrong with the operation went wrong. In the end there was only one shot fired; that was by me. Unfortunately, the person I managed to shoot was myself.' The OC paused. 'That, comrades, is the inglorious way I acquired the wound with which I sometimes try and impress people.'

The speaker limped a couple of steps across the stage, looking at the floor. Then he lifted his head and said, 'However, every one of us here has war wounds. They cannot be seen, but they exist nonetheless. So how we obtained a particular physical deformity is irrelevant. We are all equal in that area.'

Seanie was reminded of a story Slash would tell of the former Second World War soldier who ran for cover every time a crow or jackdaw flew overheard, thinking it was a fighter plane about to attack. 'There was also,' continued the OC, 'a reference made to Belfast bowsies. Let me assure you, there are plenty of bowsies in South Armagh. I know because I've had to listen to them on occasion.'

There was an outbreak of laughter at this and the OC turned to Brian saying, 'I don't know why you're laughing. There's no shortage of bowsies in Tyrone either.'

From among the crowd a voice shouted, 'Up the Falls.' This was followed by someone shouting, 'Up Ballymurphy.' Someone else shouted, 'Up the Ardoyne,' and finally, in a different accent, someone shouted, 'What about Lurgan? Up Kilwilkie.'

The OC went over to the table and took a sip of water from a glass before continuing. 'Comrades, this meeting was not instigated by a little squabble between two individuals. Discipline in the ranks broke down that evening. This is something which cannot be tolerated. There must be consequences. Before I outline my plans in this regard, I want to address the importance of order.'

Seanie's friend gave him a nudge.

'We all know,' said the OC, 'the Diplock train is hurtling towards us at breakneck speed. This generation of Irish Republicans are going to be called upon as much as any generation that has gone before. I don't know what form the resistance will take, but surely for some it will involve the supreme sacrifice. If this martyrdom is not to be squandered there must be discipline. Comrades, when under pressure, there must be discipline. When we lose people, there must be discipline. If it should come to the point where we have to watch a comrade die the appalling death that attends the hunger striker, we will need discipline. When we see his hair fall out, when we see his teeth fall out, when we see his eyes go blind, when we see his body eating itself in a desperate search for nourishment, when we see his flesh starting to decay and rot even before he is dead, we will need to be disciplined.'

Only the OC's words broke the silence in the room. 'These unspeakable things must be turned into words, into images, into language, and articulated, so that the world knows what's going on. However, it is never easy to go against the prevailing sentiment. We will need people with a different kind of courage. Perhaps the kind of people who are prepared to declare Cromwell was a Republican. Whether he was or not is immaterial. "Republican" is a broad term. The American president Richard Nixon is one. You can make up your own minds about him.'

The OC took another sip of water. 'It took me some time to construct a proper response to the breakdown in order; in other words, what sanctions were to be applied to those who participated. During a discussion this morning it became clear what should have been obvious all along. It struck me that society wishes people to be responsible for their actions, especially if they are deemed to be incorrect in some way. Unfortunately, this sense of responsibility is usually promoted by leaders who are often reluctant to apply the same moral judgment to their own behaviour. It always seems to be the lowest in the scale of things who are encouraged to act responsibly. This is not something new. The Romans, as we know, busied themselves extensively with things military. It's noteworthy how they dealt with soldiers who rebelled or didn't perform as expected. They had a punishment whereby every tenth man in the ranks was taken out and executed. It was known as 'decimation'. The generals weren't decimated.

'Comrades, it is my intention, as Officer Commanding, to accept full responsibility for the aforementioned disturbance. I have therefore set in motion plans for my return to the ranks and for the vacant position to be filled as soon as possible. This action that I inflict on myself, I will deem sufficient punishment necessary for the entire affair.'

At this, a voice shouted up, 'No.' This was followed by a chorus of noes. People began to stamp their feet.

The OC straightened his shoulders. 'Volunteers,' he ordered. 'Stand to attention.'

Everyone, including Seanie, immediately jumped to their

feet and stood to attention. The OC began to sing '*Amhrán na bhFiann*'. All joined in at the top of their voices. Seanie bellowed it out as lustily as the rest. When it was over, the OC gave the order, 'Volunteers. Dis . . . miss.'

After the meeting, Seanie went to the Crab and apologized. The Crab said everybody had learned from the incident.

'We are going to fight this thing tooth and nail,' said Gerry, who had the smell of drink on him. As Seanie's solicitor, Gerry was entitled to privacy with his client. The room where meetings were held contained only four plastic chairs and a wooden table. A warden waited outside the door. The trial was due in four weeks.

'Who's the judge?' asked Seanie.

'His name is Judge White, which from our perspective is good and bad. It's good because he's the only Catholic judge in the North, but bad because of that very reason. If you want to stop the poaching, make the poacher the gamekeeper. The other problem is, London wants convictions.'

'So where are we at?'

'The forensics are our bogey and we can't press the notion that the evidence was planted.'

'But what if it's true?' said Seanie.

'Judges cannot take it on board that the police or the army would lie, because they feel that if they did then the whole system of justice would fall apart. So to concentrate on the idea that the stuff had been deliberately put on your hands would be counterproductive.'

'They're a shower of gangsters,' said Seanie.

'Let me explain how it works,' said Gerry. 'Each side

advances its own arguments. But both parties are obviously biased. So who does the judge listen to? He listens to people who have no interest one way or another. Unfortunately, in your case these people are the forensic experts. Supposedly they don't give a hoot who they are favouring, and because they are experts in the field, the judge as a general rule accepts their evidence as fact.'

'I can't be locked away. I'm innocent don't forget.'

'Unfortunately, *a mhic*, that's not what trials are about.'

'What are they about?'

'Winning and losing. Neither the prosecution nor the defence has ever the slightest bit of interest in the guilt or innocence of an accused person. The only thing they are thinking of is their own careers.' Gerry loosened his tie. 'God it's hot in here. I'm parched with thirst.'

Seanie had it on the tip of his tongue to tell Gerry he had plenty of liquid in him, but didn't. 'Gerry, can we not get some more legal advice somewhere?'

'We have another solicitor working on the case with us.'

'That's great. Who is he?'

'Phonsie, my assistant.'

Seanie jumped out of his seat and kicked over the chair. He leaned over the table and said into Gerry face, 'For fuck's sake. Is that the best you can come up with?'

'Calm down,' said the solicitor.

'Calm down my arse. I want out of here.'

Gerry rose to leave. 'I'll be in touch with you. My God, how do you stick the heat in this place?'

Two days later the letter came. The first lines read, 'Hello Daddy O'Rourke. You've a healthy son born four hours ago weighing in at six pounds, twelve ounces.'

Seanie let a holler out of him and ran to the workroom, roaring and shouting, 'I'm a daddy.'

Everyone gathered around congratulating him. One prisoner said, 'Another wee Provo.'

Eileen said she had gone into labour unexpectedly. It was the middle of the night and she didn't know how long it would take for an ambulance to arrive. She thought of her Northern neighbour. Fortunately, he was at home and he drove her to hospital. He was in an awful panic in case it would be born in the car. He was almost as stressed as herself. He asked her if she wanted him to contact the father or anyone, and was very diplomatic when she said no. When she got to the hospital, the baby was born almost immediately. She wanted to catch the post with the letter. She wrote that she was fine. The baby was the image of his father, and he definitely had the same stubborn personality, but he was beautiful. Enclosed was a polaroid photo taken by a nurse. She would like to name him Patrick.

'This calls for a celebration,' said Brian. After getting the go-ahead from the OC, a number of people with whom Seanie had become friendly gathered in his cell. Brian supplied a cardboard box full of goodies. In it were oranges, apples, lemons, pastries, crisps, and a bottles of strange looking liquid. After jabbing a small hole in an orange with a pencil, he said to Seanie, 'Here suck on this.'

'That's a strange-tasting orange,' said Seanie.

'You never got vodka and orange like that in your local,' said Brian.

'How did you get the vodka into it?'

'Syringe. A medium-sized orange will hold a half one of vodka, and there's no tell-tale marks. All this fruit has been injected with spirits and taken in as food parcels. Gin in the lemons. An apple is very dense and won't hold much, but it can be laced with brandy or whiskey. There are other ways of getting stuff in, although I personally believe Nelson's eye is sometimes involved. The mother with a baby sucking on a bottle might not be all it seems. The teat may have no hole in it, and if it did the baby would discover the Cow and Gate had a funny taste. We also have homemade wine made from fermenting grapes, adding sugar and pieces of bread for yeast.'

'What's that stuff?' said Seanie, looking at Coke bottles with thick black liquid in them.

'Made from the alcohol in boot polish,' said Brian, holding aloft one of the bottles. 'Pure rocket fuel. We call it the Crumlin Cocktail. A toast. Let's drink a toast to Seanie's son, that he will bring pride and joy to his family, and carry forward the Republican ideals to a new generation. Everybody on their feet. *Chun Seanie's mac.*'

In unison, everyone said, '*Chun Seanie's mac.*'

Even in his exhilarated mood, Seanie could see the bizarreness of the situation. Ten men crowded into a jail cell, drinking a toast to his son by sucking on an orange or taking a bite out of an apple. Yet it didn't feel odd.

'Can I call a toast?' he asked.

'Sure.'

'To my new baby. That he will be his own man.'

Again the prisoners shouted out, 'That he will be his own man.'

Seanie took another bite of the apple. Then the realization hit him. He wouldn't be there to help shape him towards being a man. He wouldn't be there when he took his first steps. He wouldn't be there when he spoke his first words. He wouldn't be there to take him to his first football match.

He wouldn't be there to take him to any football matches.

Brian gave him a dig that brought him out of his reverie 'Do you fancy some Mellow Yellow?' he said, producing some black-looking material from the box. 'Banana skins, dried slowly on the radiator. They're great for producing a high when smoked. That's if you can tolerate it.'

Only one inmate decided to try it. He began to choke, and wasn't impressed by the result.

'It's an acquired taste,' said Brian.

Seanie put away his morbid thoughts. The Crab gate-crashed the party and Seanie welcomed him to join in the celebrations, all past grievances forgotten. Crab won the hearty handshake competition. A guitar and an accordion were produced and soon a singsong was in full swing, with mostly Republican songs and ballads. One prisoner had obviously got singing lessons. He sang 'The Last Rose of Summer' and then '*La Golondrina*'. Some of the men had tears in their eyes, but everyone kept their heads down and pretended not to notice. When the fruit was all eaten and homemade wine finished, the bottles of boot polish brew were uncorked. Seanie decided it didn't taste so bad after all.

After a couple of hours the prisoners drifted off to their own cells, leaving just Seanie and Brian alone. 'You know it could be worse,' said Seanie attempting a little waltz with Brian.

Brian had his arms around Seanie. 'Never entertain those thoughts even for a second, my friend.'

Seanie, in a serious voice, asked, 'Why do you say that?'

Brian slumped down on Cormac's empty bunk. 'The day you start to think like that will be the day you've become institutionalized. I have a fear of that happening to me because of the number of stretches I've done.' He paused for a few moments and then added, 'And all for what? That's what I sometimes wonder.'

'For what you believe in.'

Brian just grunted and said, 'We almost all sell out in the end.'

Seanie took a swig from the bottle, grimacing as he swallowed. On the bed, Brian twisted himself onto his back and stared at the ceiling. 'God knows, I've had plenty of time to study Irish history. Almost every period of trouble ends the same way. It wasn't for nothing Brendan Behan said the first item on the agenda at a committee meeting in Ireland is the split.'

'Oh yeah?' said Seanie.

'When the uprising is near over,' said Brain, 'and again the goal is not achieved, one side grabs whatever spoils there is going, and makes speeches about dead heroes, while the rump fights on and causes more futile bloodletting.'

Seanie, trying to focus, had one eye closed. 'So what?'

'Will this time be any different?' said Brian.

Seanie jabbed a lemon with a pencil and sucked at the hole. 'Is everybody wrong then?'

'What are you on about?'

'You seem to be saying that whatever position either side of the split adopts, it's wrong.'

'It's according to how they accept defeat.'

'I'll never see a lemon again without wanting to suck on it,' said Seanie.

'There are circumstances,' said Brian, almost talking to himself, 'where some won't accept defeat.'

'What are you mumbling about?'

'There's a difference between defeat and personal victory.'

'Tell me.'

'Say someone goes on hunger strike. At that stage it's not about dying for Ireland. It's about one's own personal ideology, beliefs, standards, creed, duty, call it what you will. It's about not surrendering these principles under any circumstances. In that there is victory.'

Seanie said nothing for a few moments, thinking of his own father's lifelong beliefs and the conflict this caused in him. 'But you can't say these are somebody's *own* beliefs and principles. Most likely they have been born into it, or reared up to take all this stuff on board. They're not really their own.'

'Hand me one of those bottles of poison,' said Brian. 'It'll cure me or kill me. Listen, I don't care if you get your belief system – whatever that happens to be – from your parents, you buy it out of a Littlewoods catalogue, or you catch it off the seat in a jacks. It's yours. It belongs to you and it's up to you to decide what you do with it. You can discard it, or you can run with it. But if you run with it, how far are you prepared to go?'

Seanie sat on the bunk, lying with his back against the wall. He began to sing, '*In Dublin's fair city, where the girls are so pretty, I first set my eye on sweet Molly Malone. As she wheeled her wheelbarrow, through streets broad and narrow, crying cockles and mussels, alive, alive, O.*'

Brian joined in the chorus, and the two of them belted out raucously, '*Alive, alive, O. Alive, alive, O. Crying cockles and mussels, alive, alive, O.*'

'I think I'm drunk,' said Brian.

Seanie tried to rise off the bunk, but fell back again. 'You're my one true friend, my, my comrade and my helper in need,' he said.

'I think you're drunk too. What about Cormac?'

'Oh, well, you're second after Cormac then . . . But you're both equal.'

There was silence between the men for a few minutes. Then Seanie said, 'How far are you prepared to run?'

Brian studied the bottle of liquid in his hand, and then drained it down. He grimaced and said, 'I think of these things. Would I stay with it to the bitter end, if that be the case? Or would I just throw in the towel and surrender?'

'Well, what's the answer?'

'I don't know.'

'What about finding a way out with your ideals intact?'

'Is there any fruit left in the bag? I doubt if that would be possible.'

Later on, Seanie didn't want to sleep. In spite of being in jail, it had been one of the most joyful days of his life. He felt drunk, but his mind was crystal clear. For himself, any remnant of his own father's Republican indoctrination would be discarded. If he didn't 'run with it' there could be no 'sell out'. And as for his son, he would not become another 'wee Provo', or wee anything else, because of a father's influence. The boy would be allowed to determine his own path.

21

The British royal coat of arms was affixed to red velvet drapes above the judge's bench. Just in front of this, at a lower elevation, were the court recorder, officials and news reporters. Situated to the right of the judge's seat stood a hexagonal-shaped witness box with a tattered Bible resting on one edge.

Seanie, dressed in his law suit, had been transported on the morning of the trial in a prison van. He sat with a prison guard beside him watching the proceedings from one of the side boxes. There were a number of other people in attendance: Gerry, his solicitor; the prosecuting barrister; Cormac, in the area assigned to members of the public; and a young girl with a notebook, below the judge facing the court. She was probably a trainee reporter. The case was unlikely to be newsworthy. Maybe if there was a 'not guilty' verdict it would merit a few column inches. Generally, only the unusual got reported. The court attendant stood just inside the rear door with his hands behind his back.

A door to the right of the judge's chair opened. His Lordship's tipstaff appeared and announced, 'Everyone stand.'

The judge came out and walked briskly to the podium. He sat down, glanced around the room and stated that the court was now in session. He seemed slim and of medium height, but due to his robes and wig it was difficult for Seanie to form an impression of him. He disliked him anyway. The prosecution counsel rose to his feet. He was extremely tall and skinny. He had a long thin neck, and there was a space between his throat and the tie knot.

Seanie listened intently to him saying, 'The case being the State versus John O'Rourke.' He spoke with a slight lisp, which made the words sound even more precise and modulated. It reminded Seanie of an ice cream man shaping wafers in a shiny steel mould.

'John O'Rourke is charged, that he on March twenty-ninth of this year did have in his possession and under his control named explosive substances, with intent to murder members of the Crown forces. And on a second count, that he violently resisted arrest.'

The lawyer then went on to claim that evidence would be produced to prove the defendant guilty on both counts. His speech was so matter of fact that it made the charges seem incontestable.

When he had finished, Gerry, dressed in his usual crumpled suit, rose. He said that his client pleaded not guilty to both charges.

The prosecutor began by calling a number of soldiers to give evidence. After taking the oath, they all repeated the same story. The car had been spotted being driven in a suspicious manner not far from where a bomb explosion had just killed two of their comrades. A helicopter had tried to intercept it, but the driver had attempted a getaway. It was only when a foot patrol managed to ambush the Ford Escort that the occupants had been arrested. Even then they had resisted, and as a result received injuries.

Seanie despaired. It all sounded so plausible.

Gerry cross-examined each of them in turn.

'In what way was the car being driven in a suspicious manner?' he asked the first soldier.

'The headlights were switched off and it had come off a little-used byroad.'

'Might it be they were afraid of being stopped and abused by Crown forces?'

'Why would they be afraid?'

'How did the accused suffer such severe injuries?'

'He resisted arrest and it was necessary to use minimum force to restrain him.'

'Such minimum force that would necessitate a prolonged stay in hospital?'

'I know nothing of how long he was in hospital.'

'Is it believable he would have received such severe injuries simply by resisting arrest?'

'I believe he fell and hit his face on the personnel carrier during the struggle.'

'Did you or any of your colleagues have access to explosives that might subsequently be used to incriminate others?'

'We would have no reason to access explosives.'

So it went on. Each witness repeated the same story. It was as if they had been coached in what to say. At the end of the session, Gerry had a word with Seanie and told him to keep his chin up. They had witnesses also.

The next day was taken up by various members of the RUC giving evidence of the formal arrest and charge. One of them gave testimony as to how he took the fingerprints and swabbed the hands for forensic testing. Then doctors who had treated Seanie also gave accounts of their contact with the accused.

On the third day it was the turn of the forensic expert. He sounded confident and assured, describing the nature and technical qualities of the substances tested. Gerry cross-questioned him. 'How scientific is the methodology?' he asked.

'The process used has been tested and tried in the laboratory,' the expert said. 'If one has handled the materials in question, there will be residue on the hands. In this case, traces were also found under the fingernails.'

'Could you be mistaken in your findings?'

'I have complete confidence in the methods used.'

'Have you had experience of being wrong in your analysis?'

'No.'

'Could there have been contamination from other sources?'

'Highly unlikely, from my investigations.'

'Would it be possible for the substance to be put on the defendant's hands maliciously?'

'How it got there is not part of my brief.'

'It's surely relevant to my client's case.'

'I can't comment on that.'

Gerry was clearly about to pursue this line of questioning further when the judge intervened. 'What the defence appears to be alluding to is some fantastical conspiracy. Perhaps learned counsel will direct appropriate questions to the expert witness.'

'May it please Your Honour,' said Gerry to the judge before turning back to the forensic expert. 'Is it possible that the incriminating substances could have been obtained, for example, from working with garden pesticides or fertilizer?'

'To my knowledge, the chemistry of these products is not

of such a nature that would produce findings consistent with what I have discovered in my sample analysis.'

'To your knowledge?'

'Chemistry is an ongoing science and new discoveries are being made all the time.'

'Quite. Definitive proof that the substances found on my client's hands could *only* have come from handling explosives is not possible. Would you agree?'

'Anything is possible, but some things are very unlikely.'

'I put it to you that in the present circumstances the term *unlikely* is hardly sufficient.'

'On that there is nothing more I can say.'

'No, there is isn't. Finally, however, will you agree with me that the vast majority of IRA bombs are primarily made from common farm fertilizer?'

'That is my understanding.'

'I have no more questions, m'lord.'

This completed the case for the prosecution. Afterwards, Seanie told Gerry he hadn't handled garden products before his arrest. Gerry said he wanted to promote the notion in the judge's mind that lots of common stuff can be used in the construction of bombs, and perhaps leave incriminating traces when innocently handled.

The next day it was the turn of the defence. Gerry called his main hope, the soldier who had been reluctant to drive the army Saracen. This was an eye-witness that would tell the truth. But when asked to take the oath, the soldier refused. He said he was a non-believer. Seanie saw Gerry's body visibly slump. To a conservative Catholic judge, an atheist's evidence would be of little value. It was such an unusual event that the court attendant who conducted the oath procedure was at a loss to know what to do. He looked at the judge. The judge shuffled his robes impatiently, and said in an exasperated voice, 'Get him to promise to tell the truth.'

'Why were you reluctant to drive the vehicle on the night in question?' Gerry asked the soldier, putting on a show of confidence.

'It was clear to me the two men had been badly beaten and I wanted no part of it.'

'What did you do?'

'I told them to get another driver.'

'There was no other driver available on the night?'

'No.'

'You eventually agreed to drive?'

'On the condition the abuse would stop.'

'What was occurring in the rear of the vehicle as you were transporting the defendant?'

'He was being abused by members of the regiment.'

'Did you ask them to refrain?'

'Yes.'

'Is there anything more you can say?'

'No one should have those things done to them.'

Then it was the turn of the prosecutor to cross-examine. He started off by asking, 'Why do you not believe in God?'

'Because I have never seen God.'

'None of us has seen God, yet many of us believe in him.'

'When I see him with my own eyes, then I'll believe in him.'

Gerry was on his feet. 'Your Honour, this line of questioning has no relevance.'

The judge agreed and told the prosecutor to confine himself to pertinent matters, and not a useless academic discussion only heathens engage in.

'Is it because you are afraid of perjuring yourself that you didn't take the oath?' said the barrister.

'That is not the reason.'

'Did you see the soldiers beat the accused?'

'I didn't actually see them beat the men, but it was obvious they had been beaten.'

'When driving the vehicle, could you see into the back of the carrier?'

'I couldn't turn around as I had to keep my eyes on the road.'

'I put it to you that you concocted this story of the prisoners being abused, for reasons best known to yourself.'

'What I said is true.'

'Yet you won't swear it is true on the Bible.'

'Because I don't believe in the Bible or God.'

'Ah yes, you only believe what you can see with your own eyes. Yet in your evidence to this court, you have stated you didn't see with your own eyes the prisoner being abused.'

The soldier made no reply to this statement.

'Can you explain this discrepancy? On the one hand, you refuse to believe in the Lord because he hasn't decided to let you personally see him, while on the other hand you surmise things happened that you clearly could not have seen happen.'

'You are twisting things around. I could hear their screams.'

'When you first saw the prisoners you were reluctant to drive because of their condition, which you inferred had been deliberately inflicted on them but didn't actually see happen?'

'Yes.'

'An argument between you and the rest of your mates then ensued. Is that correct?'

'Yes.'

'When you were driving the vehicle, might it have been the case that your colleagues, aware of your tender sensitivities, were ribbing you by screaming and pretending it was the prisoners?'

The soldier didn't answer.

'I put it to you again, your evidence to this court is malicious in intent.'

'No,' said the soldier.

The barrister directly addressed the judge.

'I am minded, Your Honour, to ask you to treat the witness as hostile.'

'Are you finished questioning the witness?' asked the judge.

'Yes, m'lord.'

'Does the defence wish to add anything more?'

'If it may please you, Your Honour,' said Gerry. He stood up and addressed the witness. 'You say you don't believe in God. Is that correct?'

'That is correct.'

'Do you believe in sin?'

'I believe in right and wrong.'

'If you don't believe in God, how do you know what's right or wrong?'

'I don't need to believe in God to know it's wrong to abuse anyone the way that man over there was abused.'

Gerry looked to the judge and said, 'I've no more questions, m'lord.'

'The witness may stand down,' said the judge.

Finally on Friday morning, Gerry called for Seanie to take the stand. Seanie had lain awake most of the night. Brian had told him to relax, to speak clearly and the truth would come through. He wasn't so sure that the judge would heed anything he said. Like everyone else, Brian was of the opinion it was a hanging court. However, he argued that it was important for the record that he state his case.

Seanie stood in the witness box and took the oath. Gerry began by asking him to describe the events as they happened that night.

Seanie told of how he and Cormac were on a business trip to Castleblaney. He went over all that happened. He described how he was afraid of the army because of rumours of brutality, and of trying to get home after he realized violent incidents were occurring in the vicinity. Gerry asked him if he was now, or ever had been, a member of the IRA. Seanie said no. Gerry asked him if he resisted arrest. Seanie replied by asking how could one resist arrest against such superior numbers. Gerry asked him to explain the findings of the forensic expert and the substances in the car. Seanie said either the finding was incorrect, or the substances had been put on his hands by members of the security forces. If the explosives *were* in the car, they had been planted there. Gerry asked him if he condemned the violence of the IRA. Seanie said he condemned all violence. Violence had been perpetrated on his own person. He condemned that also. Finally, Gerry asked him if he was guilty of the charges against him. Seanie said, 'I am definitely not guilty.'

The prosecuting barrister rose out of his seat, slowly uncoiling his long body. 'John O'Rourke, among other things you have been accused of having in your possession materials that were invented for the good of mankind. These substances can be used to blow mountains apart, but they can also be used to blow human bodies apart.'

The judge interrupted. 'This is not the time for a closing speech. Do you wish to cross-examine the witness?'

'May it please m'lord,' said the barrister. 'I merely wanted to contextualize my questions.'

'The context is quite clear to me,' said the judge.

'May it please m'lord,' repeated the barrister. 'You say you're not a member of the IRA,' he said addressing Seanie, 'yet you have, it seems, chosen B Wing of Crumlin Road Gaol when you had other options open to you. Is that correct?'

'That is not correct,' said Seanie.

'Oh? Perhaps you will correct me then.'

'The prison warder decided where to put me when I told him I was from South Armagh.'

'And you could, could you not, have chosen other options?'

'I was too scared.'

'Ah, I see,' said the barrister bending down as if he was talking to his notes. 'You were too scared.'

Seanie didn't reply to this. It wasn't a question. The lawyer peered at his papers and shuffled a few pages as if searching for something. Then, with knuckles resting on the edge of the table, he said to Seanie, 'I want to get a picture of the night in question. Let me see. You were going across the border on business. Is that correct?'

'Yes,' said Seanie.

'Would you care to elaborate on the nature of the business?'

Gerry sighed loud enough for the judge to hear him and rose to his feet. 'What is the relevance of the question?'

Seanie knew Gerry's weary objection was a bluff. In reality, the lawyer was concerned that the prosecution would know that Seanie was a smuggler, and attempt to paint a picture of him as someone with no respect for the law.

The judge asked the barrister for an explanation of the question's relevance. 'The aim,' said the barrister, 'is to ascertain if the accused man's journey on that night was in pursuit of lawful business.'

Gerry was on his feet again. 'M'lord, the facts are, the accused is either guilty of the crimes as charged or he isn't. If he is, then so be it; but if he is not, then like any other citizen he should be free to come and go as he pleases without questions being asked as to his business for being abroad.'

The judge looked at the barrister and said, 'The right of free unhindered passage is as old as civilization itself, would you agree?'

'Quite so, m'lord.'

'That being the case, unless you can connect the business the accused was engaged in on the night in question with the charges, I direct you to leave that line of enquiry in abeyance.'

'May it please Your Honour,' said the barrister, bowing his head in false remorse. Then as if the reprimand had never happened, he fixed his glare on Seanie again. 'You met a car that flashed its lights at you, which made you turn back, is that correct?'

'Yes.'

'On your way back another light was waved at you, and this light caused you to stop, am I correct?'

'Yes.'

'The person waving the light told you there had been an explosion further up the road. Am I correct in this?'

'Yes.'

'Finally, you then entered a byroad which ultimately led you to Crossmaglen. Is this correct?'

'Yes,' said Seanie.

The barrister leaned over the table and stared at Seanie

through his heavy spectacles.

'I put it to you, there were never any lights flashing. There was never any man out on the road with a lamp. I put it to you that the reasons you have presented to this court for being out that night are a tissue of lies. I put it to you that you violently resisted arrest. I put it to you that your claims to have been abused are false allegations.'

The barrister paused a few moments and drew in a breath. Then slowly and deliberately he said, 'Finally, John O'Rourke, I put it to you that the reason you were abroad that night was to cause destruction, mayhem, and loss of life.'

Seanie answered quickly. 'It was not.' He felt as if his head was spinning by the relentless accusations.

The barrister, pretending he didn't hear him, looked up at the judge. 'No more questions, Your Honour.'

The judge asked Gerry if he wanted to respond.

'Just one question, m'lord,' he said, turning to Seanie. 'Why did you not produce the man with the torch to testify on your behalf?'

'He resides just on the border, an area where there is a lot of British Army activity. He said he had a large family and couldn't be getting involved in giving testimony that the British soldiers may not like. He was decent to us that night. It would be wrong of me to put him in danger.'

'That concludes the defence, Your Honour,' said Gerry.

All that remained was the closing address by both sides. The prosecuting barrister began by saying he wouldn't detain the court longer than was necessary. It was a straightforward case. The accused had been on a nefarious mission to maim and kill. He wanted to remind the court of how much ordinary citizens owed to the police and army. Every minute of every day they risked life and limb to protect the public.

They were under constant attack from people such as the defendant. Just hours before he was arrested and found to have explosive materials in his possession, two regiment members had their lives snuffed out by similar substances. The defence had offered no explanation as to how the materials came to be in the possession of the accused, except to hint at some fantastic scenario which suggested it had been placed in the car by someone else. 'The someone else, Your Honour,' he continued, 'is none other than members of Her Royal Majesty's armed forces.'

The barrister took a sip of water. 'I ask, who is it that plants these dastardly traps that kill so indiscriminately? It is surely not faeries and leprechauns who come out at night.'

Seanie could see the newspaper headline. *Lawyer states in court it is not Faeries and Leprechauns who plant bombs*. Maybe he was looking for publicity. The barrister lisped on relentlessly. 'No, it is human beings intent on destroying lives. When apprehended they must suffer the full rigour of the law. The evil involved can only be described as the work of Satan.'

He picked up some documents. 'Let us examine the evidence. A number of witnesses, members of the security forces, gave testimony to the fact that the accused was acting suspiciously. He was driving his own car accompanied by a friend.'

At this point the barrister looked up from his notes and addressed the judge directly. 'It is worth noting, this friend is not presently before this court, but perhaps in other circumstances he might have been.'

Seanie looked across at Cormac, who attended court each day. The bastard of a barrister was trying to plant in the judge's mind that there were two of them and one had got away with it. However, the judge interrupted. 'There is a lack of clarity as to what you're referring to. Perhaps it is a wiser course if counsel addresses only what is before the court today.'

The barrister gave a bow as if properly reprimanded, and said, 'May it please you, Your Honour.'

Gerry wasn't happy. His peer had been chastised, but prior to making the statement he knew he would be. The seed had been planted and could not be unplanted. It was a ploy often used in jury trials, and he could only hope an experienced judge wouldn't be as susceptible to such a cheap trick as a jury might.

The barrister continued as if there had been no interruption. 'It was the suspicious movements of the defendant that first drew the attention of the security forces. But before we proceed we need to situate the episode in context. Your Honour, due to rampant terrorism prevalent in the aforementioned area, very few people dare venture out at night. Yet here was the defendant, a long way from his own home, seemingly unaffected by such terrorist activities. However, if he himself was one of these people, then no other explanation is required. Unlike all decent, God-fearing people, *he* had no reason to be frightened of being abroad during such cruel times.'

As he was articulating these words, the barrister leaned his long skinny frame towards the judge. 'A man acting like a lighthouse keeper, out on the middle of the road to warn of danger ahead, is surely not believable. But if such a person exists, why is he not here? He is not here because figments of the imagination do not give evidence in a court of law.

'When we come to the arrest of the defendant, the question must be asked, why should he resist so violently if he was innocent? To say he was overcome by sheer weight of numbers and couldn't resist is asking the court to believe a citizen going about his daily business was set upon by Her Majesty's forces for no reason.'

The prosecutor stopped talking at this point and laid the documents on the desk. Then he unwound himself fully and clasped the lapels of his jacket with both hands. He looked at the judge and spoke in an authoritative tone. 'I have, Your Honour, tried to keep my closing address precise and to the point. The facts are clear. There are no extenuating circumstances in this case. A message must be sounded to terrorists who plot to kill, maim, and destroy our heritage. I ask that the full rigour of the law be applied, and the maximum allowed sentence be handed down. Thank you, m'lord.'

The barrister sat down, and the judge asked Gerry if he wished to begin his final submissions or wait until Monday morning. Gerry said he would wait, and the Judge adjourned the case for the weekend.

Seanie said it looked hopeless. Gerry didn't try to convince him otherwise. He said he would do his best to convince the authorities to let Eileen and the baby visit him immediately after the trial.

Gerry travelled to Clogherhead on Saturday evening to prepare Eileen for the bad news to come on Monday morning. She greeted him at the door. Gerry was taken aback by her appearance. Her expression was dull and her eyes glassy. He pretended not to notice and said, 'Congratulations, Mrs Seanie O'Rourke. How is the latest addition to the ancient and honourable O'Rourke clan?'

Cormac was in the room. Eileen gently parted the blanket covering the baby's head with her index finger and revealed a tiny face. 'Oh God,' exclaimed Gerry. 'He's the spitting image of myself.'

Cormac smiled. Eileen said nothing. Gerry chuckled at the baby. 'Do you see him laughing at me?'

'I'm going to let him sleep now,' said Eileen.

Gerry took out a pound note and put it into the baby's hand. The baby immediately clasped it with little fingers. 'Ah, he's Seanie's son all right,' said the solicitor.

Cormac wasn't impressed by Gerry's level of generosity. Eileen seemed not to notice. She covered the baby up and listlessly asked Gerry if he wanted tea. At the mention of tea, Gerry shuddered as if someone had made a horrific suggestion to him.

'I think it's important to celebrate the new arrival,' said Gerry. 'If you had a wee whiskey that might be more appropriate for the occasion.'

Eileen poured a generous measure of whiskey for her uncle-in-law and one for herself, but forgot to ask Cormac if he wanted one.

Gerry didn't know what to say. He had often seen Eileen's symptoms manifested in young wives whose husbands were imprisoned for the first time. Eileen just sat on the sofa, not speaking. She held the full glass of whiskey in her hands and stared into it.

'Tell us about the court case,' said Cormac.

Gerry didn't want to make Eileen even worse, but telling lies wouldn't help either.

'The problem is simple, really. The forensic evidence is almost impossible to surmount, considering all the circumstantial stuff, such as being in that area, and an explosion recently occurring. The fact that Seanie was beaten up is a side issue. It won't have any bearing on the substantive charge.'

'What are you to going say on Monday?' said Cormac.

Gerry finished the whiskey and made a show of putting down the empty glass before continuing. 'If it were a jury trial it might be a little bit easier. A jury composed of a number of individuals becomes a separate entity. It is no longer a group of people, all with their own prejudices and hang-ups, but a totally different animal, open to see and perceive things that one person on his own is blind to. However, London wants convictions. That's our dilemma.'

'So the judge is corrupt?'

'I wouldn't go that far. But he is actively seeking reasons why he should convict. It can be argued that there is nothing wrong with this. If he doesn't find the reasons then that means the person is innocent, and he will decide accordingly. I would need to have the judge in a position where he is actively looking for reasons to find Seanie *not* guilty.'

Nobody spoke for a couple of minutes. 'Gerry,' said Cormac. 'Be honest with us, what's the chances?'

'Honestly?'

'Yeah.'

Gerry shook his head. 'Only a miracle.'

'What are we going to do, Cormac?' asked Eileen, her voice almost pleading.

'Try to spring him is all I can think of,' said Cormac.

'Could we do that?' said Eileen.

'We could get a gun from Dickie Stone and smuggle it into the courthouse, release Seanie at gunpoint, and have a car waiting to take us to the border.'

'It might work,' said Eileen, suddenly more animated.

Gerry sat listening to the conversation. 'I know how desperate you are, Eileen,' he said. 'But what you're discussing is crazy.'

'We must do something. Will you please help us, Gerry?' said Eileen.

'You could get the gun in for us,' said Cormac. 'They won't search you and you could say you were forced to do it.'

'Even if I got the gun into the courtroom you wouldn't get away.'

'Gerry, we have to do something,' said Eileen.

'This will be our best chance,' said Cormac. 'We must at least try.'

Gerry shook his head sorrowfully, and rose from his seat. 'I'm getting a drink.'

He walked out into the kitchen where the whiskey was kept. Through the back window he could see a car with a Northern registration pull into the drive next door. The driver's door opened. A light came on illuminating the pathway. A man stepped out of the car. Gerry blinked to make sure what he was seeing. 'Jesus,' he whispered.

The whiskey now forgotten about, he followed the man with his eyes until he entered the house. Then he plonked himself down on a chair. Cormac came into the kitchen suspecting something was up. He saw Gerry deep in thought and the whiskey untouched. 'What's happening?' he asked.

Gerry looked up at him. 'Forget about rescue attempts. Get on your knees and pray that on Monday morning the judge lets me call one more witness.'

22

On Sunday night, Seanie went to the OC's cell to thank him and say goodbye. Regardless of the verdict, Seanie wouldn't be back to B Wing as it was mostly for holding prisoners on remand. The OC was sitting at a desk writing. 'I like scribbling verse,' he said. 'It's therapeutic.'

He wished Seanie good luck at his trial, and Seanie asked why, despite everyone wanting him to stay on, he felt it necessary to step down. The OC said he believed there were terrible times ahead, and he decided to do something a little bit dramatic. 'To steel the lads.'

Then he asked Seanie about his new son. Seanie felt the older man was just being polite, but he showed him the Polaroid image he carried in his pocket. The OC gazed at it for a few seconds. 'I lost a boy,' he said.

'How?'

'Shot dead. He was just nineteen.'

'I'm sorry.'

He gave Seanie back the snap and turned away. Seanie could tell it was to hide tears that were welling up in his eyes.

'I sometimes think of Joyce's words about the old sow that eats its own farrow,' said the OC.

'I'm not sure what Joyce was referring to,' said Seanie.

'Over the ages, Mother Ireland has sacrificed countless children in her name. Is she giving them a noble cause to die for, or is she just devouring them?'

'Perhaps the martyrs would believe they died for a noble cause, and it's those who grieve that wonder was it worth it.'

The OC blew his nose into a handkerchief. 'The pain of losing one so young is difficult.'

Seanie didn't know what to say. He looked around the cell full of books and wondered what was driving this man. 'Can I ask why you still back the cause so strongly when you have doubts?'

The OC sat down and hung his head to think before answering. 'Only the fanatic doesn't have doubts, and he's usually crazy. Even Jesus wavered in Gethsemane. I think it's important to have a higher aim to strive towards. For me, that's to see my country united. One nation, sovereign, and free from foreign occupation.'

'Not everyone wants the same as you,' Seanie ventured to say.

The OC lifted his head and looked at him. 'Seanie, tomorrow morning you will be found guilty of a crime that you didn't commit. I don't need to remind you of our history, or that your experience is but a tiny drop in that ocean of injustice. It's time for English rule in Ireland to end. Until that happens, there will always be those who rebel.'

'Can the IRA win?'

'While the union flag flies over Belfast there will be conflict.'

'Would replacing it with the tricolour stop the conflict?' said Seanie.

'The tricolour is the flag of this country, and as such must be given proper recognition.'

Just before Seanie left for the courthouse the next morning,

Brian called to say goodbye. Seanie thanked him for all his advice.

'What did I tell you, besides to pump up your wrists before they cuff you?' said Brian.

'And not to catch flying objects when I'm being questioned,' said Seanie.

Brian threw himself down on Cormac's empty bunk and lay back with his hands behind his head, looking at the ceiling. 'You taught me things also.'

'Such as?'

'People have different values. If a person who preaches non-violence picks up a gun, he would be betraying *his* values.'

'What about those who preached armed resistance and now advocate non-violence?'

Brian jumped up. 'Maybe we should have a farewell swig?'

'No way,' said Seanie. 'My stomach still has to recover from the last session, and I never want to see another banana as long as I live.'

'Some of those people,' said Brian, 'remind me of the drunk who gives up drink. He's fucked and beaten, but he turns his surrender into some kind of victory.'

'So what do you do if you're fucked and beaten?'

'If you can't continue that's fine. But don't go on a crusade pretending you won something for personal glorification.'

Crab came into the cell also to say good luck.

'We were chatting about changing our way of going on,' said Brian.

'I often wondered what way my life would have been if I hadn't lost my fingers,' said Crab.

'Suppose you woke up tomorrow morning and you had them back,' said Brian. 'How would you feel?'

'I wouldn't be me,' said the Crab.

Brian grasped Seanie's hand and shook it warmly. 'Be who you are, Seanie.'

The courthouse was full. Ballyduff GAA club had organized a bus load of supporters for the final day of the trial. Club flags and jerseys had been hung out through the windows during the journey, but were folded away on arrival. Seanie had enough going against him without causing resentment because of noisy supporters. McIver donated carry-outs for the trip, half of which were left on the bus for the return journey. Slash and Wee Pat were in charge of distribution. Slash had to be persuaded to leave the vehicle and attend the trial.

When Seanie came in, Gerry gave him a fingers crossed sign. Seanie's friends crowded into the public seats. They were quiet, as if silenced by the solemnity of the occasion. The young newspaper girl had a male companion. Every so often they whispered to each other. The same prison escort Seanie had for the whole trial sat beside him. He rarely spoke. Seanie sometimes wondered what he thought about. The atmosphere was different, more tense than on previous days. Seanie focused again on his uncle. Was there a touch of excitement on his face?

'Everyone stand,' announced the tipstaff. The judge marched briskly out and glanced around him. He pulled his cloak tighter around his shoulders, as was his custom, and took his seat. 'Court is in session,' he declared as he sat down.

Gerry was on his feet immediately. 'Your Honour,' he began, 'there have been developments over the weekend. Before I make my closing address I would like permission to call a final witness.'

The prosecutor jumped up. 'Your Honour, this is most unusual.'

'Why is the court only being made aware of this now?' asked the judge.

'During the witness's testimony, the reason for the delay will become clear,' said Gerry.

'Your Honour, the prosecution objects strongly to a witness appearing at such an advanced stage in the proceedings.'

'If he is convinced of the righteousness of his case, then my learned colleague has nothing to fear,' said Gerry.

'It is simply a matter of procedure,' said the barrister.

'When should procedure take precedence over justice?'

'Enough,' declared the judge. He then said to Gerry, 'You may state the reasons why the court should facilitate this aberration.'

'Thank you, m'lord,' said Gerry, and then he paused to make a point of looking at his watch. 'Your Honour,' he began, 'it is now half-past eleven on a Monday morning. The good Lord has granted us another day. By twelve o'clock midday my witness will have concluded giving evidence.'

Gerry then slowly placed both hands flat on the table in front of him and leaned forward.

'Because it is crucial to the argument I will make in my closing address, that evidence may mean that my client does not have to spend many, many Monday mornings between half-past eleven and twelve o'clock midday locked in a dank, musty cell. That evidence may mean he does not have to spend hundreds of Monday mornings isolated from family and friends. That evidence may mean on future Monday mornings, his wife and child can enjoy his presence at home. That evidence may mean, Your Honour, that my client, on *this* Monday morning, has been allowed to avail himself of *every* opportunity to present his case.'

Gerry lowered his voice almost to a whisper. 'One half hour is all the time I beg the court in its wisdom to grant me.'

The judge looked at the prosecuting counsel. The barrister rose to his feet. 'We will respect Your Honour's decision,' he said.

'You may call your witness,' said the judge.

Gerry was on his feet again. 'I thank the court for its gracious indulgence,' and then, holding himself upright, he announced in a loud voice, 'I call to the stand, Mrs Eileen O'Rourke.'

Eileen had been sitting in a side recess adjacent to the courtroom waiting on the call to come. Gerry had coached her on how to make her entrance. She felt rather than heard the court attendant lean over and whisper, 'Mrs O'Rourke, follow me please.'

Eileen walked steadily behind the man. They entered the courtroom.

Seanie stared at his wife. Gerry hadn't told him about this. All the suppressed loneliness almost overwhelmed him. How he ached to hold her. She looked even lovelier than ever. She waved to him. He watched her look straight ahead and enter the witness box. He could see her seek out Gerry's face directly in front of her. The court attendant read out the oath and she repeated the words after him.

Then Gerry rose, saying, 'Mrs Eileen O'Rourke, wife of the defendant, will you please explain to the court why it is only now possible to have you here as a character witness for your husband.'

Eileen opened her mouth to speak, but the words dried up and came out in a whisper.

'Please address the judge and repeat your answer,' said Gerry, sharply.

Eileen turned towards the judge. The man in robes facing her was her Northern neighbour.

From the moment Eileen entered the room, Gerry had been watching the judge's face. He would know Eileen's gasp of surprise was not faked. Would he discharge himself from the case? There were two things Gerry had learned about judges. One was they all had an inflated conviction of their ability to be fair and just, regardless of the circumstances. The second thing was that once a case had started they hated to abandon it until they themselves had delivered a verdict.

'Do you wish to have a drink of water?' Gerry asked Eileen. He turned to the court attendant to ask for a glass of water, but he was already on his way with one. Eileen sipped it.

'If the witness is composed, I will continue if I may,' Gerry said to Eileen.

'Yes, I'm OK now,' said Eileen.

'Do you wish me to repeat the question?'

'No. I was in hospital having a baby and only got discharged last Thursday.'

Gerry was pleased. Her voice was low and weak, but all the better. He knew she was saying to herself: the judge knows this. But he had instructed her, no matter what occurred, to answer the questions she was asked.

'Where do you reside at the moment?' said Gerry.

'I live in Clogherhead.'

'You relocated there?'

'Yes.'

'Why?'

'My husband and I wanted to be away from the Troubles

and to be able to rear our child in a place where he wouldn't get involved when growing up.'

'Was your husband ever a member of the IRA?'

'No.'

'Did he have explosive substances in the car on the night he left to go to Castleblaney on business?'

'No, he did not.'

'Finally, Mrs O'Rourke, could your husband kill British soldiers?'

'He couldn't kill anyone.'

'How do you know that?'

'Because I know my husband.'

Gerry turned to the judge. 'I promised I wouldn't delay the court. I have no more questions, m'lord.'

The judge turned to the prosecution barrister. 'You may cross-examine the witness if you wish.'

'Just a couple of questions, Your Honour.'

The barrister rose slowly to his feet, adjusted his glasses, and fixed his eyes unwaveringly at Eileen. 'You say your husband hadn't explosives in the car on the night in question. How do you know that?'

Eileen tried to meet his stare. Gerry had warned her how intimidated she would feel.

'Because I'm certain they weren't in it when he left, Your Honour.'

The barrister's lips transformed into a sickly smile. 'There is no need to address me as "Your Honour". By doing so, you have promoted me to a status I have not yet attained.'

'I'm sorry, Your Honour. Oh, I'm sorry,' said Eileen, flustered. 'I said it again. "Your Honour to be" I should have said.'

Gerry was watching the judge. Did he smile? The smirk

had gone off the barrister's face.

'You say you believe your husband could not kill British soldiers.'

'I didn't say that.'

'Oh, perhaps you would tell the court what you *did* say.'

'I said I know my husband could not kill anyone.'

'You have a way with words, have you not?' suggested the barrister. Then with an expansive wave of his arm, he said, 'Would I be imposing upon you to ask if you might care to enlighten this august court as to the subtle difference between believing and knowing?'

Eileen's eyes darted from the barrister to Gerry. Her two hands clenched the edge of the witness box. Seanie stared at her. He could see the whiteness of her knuckles. He's trying to make you look stupid, Eileen. Say something simple. Say you're not a lawyer.

Eileen took a deep breath and began, 'If you come in out of the rain, Your Hon—' She stopped herself just in time. 'If you come into my house and tell me it's raining, I *believe* it's raining. If I'm standing out in the rain, I *know* it's raining. I *know* my husband could not hurt anyone.'

The barrister stood for a few moments clearly considering his next move. Finally, he said, 'I've no more questions, m'lord.'

'The witness may stand down,' said the judge. Then he looked at Gerry. 'You have, I presume, your closing address prepared by now?'

Gerry jumped up, 'Yes, m'lord.'

'Following final submissions, I will deliver the verdict of the court,' said the judge. 'The court will recess for fifteen minutes.'

Seanie caught Gerry's attention and the lawyer went over

to him. 'Will you tell me what's going on?' said Seanie.

'The judge is Eileen's Northern neighbour.'

'Jesus!'

'I haven't touched a drop since I saw him.'

'What does it mean?'

'Instead of him looking for reasons to convict, we surely now have him in a position where he should be looking for reasons *not* to convict.'

'What are you going to say?'

'You'll soon hear.'

When Gerry went back to his seat, the barrister leaned over to him, 'That was a smart stroke you pulled, keeping the grieving wife to the very last minute.'

'I don't do smart stokes. I'm not a barrister.'

'Was the devil's buttermilk the reason you never made it to be a barrister?'

'I wouldn't want to belong to a profession that wears a gown with a pouch in the back for tips.'

'You've lost anyway.'

'I still have my closing speech.'

'So what? Are you going to hypnotize him?'

'No, I'm going to present reasons why he should find my client not guilty.'

'The evidence is indisputable.'

'Sometimes there are other variables.'

'Five to one you lose.'

'A hundred quid to twenty.'

'Wow! I'd have to do a lot of talking for that kind of money.'

'Is Her Majesty's table not a broad one?'

'OK, I'm going to enjoy this.'

*

'Everyone please stand,' announced the tipstaff.

The judge came out, glanced around him, pulled the robe tighter across his shoulders and sat down. 'Is the defence ready to continue?'

Gerry was on his feet. 'Yes, Your Honour.'

'You may proceed,' said the judge.

Gerry stood up and surveyed the room. Seanie knew his tactics by now. He would say nothing until he was sure everyone was attentive and waiting on his words.

'Your Honour,' Gerry began, 'standing here, on this hallowed spot, I am struck by the enormity of the calling those of us in the legal profession are privileged to answer. But what does this calling involve, and why is "hallowed" the term I use?'

Gerry stopped to let the questions sink in. 'My answer to the first question might be "justice". I could suggest, that because we seek justice it makes the place we seek it in . . . sacred. Your Honour, that would be a *wrong* answer. What our calling commands us to seek is *truth*. There can be *no* justice until we first have truth.'

Gerry let his eyes wander around the room, 'This space is *not* about justice. This space is about *truth* and *that* is why it is hallowed.'

Gerry walked over to the witness box and picked up the Bible. He held it aloft and said, 'Here is a book *so* important that we hold it in our right hand when we swear to tell the truth. And in this holiest of books is a story. It's a story about another trial. A trial in an insignificant little province of a huge empire. The man being tried was deemed to be causing political trouble, so the rulers in the capital of the empire wanted him found guilty.

'There was no jury. The defendant, whose body had been twisted and broken by his captors, stood before the judge. The judge asked him to tell him the truth. This peasant man from a lowly background looked at the judge. He simply said, "What is truth?"'

Gerry paused. He was twenty-one again. He was on the stage. He didn't need notes. The lines would come to him. 'Pontius Pilate,' he shouted, 'did not have an answer to this question.'

His voice became quiet again. 'Your Honour, justice is easy. Justice is what's dispensed after the truth has been revealed. Justice is the price paid by the guilty party. Justice is compensation to those who have been wronged. *Truth* is never easy.'

Gerry stopped and closed his eyes. He breathed in and stood still for a second. 'Maybe we are being too harsh on that governor whose task it was to sentence unruly elements? Maybe he could not understand truth? Perhaps truth cannot be understood. Perhaps truth cannot be explained. Perhaps truth cannot be described. Perhaps truth can only be *recognized*.

'How can truth be recognized? Why could that cruel lackey of Rome not recognize truth? Why could he not see the Galilean peasant's innocence?

'Your Honour, thousands of years ago in Greece they knew how to recognize truth. In ancient Rome they knew how to recognize truth. At the time of the Magna Carta they knew how to recognize truth. In the birthplace of civilization, Athens, five hundred people were called upon in cases of serious crime to pronounce a verdict. The guilt or innocence of a man charged with a crime against his fellow man has *always* been determined in this way. In our own so-called modern age, just twelve people are given that responsibility.'

Gerry's voice fell away and became sorrowful. 'That Roman governor's decision resulted in the greatest crime in the history of all mankind.'

Then Gerry became more businesslike. 'I want to address the specifics of this present case. Your Honour, I will concentrate first on the lesser charge, which is one of resisting arrest. We have heard evidence from the arresting soldiers that there was no brutality involved in the arrest incident. However, if we can show there *was* brutality involved, then that would surely invalidate the charge against my client. To this end I called to the witness box a soldier who claimed the defendant had been badly beaten. My learned colleague made much of the fact that this soldier did not swear on the Bible that he was telling the truth. And it is true, he said he did not believe in God. However, he also stated he believed in right and wrong, and he maintained that one didn't have to believe in God to know the difference between right and wrong. Are any of us in a position to dispute this statement? The salient fact in this witness's evidence is not what he said, but that he had the courage to say it. We can only imagine the odium and loathing that has been directed towards him from his peers because of his lonely stance. There is surely no conceivable reason for him to give the evidence as presented other than to do his duty as a fellow human being, and to fulfil his commitment when he joined Her Majesty's armed services to act honourably at all times.'

Gerry took a sip of water. 'In respect of the more serious charge my client faces, the prosecution has fostered the notion that the evidence against the defendant is overwhelming. However, it consists of only two *suppositions*.'

Gerry held aloft a document in each hand. 'One, that the soldiers found explosive substances in the car; and two, that there were traces of this explosive substance on the defendant's hands.'

He dropped the documents onto the table. 'Let us consider them in turn. It is stated by the soldiers that there were explosives found in the car. It is stated by the defendant that there were no explosives in the car. Clearly, there is a conflict of evidence. What can be said? On the one hand, if the defendant were guilty then it would be in his interest to say the explosives were not in the car. But on the other hand, if the soldiers abused the defendant it would be in their interest to say they found the explosive substance in the car. We have shown that the defendant *was* ill-treated by the soldiers.'

The solicitor paused. 'And so we come to the expert witness. He said that the samples tested contained traces of explosive substances. We do not wish to impugn his findings. No one can doubt the veracity of his tests. But there are certain lacunae in his evidence. There are missing parts. He could not offer a definitive answer when asked if other commonly used materials could have been responsible for the results. When asked if he knew how the swabs were taken, he answered . . .' Here, Gerry consulted his notes. '"*That is not part of my brief.*" Your Honour, it has not been proven how the substances got on the hands, or even what these substances were. The witness unambiguously admitted to the possibility that other unknown materials might produce a result similar to his findings. The court is being asked to *infer* from what are at best very dubious circumstances, the defendant's guilt in this respect. I don't need to remind m'lord that to *infer* something and to *prove* something have little if any relationship to each other.'

Gerry said nothing more for a few moments. He absent-mindedly arranged the files on his desk with one hand, and held the other hand behind the small of his back. Then, still looking down at the documents, he started speaking again.

'Your Honour, all of us have responsibilities. We have a responsibility to ourselves. We have a responsibility to our fellow man. We have a responsibility to God. It could be said that if we perform the first of these two responsibilities, then the third will be fulfilled.'

Gerry lifted his head. He leaned forward, slightly bent, fingertips of both hands pressing into the table. Looking the judge in the eye, he said, 'You, m'lord, have an unenviable responsibility. It is *incumbent* upon you to abandon your role as the sole decision maker in this case. It is *incumbent* upon you to set aside your function as dispenser of justice, until truth has first been recognized. It is *incumbent* upon you to assume the mantle of a jury of twelve ordinary citizens, so that you might be in a position to recognize truth. *Truth,* Your Honour, can be recognized in the actions of one neighbour helping another. *Truth*, Your Honour, can be recognized in the cry of a newborn baby.'

Gerry straightened himself up. He flung his arm out and pointed his finger at Eileen. In a raised voice, he declared, '*Truth,* Your Honour, can be recognized in the words of a wife who doesn't have to *believe* her husband is innocent, because she *knows* her husband is innocent.'

His voice returned to normal. 'Ordinarily, a judge is not required to recognize the simplicity of these things. That is the function of the jury. Their absence is why you have such a burden to bear in deciding the guilt or innocence of the accused. Thank you, m'lord.'

The judge said, 'Thank you, counsel. The court will rise and resume again in one hour.'

There was a hubbub in the courtroom as soon as the judge left. Seanie tried to get Gerry's attention, but his uncle pretended not to notice and kept reading his documents. Then Seanie asked the guard if he would allow Eileen to speak with him. The guard said it wasn't permitted, and motioned to him that they would have to go down below to the cells. Eileen waved over and shouted that she loved him. Seanie waved back as he was being taken away. Slash said he had to go and check on the carry-outs. Gerry's colleague left to make phone calls. The two reporters sat talking. The court attendant waited by the exit, ready to be of service if required. A couple of RUC men with peaked hats under their arms stood chatting beside him. Outside in the foyer, British Army soldiers carrying machine guns casually patrolled the building.

'Everyone rise,' said the tipstaff. It flashed across Seanie's mind whether the tipstaff already knew the verdict. During the break, Slash had threatened not to stand for the judge. He said he would not rise for someone who was only a poodle of the English. Eileen asked him not to make a scene. She told him she knew the depth of his patriotism, but to cross his fingers and do as he was asked. Slash said he would swallow his pride on this occasion, but wanted it clearly understood he was prepared to go to jail if necessary.

The judge took his seat. All eyes in the room were focused on the man in robes. Even Seanie's guard, the RUC men, and the court attendant momentarily forgot their own private concerns.

'Normally,' began the judge in a brisk voice, 'in cases of the kind before us today, the foreman of the jury comes in and delivers the verdict to the judge. The judge does not ask how the jury reached that verdict. He does not enquire what facts, what arguments, what criteria were used in coming to their decision. This information is for the anonymity of the jury room. It is not my intention to modify or change this process. I find the defendant not guilty as charged. He is free to go. The court will rise.'

23

Eileen maintained later that Seanie threw his arms around the prison guard and kissed him, but Seanie had no recollection of it. His memory was of Slash, with his belly sticking out, standing across from him on the public bench, waving a football jersey and shouting, 'Up Ballyduff!'

Although he and Eileen wanted to get home to the baby, Seanie felt they had a duty to join his supporters on a triumphant trip back to McIver's. Word had reached Ballyduff by the time the bus arrived, and a crowd had gathered. It wasn't just winning a court case that was being celebrated. Every local who had ever been hassled by the British Army would take satisfaction in the outcome. Dickie Stone greeted Seanie warmly and whispered in his ear that they could talk later. Sandwiches were made. Cormac, on Seanie's instructions, arranged a free round of drinks for everyone. Wee Pat put off checking the racing results until later. Sober sat in the corner with an unlit Woodbine hanging from his mouth, telling everyone who was interested that he was sober. McIver, surveying the full house, decided that besides it being a neighbourly act to offer free carry-outs, it was also a worthwhile investment.

Slash had cornered Seanie. 'Did your father, God rest his soul, ever tell you about the time him and me were put on trial in Mexico for gun smuggling?'

'No,' said Seanie.

'God, he kept a lot of stuff to himself.'

'Yeah, maybe.'

'We refused to recognize the court,' said Slash.

Dickie Stone came over and drew Seanie aside. 'Well, how was it?' he asked.

Seanie thought for a moment. 'In a word: educational.'

'Yeah, I bet it was. Nowadays everyone's talking about having fifteen minutes of fame. I think fifteen weeks, or even fifteen days behind bars would be more beneficial.'

'I agree.'

'Anyway, that's not what I wanted to talk about.'

'What's on your mind?'

'I have been getting reports of strangers looking for Big Frank Ratigan in Monaghan pubs, and of Big Frank requisitioning weapons for unspecified missions.'

Caught off guard, Seanie grimaced and plopped himself down on a chair. He didn't answer for a few moments, but finally said, 'What can I say?'

'You can explain what's going on.'

'If there ever was anything going on, other than a rush of blood to the head, it's over.'

'I'm glad to hear that.'

'Believe me, it's finished.'

'You sure?'

'I'm sure.'

'OK, I believe you,' said Stone. 'I doubt if you'd ever have carried it through anyway.'

'I wouldn't like Ratigan to be in trouble.'

'Every army has their Ratigan. He'll be OK.'

'Thanks for that.'

Stone clasped Seanie by the hand. 'You're not cut out for

what you had in mind, Seanie. You have to be yourself.'

It was just coming dusk when the couple managed to get away. Seanie got Cormac to drive them home. He needed his help to do something. When the trio got there, Seanie spent the first hour being amazed at the new baby, then he took Cormac to the attic. He pointed to a trunk in the corner. 'My mother insisted on me taking that with me. I want you to return it to her tonight, or whenever suits you.'

Cormac looked at Seanie, flabbergasted. 'What the hell is in it?'

'Just some old stuff from dad's army days.'

'What kind of stuff?'

'Nothing much really.'

'What's the rush? Could it not have waited?'

'Give me a hand,' said Seanie. 'Let's get it shifted.'

Later, Seanie and Eileen were having supper. 'You're very quiet, darling,' said Eileen. 'What's in your thoughts?'

'Nothing really.'

'You're thinking about today?'

Seanie got up from the table and walked over to the pram. He gently parted the blanket partially covering his son's face. 'I'm thinking about tomorrow.'

ACKNOWLEDGEMENTS

I want to thank my wife Patricia and my cousin Noel who shared this unforgettable, if sometimes traumatic, journey with me. The story literally couldn't have happened without them. I also want to acknowledge the contribution of a little Dublin-based group of writers. The leader is the well-known author, John Givens. He has an encyclopaedic knowledge when it comes to the art of transforming a story you want to tell into one that's fit for print. Also I want to thank the author Andrew Hughes. Due to some innate skill he always knows the right word and, just as importantly, where to put it. In addition, I want to thank the author Caroline Madden, whose massive contribution to the novel included a feminine perspective into the emotional and psychological aspects of the book's characters. There are, of course, many others who helped along the way, but it would be unfair to single any one of them out. However, they know who they are and I thank each one of them most sincerely.

57609159R00171

Made in the USA
Charleston, SC
20 June 2016